FRAME
of
REFERENCE

AMBER GABRIEL

Scrivenings
PRESS
Quench your thirst for story.
www.ScriveningsPress.com

To those with doubts, may you find grace

"The Lord shall preserve thee from all evil: he shall preserve thy soul." (Psalm 121:7 KJV)

"Every good and perfect gift is from above, coming down from the Father of the heavenly lights, who does not change like shifting shadows."
(James 1:17 NIV)

"And we know that in all things God works for the good of those who love him, who have been called according to his purpose."
(Romans 8:28 NIV)

CHAPTER 1

Friday, November 4, 2017
Kyiv 14:50 New York 7:50 a.m.

The crowd in Independence Square swelled as the protestors chanted louder. Natalia's heart burst with pride as Danylo addressed the onlookers.

"We are fed up with corruption! Fed up with cronyism! We call on Parliament to establish an independent anti-corruption court," Danylo thrust his fist in the air.

Natalia hoped he'd finish his speech before she had to leave, since Iryna expected her to see her off at the airport. She checked the time on her phone. It would take fifteen minutes to reach the airport by metro, and Iryna would not arrive for over half an hour. *I can stay a little longer.*

As Danylo continued his impassioned oratory, the spectators grew more agitated. Someone bumped into her, and Natalia backed away.

"Out with Poroshenko!" cried a protestor.

A rock flew toward a nearby police officer. People started yelling.

No, no, no! This is supposed to be a peaceful protest. Saying a brief prayer that God would keep Danylo safe, Natalia edged toward the nearby office building. She could lose her role as prima in the upcoming Grand Kyiv Ballet season if she appeared in a news report or got arrested.

Natalia turned to face the center of the square, where Danylo fought to maintain control of the crowd. He'd understand if she couldn't stay to the end, though he'd be disappointed. It was important to him that she support his goals, but he supported hers as well. That's what made him such a great boyfriend.

A smile tugged at her lips despite the surrounding tension. Soon, she would have to introduce Danylo to her father. As she walked toward the street, she pulled out her phone to text Danylo she was leaving.

Intense pain jolted her system, and she crumpled to the ground.

"One down, two to go" were the last words she heard.

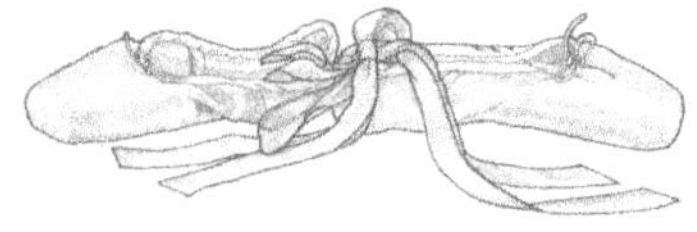

Kyiv 15:30 New York 8:30 a.m.

Iryna glanced at the clock on the wall above the ticketing counter. *Where is Natalia? She said she would be here to say goodbye.* All around her, other dancers embraced their spouses, children, or friends. But Iryna was alone.

She shook herself. It wasn't like this was her first time touring. *I'm a professional. I'm a prima. This is my job, not my first day of primary school.*

Besides, she and Natalia had spoken at rehearsal yesterday. Iryna's parents had dropped her off at the airport that morning —quite a sacrifice on her father's part since the political situation was so unstable and his job as a cabinet minister constantly in jeopardy.

Still, it would be nice to have someone in her circle of family and friends here just for her. She fingered the cross on her charm bracelet. *The Lord is with me.*

"Let's go, *Irynochko*," called Viktor, the director of the touring half of the ballet company. His normally stern visage sported a deeper frown than usual. Traveling was stressful, and traveling while in charge of a large group of people had to be wearing.

Iryna clutched her ticket and passport to her chest and grabbed the handle of her carry-on as she followed her troupe toward the security line. Fortunately, they qualified for expedited screening.

"Do we have everyone?" Katherine, one of the trainers and Viktor's occasional secretary, asked as she scanned the sea of faces before her. "I don't see Fyodor."

Olena rushed up to Viktor. "The ticket counter wouldn't print a boarding pass for me. The flight is overbooked."

Viktor scowled. "When is the next flight?"

"Tomorrow morning. Anyone else who isn't here yet will be bumped."

"Be sure you're on that flight." Viktor held up his passport for the security officer while speaking to Olena over his shoulder. "We need our choreographers."

Katherine gave Olena a quick hug. "Don't worry. It will be fine. Let us know your flight number, and we'll send someone to pick you up."

One by one, they passed through the screening area, leaving Olena behind. Iryna was glad she didn't get bumped since she was already nervous, and not only because of traveling. This was the first time she would see Rick since the Carters left Ukraine.

Since Cassie had died. It was still hard to believe her lively, mischievous little friend was gone. She hadn't even known the severity of Cassie's illness until after they had returned to America. How hard that must have been for her brother.

Her heart sped at the thought of meeting him again. She adored Rick when she was little. The brown-haired boy with eyes like a steaming cup of chai with the leaves still in it had been so kind, so smart, so … *cute*. How much had he changed? Would he remember her? She cringed at the memory of her starstruck, attention-seeking behavior. Maybe it would be better if he didn't.

"Our gate is this way," Katherine said once everyone with a pass had completed their security check.

The troupe lumbered down the terminal, toting their overstuffed carry-ons, until they reached their assigned gate.

"Everyone, find a seat," Katherine said in a shrill voice. The dancers squished into the last available seats, though Iryna would have preferred to stand. But performers were always a superstitious lot, and Katherine was a prime example. Sergei, one of the younger dancers, lounged against a pillar. "Sit down." Katherine made a downward motion with her finger.

"Where?" He gestured to the packed waiting area.

"On the floor if you have to. And be quiet."

Sergei flopped onto the floor at Iryna's feet. "Do you know how long the flight is?"

"Hush!" Katherine said. "Everyone must sit quietly so we will have a safe flight. Now you must spit over your shoulder three times." The trainer mimicked spitting over her left shoulder.

Sergei repeated the action without enthusiasm then rolled his eyes and pulled out his phone.

Iryna smiled at the younger dancer's antics, but her smile faded as her thoughts returned to Natalia. Was the metro running on time? Had there been an accident or closure? She hoped nothing serious had happened. Natalia never let her friends down if she could help it. When the intercom announced boarding was beginning, Iryna said a quick prayer, entrusting both her journey and Natalia's safety to God. *Your will be done, Lord.*

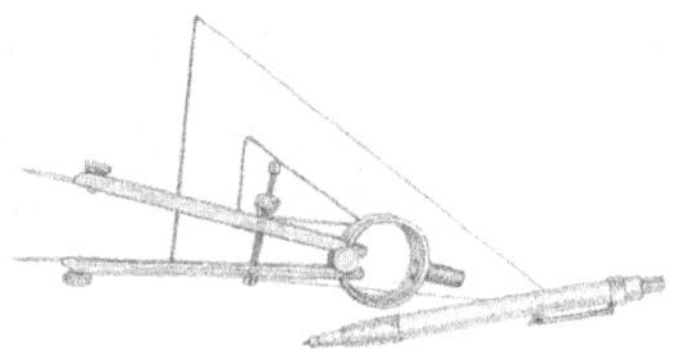

New York 5:15 p.m.

"Yes, Mother, of course I'm staying for the party," Rick spoke into his hands-free device as he wove his black sedan through the Friday rush-hour traffic headed to Manhattan. The heavy traffic had turned a quick drive into a significantly longer one. He ground his teeth, wishing he'd taken the subway.

His mother raved on, despite his inattention. "—and of course Iryna is the prima ballerina! It's been so long since we've seen her! She was such a pretty little girl. I wonder what she's like now?"

The Ukrainian National Ballet was coming to town, and as the consulate had no rooms big enough to throw a large party, Rick's parents were happy to host a welcome gala in their spacious mansion. His great-grandparents had purchased their house in the 1930s for a song when everyone else was moving to upper Manhattan, and succeeding generations had managed to keep it in the family despite numerous offers to repurpose it.

Rick focused on what his mother was saying. She had been talking about this event for weeks, so there was no way he could forget the date of the party. He suspected it was another attempt to introduce him to eligible females. At nearly thirty, he had yet to provide his parents with any hope of grandchildren. He dated casually, but no one had really piqued his interest. However, because he desired to make his parents happy whenever possible, he came when called.

"—and she'll be staying with us. Your father promised Vasyl we would look after her while she's in New York. We're right around the corner from the consulate and only thirty minutes from the theater, so it should be very convenient. I don't suppose you'll be able to show her around town while she's not rehearsing?"

Aha. There it was—the expected setup.

"Well …" He was torn between disappointing his mother and enduring the torture of escorting some entitled dancer around town. "I've got a lot of projects in the works right now. I'll have to see." *Good thinking. Put the decision off until after you meet her.*

Of course, he *had* met her before, when his father was the US ambassador to Ukraine in the nineties. Her father was a government official, and their parents had become friends, though his dad had worked with Vasyl in Poland previously. He searched his memory for a glimpse of Vasyl's daughter. Surely at least fifteen years had passed since they'd returned to the States for Cassie's unsuccessful cancer treatments. He shrugged off the somber feeling and searched his mind for images of his life in Kyiv that did not directly involve his sister.

There *was* a little girl. Their families had exchanged dinner visits. A little dark-haired girl, with startling blue eyes and an impish smile. She'd challenged him to a game of chess, stating, "I will win you," and trounced him in an embarrassingly low number of moves before throwing her hands in the air and dancing around the room. He had laughed at her antics and congratulated her politely. *Such a funny little thing.*

The memory left Rick rather unsettled. Was that girl Iryna? He must have blocked her out of his mind along with Cassie.

He had a vague impression of other informal meetings, family dinners, and passing the girl in the hall at the diplomatic school he'd attended, but he hadn't really spent any time with her. He heard Cassie's voice exclaiming *"Iryna ballerina!"* with childish delight. His throat tightened.

"I'm going to hang up, Mom. I'm almost there."

"Okay, sweetie. We'll see you in a few minutes! Peters can park your car for you."

He pulled up in front of the house and double-parked, tossing the keys to Peters on the way up the steps. Beth Carter's idea of economizing was to have one all-purpose butler/chauffeur/handyman, one cook, and one maid on staff, hiring a cleaning or catering company when more was required. They would have to hire at least a dozen valets just to shuttle vehicles around for the party guests without chauffeurs.

Beth greeted her son at the door with a wide smile and open arms.

"Hi, Mom." Rick hugged her and kissed her on both cheeks, a habit picked up from living most of his youth in Eastern Europe.

"You didn't bring a bag?" she asked in an accusing tone.

"You know I keep half of my clothes here. I'm here almost every weekend."

"I hope you have a nice tuxedo. It's white-tie."

"Peters took it to the cleaners for me when I was here last Saturday. I bet he already picked it up. Don't worry—I'll be as dapper and charming as ever," Rick said with a hint of sarcasm.

Beth sighed. "You know very well you can be irresistible when you wish, and there won't be anyone here even half as handsome as you."

"Well, I hope you invited a doctor to attend to all the ladies who faint when I walk in the room." He snickered.

Beth rolled her eyes. "One of these days, son, you will be the one to faint, and that will be the happiest day of my life!"

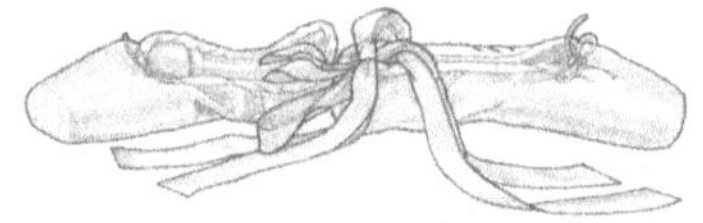

New York 12:20 a.m. Kyiv 7:20

"*Allo, Tato,*" Iryna said as she sank with relief onto the hotel bed. It had taken her twenty minutes to figure out how to make an international call from the hotel phone. Her eyelids drooped.

"Hello, my *Irynka*. How are you? How was your flight?" Vasyl Schevchenko's deep voice swaddled her and eased the tension in her shoulders.

"Good. I slept for an hour or so. Then the turbulence woke me up. It's probably a good thing I'm not going to the Carters' until tomorrow. I can't stay awake another minute." Iryna stifled a yawn.

"Matt and his family will take good care of you."

"I'm excited to see them again." She especially looked forward to dancing at the party, hopefully with Rick. "How was your day?"

Vasyl sighed. "More of the same. The protests downtown got a little tense. Russia continues to build up its forces in Crimea. The economy is on the brink of collapse. Some days I think I should just retire and move to America."

Iryna laughed softly. "You know you love Ukraine too much for that." His reference to the protests stirred something in her mind. Hadn't Natalia said something about them?

"*Irynka?*"

"Hmm?" She forced her eyes open. "I must have dozed off."

"I will let you go. Get some sleep."

"Okay. Love you. Bye."

"Bye."

Iryna fumbled to replace the phone with half-closed eyes. *I should call to check on Natalia.* Before she could act on the thought, she fell asleep, still wearing her travel clothes.

In her dreams, Natalia appeared with her hand outstretched, urgently calling Iryna's name.

CHAPTER 2

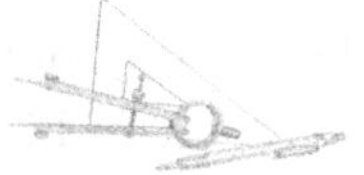

Rick crossed the hall to his parents' bedroom the next evening and knocked on their door.

"Come in," Beth said. He opened the door to see her lips pursed in concentration as she straightened his father's tie. Then she smiled, patted him on the chest, and turned to study her son's attire. "Oh, Rick, you look perfect!"

"And you look absolutely lovely, Mom."

"She certainly does." Rick's father, Matt, stood behind her, smiling with admiration.

Beth wore a beaded cream evening gown that perfectly suited her lightly tanned skin and blonde highlights. She twirled, grinning like a child while her husband and son gazed at her affectionately. She took both of their arms and said, "Now you two handsome men, let's go throw a party!"

As they descended the stairs, jarring notes from a variety of instruments wafted from the fourth-floor ballroom where the chamber orchestra tuned up. The house sparkled, and fresh flowers adorned nearly every surface. A cleaning crew, decorators, and caterers had been busy all day working their magic, and it showed.

The first guests were old friends, the Greens, who arrived

promptly at seven. Peters opened the door for them, dressed immaculately for his role as butler.

"Hello, Beth," Mrs. Green gushed. "I've been so excited for this evening! Thanks for including us."

"Darlene, you know I couldn't throw a party without my favorite co-hostess." Beth and Darlene chatted while her son, Andrew, and Rick exchanged pleasantries.

Many guests arrived soon after. Maids took coats and wraps. Andrew and his mother helped direct people up the stairs while Rick and his parents stationed themselves in the ballroom to form a receiving line.

The Ukrainian consul arrived with the ambassador himself, who had flown up from DC to offer an official welcome to the ballet company.

"I apologize for my bad manners in bringing an uninvited guest. I hope it is not an inconvenience." The consul bowed over Beth's hand.

"Not at all. Of course, we are delighted to have the ambassador," Beth assured. "You did exactly as I would wish."

Introductions were made. However, at the first opportunity, Beth signaled for the waitstaff to oversee the rearrangement of the dinner settings to ensure they observed diplomatic rank properly.

Rick was glad he remembered enough Ukrainian to greet the ambassador and other officials in their native language. Matt, of course, was fluent in Ukrainian and several other languages, but Beth didn't speak enough of it to be comfortable, so she used English.

A great chattering commenced below, growing louder as the voices ascended the stairs—musical voices speaking in Ukrainian, Russian, and heavily accented English—announcing the arrival of the celebrated dancers. Everyone crowded around the doorway to welcome them, and Beth grabbed Rick's arm and squeezed it in excitement. His heart pounded in sympathetic anticipation. The emotional buildup was contagious.

A young woman with raven hair, artistically arranged, appeared at the top of the stairs. High cheekbones and a creamy complexion complemented her elegant profile. Her graceful, slender figure swayed as she climbed the steps. Folds of flowing black fabric swished around her legs while a snug halter top left her arms and shoulders bare.

She was looking at the man next to her, laughing while he grinned. Her hand glided along the railing, and as she stepped onto the landing, she turned her head to survey the waiting crowd with a radiant smile. The way the rest of the company lined up behind her to offer a collective bow indicated she was the prima. This was Iryna. She turned her sparkling blue eyes on her host and hostess, and as she moved to greet them, her gaze rested briefly on Rick.

A jolt of electricity ran through him. His pulse throbbed in his ears, overwhelming all other sensations. His knees weakened as if he might actually faint. The only thing holding him together was his determination to not give his mother that satisfaction. *Breathe, man, breathe!* Now the woman was shaking his hand, and he wondered if she could feel the energy coursing through him. He was surprised there weren't visible sparks.

"It is so nice to see you again, Rrricky," she said with a slight roll of the *R*. Her accent was excellent. "You are just as perfect as ever."

Her remark caught him off guard. He replied without even knowing what he said and hoped he didn't make a complete fool of himself. Iryna's hand lingered in his for a moment before she turned away to address the ambassador. His skin tingled.

"You didn't tell me Ukrainian women were so beautiful," Andrew said, appearing behind Rick's shoulder. "Looks like I'll have to spend some time at the ballet!"

A surge of jealousy coursed through Rick, and he was saved from making a childish reply by the necessity of greeting the rest of the company. Over thirty dancers were present, plus the trainers, choreographers, and director. A number of local dancers would support the cast. He shook hands in a daze, and by the time everyone had filed in, the room was quite full.

Beth sent a big smile Rick's way and signaled the orchestra to play the music for the first dance. Matt led Iryna to the floor while the ambassador escorted his hostess to the tune of a familiar waltz. Other couples followed, and Rick saw Andrew take the floor with a pretty blonde.

Rick downed some ice water, hoping it would cool him off a bit. The daughter of a family friend approached him, a woman who his mother had previously set him up with. Her name eluded him. He avoided asking her to dance even though it was rather rude as a host, but his eyes followed Iryna's every move. At the first opportunity, he passed the family friend off to Andrew, who appeared more than happy to dance with her.

Iryna captivated him. She floated gracefully through each dance, matching her partners' moves without showing off. Rick desperately wanted to dance with her, but admirers surrounded her like water around a fish. Even if he had been brave enough to ask, approaching her proved daunting.

He chatted for a moment with a few members of the troupe who were enjoying the appetizers. Several savory Slavic favorites were available, including something wrapped in grape leaves, and he ate one without really tasting it. Many members of the troupe were originally from Russia or Georgia, but all spoke some amount of Ukrainian, so Rick made awkward conversation with his limited vocabulary.

"What do you think of America?" he asked a circle of dancers.

A slim, athletic dancer named Maxim answered smoothly, "Oh, I am all excitement to be here. I have some … souvenirs I am eager to acquire."

"I am enjoying the dancing," another dancer said. "The waltz is easy, but I am less familiar with the Latin dances. I have had no time to learn them, being focused solely on ballet."

"Iryna can dance them all," remarked another, waving toward the couples twirling across the floor.

"Even tap and hip-hop," Maxim said as he reached behind Rick to lift a glass of champagne from a tray.

"True, she dances everything. It is an honor to work with someone of such talent," said the second dancer. Heads nodded in agreement.

"But you knew her before us." The trainer, an articulate and well-toned woman named Katherine, smiled. She switched to English, to Rick's relief. "Didn't you live in Kyiv for a while?"

"Yes, my father was in diplomatic service for many years."

"So you must be able to tell us some interesting stories about her." Katherine raised an eyebrow and leaned in conspiratorially.

"That was a long time ago," Rick laughed. "But I do remember she was a good dancer, even then."

"Were you also in Poland? I heard your father was there during the Cold War."

Rick wondered where the trainer had heard that since it wasn't common knowledge. "No, that was before my time. We were in Kyiv for several years when I was a boy, then we returned to the States and my father worked with the consulates here in New York."

"There you arrre!" said Iryna, appearing magically before him. "You have not yet asked me to dance," she complained with feigned petulance.

"Ah," Rick said, searching for something to say, "I felt as a host that it was my duty to share you with your adoring fans." He managed his most charming smile. "But if you are free"—he bowed slightly—"it would be my honor to escort you for this next dance."

Iryna smiled and gave his arm a light squeeze before resting her hand on his. He led her to the floor and turned to face her. She slid effortlessly into his embrace, forming a perfect dance frame. His entire body tingled in awareness. The musicians played a foxtrot, and a Sinatra-style crooner sang the lyrics to "Beyond the Sea."

Rick stepped forward and entered a dream. Iryna followed, interpreting his lead from the slightest pressure of his hand. He limited himself to basic steps at first, to ensure his concentration and his feet didn't slip. The vibrant reality of Iryna in his arms was enough to distract anyone.

But after one turn around the floor, he led Iryna in a promenade and performed a triple twinkle. He incorporated more complicated steps as he relaxed. He was grateful, for once, for the lessons his mother made him take so he'd be presentable at occasions such as this. *As long as she doesn't make me talk and dance at the same time, I'll be okay.* Luckily, Iryna focused on her movements and did not require him to speak.

At the end of the song, he spun her out then back into a dip. It was a bold move since he had not practiced it in years, but he executed it flawlessly. Those nearby applauded.

As he raised her slowly, she murmured, "How appropriate, that song."

"Oh?"

"Now we meet on another shore," she said cryptically. "Thank you for the dance, Ricky." She moved away, smiling, leaving him to puzzle out what she meant.

"Bravo!" Someone clapped a hand on his shoulder. A middle-aged man named Alexei, one of the choreographers, stood next to him. He had met so many people at once it was hard to keep them all straight. "Eet can be very, ah, eentimeedating to dance weeth one as good as Iryna, but you deed verry well."

"Thank you, but I think she would make anyone look good."

"Oh yes, she weel make everyone look *better,* but you geeve her room to make herself look good, and not everyone can do that. You must have the good eenstincts for dance." The man handed Rick a drink and raised his own. "*Vashee zdarovye.*"

Rick replied in kind and felt he had been given a great compliment.

As the party continued, Rick attempted to be a better host and danced with a few other honored ladies, but he knew he was inattentive. He was relieved when ten o'clock neared so they could sit down to dinner. To his surprise, his mother stood beside the musicians' platform and called for attention.

"Good evening, everyone! You are in for a special treat this evening. Iryna Shevchenko, prima ballerina of the Ukrainian National Ballet, is going to perform an interpretive dance." Mrs. Carter gestured toward Iryna, who had reappeared in the center of the floor wearing her ballet slippers.

A slight flush reddened her cheeks, but besides the fact that her nose was a little shiny, nothing betrayed the fact she had already been dancing for over two hours. The lights dimmed, and a spotlight appeared. The excited buzz that greeted the announcement fell to a reverent hush. Rick held his breath in anticipation, not wanting to miss one moment.

CHAPTER 3

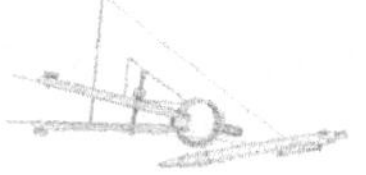

Iryna unfurled a pink dance ribbon that stood out against her black outfit. Rick had paid little attention to what she was wearing before. He was focused on her face and her vibrant personality that made outer garments hold no importance, but now he realized the black jumpsuit with halter top and split skirt was designed perfectly to allow freedom of movement, accentuating her lithe form and graceful motions.

Rick and the rest of the audience watched, enraptured, as Iryna told an entire story with her dance. Beginning in a seated position, she rose slowly until her arms stretched toward the ceiling like a flower unfurling. As if they were petals in the wind, her limbs swayed with the music. Her slippered feet flitted in ways he didn't know were possible, extending over her head and fluttering across the floor as if on wings. Every movement matched the music perfectly.

The melody changed from lighthearted to dramatic, and Iryna leapt into the air, snapping her ribbon like a lightning bolt. Crashing cymbals chased her one way then the other, searching for safety in a storm.

Rick responded to every emotion portrayed as if she were a puppeteer with his heartstrings in her hand. He was under a spell. He held his breath as the tempo decreased and the storm subsided. Iryna the flower straightened and shook off the rain, delighting in the restorative sun breaking through imaginary clouds.

A few plaintive notes crept into the song, and Iryna slowed her motions. Her arms drooped and her posture withered. Iryna dropped the ribbon. The flower died. When the music stilled and Rick thought the dance was over, a flute trilled.

Iryna spread her arms and threw her head back. Through pantomime, seeds fell from the withered flower and sprang from the ground as she picked up the ribbon and tossed it repeatedly in the air.

She spun across the room with the ribbon whirling around her and concluded her performance in a split with her head to the floor. The room fell silent for a moment as everyone processed what they had seen before bursting into thunderous applause.

Tears glistened on a few faces as the lights came back on. Rick's eyes misted. He was by no means a patron of the arts, but Iryna's talent was unquestionable.

People lined up to head downstairs for dinner. As the guest of honor, Iryna was escorted by Mr. Carter, and for the first time, Rick was disappointed that his mother's machinations had not allowed him the privilege. He held out his arm to the consul's wife after his mother and the ambassador descended the stairs.

"I fear you are relegated to escorting me." The consul's wife wore a knowing smile.

"Not at all," Rick answered, rallying all his diplomatic poise. "It is my pleasure."

The genteel woman patted his arm. They exchanged pleasantries with the ease of long practice and followed the others to the dining room, where an elaborate dinner awaited.

A full five courses, excluding appetizers, graced the menu, including soup, salad, pasta, a main course, and dessert. Waiters rushed around serving and collecting plates, and conversation buzzed around him in multiple languages. It was quite noisy, and Rick could only watch while Iryna spoke with others a few places away. Occasionally, he heard her laughter above the general din. The food on his plate remained largely untouched, as he was kept busy with his thoughts. He tried to ignore them enough to participate in conversation with the guests on either side of him.

Finally, guests served themselves chai or herbal tea from a variety of silver and copper samovars on the sideboard. Rick wondered how his mother had rounded them all up and made a mental note to compliment her on all her planning for this event. He edged toward a circle gathered around Iryna and the ambassador.

"You do your country proud, my dear," the ambassador was saying. "I knew you were talented, but nothing I've heard prepared me for your dance tonight. I can't wait to see you perform when you play in Washington."

"I am excited for the opportunity. But I am not the only talented dancer in the troupe." Iryna took another young woman by the arm. "Let me introduce Karina, my understudy. She will be dancing some of the performances."

One by one, Iryna introduced the principal dancers to the ambassador and regaled him with their accomplishments. Rick was impressed. Not every star would willingly share the spotlight, let alone shine it on someone else.

The crowd thinned when the ambassador stepped aside to speak with a consular official. Iryna turned and caught Rick's eye as he moved toward her.

She glanced down at his empty hand and smiled. "You do not drink *chay* anymore?"

"I do occasionally, although I prefer coffee." He noticed her hands were empty also. "Would you like some tea?"

He filled a cup and handed it to her. She took it with both hands, as if to warm them, then held it under her nose, closing her eyes and breathing in the aroma. When she opened them, they crinkled with hidden laughter.

Suddenly, a memory of another tea party came to mind—he, his mother, and Cassie visiting Iryna and her mother. Black and golden curls mingling over gold-edged china. The two girls giggling while he sat bored, forcing himself to sip a spicy dark liquid that nearly made him choke. Iryna laughing at him behind her cup like she was now.

He'd wished Iryna had a brother. He didn't wish that anymore.

"At the risk of echoing the words of every person you've spoken to, your dance was the best I have ever seen," said Rick.

Iryna's mouth quirked. "And how many have you seen?"

Rick let out a surprised laugh. "Um, okay, not that many. But your performance made me want to watch more."

Iryna nodded. "That is the best compliment—to instill an appreciation for the art in someone."

"*Irynka*"—the understudy, Karina, linked her arm through Iryna's and spoke in Ukrainian—"you must come translate for me."

Iryna glanced apologetically at Rick as she was dragged away. "We must talk more later."

Everyone milled around and chatted comfortably for a while longer, then Peters came and whispered in Beth's ear. After receiving instructions, Peters approached the director of the ballet company, Viktor Kravets.

"The bus to take you to your hotel has arrived," he told the director.

The director bowed toward Rick's parents. "Thank you to our gracious host and hostess for your hospitality. We could not have wished for a better welcome. Now we must take our leave so my dancers can rest before tomorrow's rehearsal." He rose from his bow and twirled his hand in the air. "Come, everyone."

The consul translated his words, and the guests moved toward the stairs. Gratitude and compliments were given to the host and hostess as goodbyes were said. Diplomats and family friends departed when their cars arrived, then the last of the catering crew slipped out quietly, leaving only the Carters and Iryna.

"Whew!" said Beth. "I'm bushed!"

"Congratulations, my dear. The party was a great success!" Matt said with pride.

"Thank you, Mrs. Carter, for your kind thoughtfulness. I am so happy to be here!" Iryna flung her arms around the older woman, who patted her affectionately on the back. As she stepped away, Iryna cast a dazzling smile at Rick that nearly made his heart stop. "I have been looking forward to seeing you all."

"And we are delighted to have you. Absolutely delighted!" Rick's mom assured her. "But you must be even more tired than I am, you poor thing! Let's get you to your room so you can catch some sleep."

"Thank you." Iryna bounced on her toes and clasped her hands. "But first I must present my gifts to my hosts and hostess."

"Oh my," said Beth. "You didn't have to bring us anything."

"I wanted to," Iryna insisted. "I can't wait to see how you like them."

"I'm sure we'll love them. This way, dear."

They climbed the stairs to the next floor, and Beth took her to a room on the right at the front of the house. Rick and his father stiffened as she led Iryna into the bedroom, explaining where everything was and expressing hope that she had everything she needed.

"I'm sure you'll enjoy the view of Gramercy Park in the morning."

"It will be perfect. I love it. Thank you, Mrs. Carter!" Rick heard from the hallway.

His mind protested strongly. *That's Cassie's room.* Sunlight streaming through the window onto her golden curls, watching her play with dolls on her pink carpet, and lying sick in bed … He closed his eyes to the memories. Even the good ones hurt.

"Oh, please call me Beth, dear! You have your own bath through here. We make breakfast ourselves as the cook doesn't live-in, so help yourself whenever you wake up. Feel free to use the TV or the library. Make yourself at home! Peters can drive you to the theater whenever you're ready. His rooms are downstairs, off the kitchen."

"Ah, here they are," exclaimed Iryna from inside the room. She beamed as she followed Beth back into the hallway, holding a small armful of packages. "Mrs. Carter, here is yours." She held out a tissue-wrapped packet.

Beth unfolded the colorful wrapping and held up a beautiful brown-and-green silk scarf that brought out her hazel eyes. "This is lovely," she whispered, draping it over her shoulders. "Thank you."

"This is for you, Mr. Carter." Iryna handed Matt a small box.

He opened it to reveal a special brand of Ukrainian Cognac. "Oh, wow. I haven't had this in a while."

"My father sent it for you. Our diplomatic status allowed me to bring it through the customs. And for you, Rick." Iryna held out a tissue-wrapped box.

Rick took the package with building excitement, like a child waking on Christmas morning. Iryna's eyes sparkled. He tore off the tissue to reveal a box of Ukrainian candy. "These are my favorite! How did you remember?" He opened the box, unwrapped a chocolate-covered wafer, and popped it into his mouth. The creamy, buttery flavor was as tasty as his memory of them. "Mm. Delicious."

Iryna let out a delighted squeal as she clapped her hands. Both her thoughtfulness and enthusiasm surprised and warmed him. Why did something as small as him eating the candy make her so happy?

Iryna turned back to Rick's parents. "Thank you again for

letting me stay here. I am sure I will sleep wonderfully. Is there a phone I could use to make an international call?"

"Oh," said Beth, raising her eyebrows. "Sorry, I didn't think to offer a phone. You are welcome to use the house phone, but it's all the way downstairs in the foyer."

"You can use my phone," Rick offered. Maybe her phone was dead or didn't allow roaming. "You can set it on the table there when you're done." He pointed at a small table holding a vase of flowers. After disabling the lock screen, he held it out.

"Oh, thank you." She took the phone. "I will just be a moment. Good night."

She waved at them all as they wished her a good night. When she closed the door, the three of them stood staring at it. Mrs. Carter looked at her husband as he let out a long breath.

"I just couldn't put her on the third floor all by herself," she pleaded in a whisper.

"I know," he sighed, and turned away. "Good night, Rick."

"Night, Dad." Rick turned to his mom, still standing in front of Cassie's room. His mind rebelled at the idea of someone other than his sister staying there. He shoved the indignation aside for his mother's sake. "You are marvelous, Mom. I don't know how you managed it all." He kissed her cheek. She smiled at him but refrained from teasing him about Iryna, though the twinkle in her eye betrayed her thoughts.

When he reached his room and tossed his jacket over a chair, something fell from a pocket onto the hardwood floor with a tiny slap. With a frown, he bent and picked up a matchbook. *Gdańsk, Poland.* "Weird," he muttered. "Wonder how that got there." He tossed it onto his nightstand and finished changing.

A door opened, and soft footsteps padded in the hallway before the door closed again. Rick opened his door, spied his phone on the table, and retrieved it. It was still warm from Iryna's use. He fingered it for a moment before plugging it in. So many thoughts swirled through his head he feared he might never be able to sleep.

The pain of someone using Cassie's room gave way to the memory of Iryna dancing in his arms. The lyrics of the song they had danced to entered his consciousness. It was a song about two lovers living on opposite shores of a sea who longed to be together. He performed a mental double take. Did that mean Iryna had a crush on him as a child and was still nursing affection for him? *No, that's ridiculous. A woman like her must have dozens of admirers. I'm reading too much into a single comment about a song lyric. She's just teasing me.* Despite the argument, his pulse quickened. He couldn't possibly sleep now.

He had to figure out a way to discover the truth behind her words.

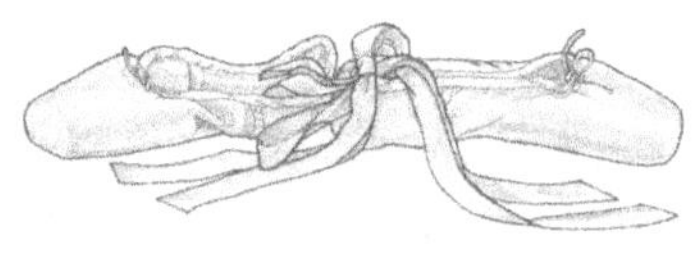

Iryna's chest tightened as she left Rick's phone in the hall and closed her door. Why hadn't Natalia answered the phone? It was after midnight in New York, which meant breakfast time in Kyiv. Natalia should be up. Maybe she didn't answer unknown numbers.

Heaving a sigh, Iryna let it go. She'd left a message asking Natalia to return her call when she could. She smacked her forehead as she remembered the time difference. Hopefully, Rick's phone would not ring in the middle of the night. She stepped farther into the room to focus on other things. Cassie's things.

A porcelain figurine on the dresser caught her attention. She remembered giving it to Cassie for her birthday—a gold-and-red firebird to match her friend's bright hair and sunny disposition. Her heart ached for the Carters and their loss, for Rick. How she and Cassie had teased him! He must miss her. Since she was an only child, Cassie had filled a void in Iryna's life, and she mourned her passing. How had Rick handled his sister's loss?

I wish she was here now so I could talk to her about him. She had dreamed of this day for months—how he would look, what he would say and do. Would he even remember her?

A spark of recognition was evident in his greeting. However, he spoke little. Ever the gentleman, his perfect manners made it hard to discern what he was thinking. But he still danced! He and Cassie had taken ballroom lessons at the same studio where Iryna practiced ballet. When Cassie first became sick, Iryna filled in for her twice. Rick tolerated her, but though worried for her friend, she was thrilled to be his partner. And nervous.

Like tonight. She was never nervous when she performed, but she had trembled when she settled into Rick's arms earlier. Did he notice? Though he lacked the flair of a professional, he led her smoothly through the dance, keeping perfect rhythm. He seemed impressed by her performance, but his responses were carefully diplomatic. If only she could read his thoughts. She conveyed her interest subtly but had no idea if he reciprocated.

Deliberately setting these thoughts aside, she rearranged her luggage. When she moved the bag holding the slippers she had used for her solo, something small and white fell to the floor—a matchbook. She bent to pick up the item and examined it. Reading the name and address of a Polish hotel printed on the front, she frowned and flipped it open. Inside, a word was printed in a language she didn't recognize above a phrase in English: *your turn soon.* Turn for what? Was this even meant for her? How did it get in her bag?

The presence of the foreign item sent a wave of uneasiness through her. *Tato will want to know about this.* She'd called him from the hotel, but now she would have to call him again. Slowly, she opened her door and peeked into the hall. Rick had already retrieved his phone. She couldn't wake him now. With a huff of frustration, she closed her door again.

Perhaps she should have given in to her friends' urging and bought a cell phone. No one ever believed she didn't have one. Her father, whose protectiveness borderlined on paranoia, viewed them as spy devices that made people too easy to track. He was finally forced to carry one for work, but Iryna hesitated to take the plunge. Everyone she knew was hostage to their electronic devices. There would be no going back once she acquired one.

She set a small framed photo of her parents on the nightstand next to the bed and laid the watch, the only piece of jewelry she wore, next to it. The arrangement made her feel more at home. In a room full of bittersweet memories and amid worries for Natalia, Iryna focused on a glimmer of hope. She had over a week to spend with the Carters, and she planned to make the most of it.

CHAPTER 4

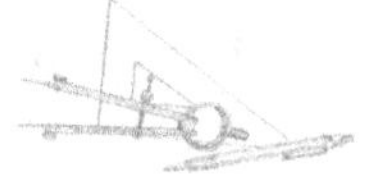

Rick eventually fell into a fitful sleep. He woke early, took a relaxing shower, and quietly headed downstairs to make some coffee, feeling vaguely unsettled. *Maybe I'll go for a jog.* Exercise always energized him.

As he reached the landing, he heard the television in the living room and wondered who was already up. Walking toward the room, he heard a gasp and "What? No! No!" in Ukrainian. Iryna sounded upset. He hesitated in the hallway, unsure if he should intrude. But when he heard a sob, his feet propelled him forward.

Iryna was staring at the television, watching the news. She was dressed in a leotard, leg warmers, and tights with a kind of tank top dress over it, but her face was ashen. A newscaster had just finished the international headlines, and the focus had switched to sports, so Rick had missed whatever upset her.

"What's wrong, Iryna? Can I do anything?"

"Oh," she cried as she wiped her eyes, "my friend Natalia! She, she …" Another sob escaped, and she struggled for control.

Rick walked over to Iryna and sat next to her. He placed a hand on her shoulder to comfort her and waited. His stomach twisted with foreboding, and he braced himself for shocking news.

"Natalia, she … her boyfriend was speaking at a protest …" Tears continued to stream down her cheeks, and Rick handed her a tissue. She dabbed her cheeks, but her eyes swam. "Natalia was there. It turned violent." Her body shuddered as she paused for breath.

"I've heard about the protests," Rick murmured, hoping to save her unnecessary explanation.

"It … the news …" She pointed at the television. "Someone threw a bottle and it hit her. It *killed* her! She was supposed to meet me at the airport, but she didn't make it. Now I know why." At this, Iryna burst into another round of tears. "She was supposed to dance the lead role in a ballet while I toured in America." Her pitch rose to a wail.

"I'm so sorry, Iryna." Rick took her hand and gave it a squeeze, at a loss for how to help. Iryna threw her arms around his neck and wept on his shoulder. What could he do? He had no idea how to help someone who lost a friend or loved one. No one had helped *him*.

As he patted her back, Iryna's tears soaked through his shirt. After a few sobs, she drew back. "Sorry, I … sorry."

"It's okay." He handed her another tissue, and she wiped her face and blew her nose. On her arm, an Orthodox cross dangled next to a pair of ballet slippers on a watchband that doubled as a charm bracelet. "Would you like me to pray with you?" he said, surprised to hear the words coming out of his mouth. He hadn't prayed since he was fourteen when his parents stopped attending church.

Iryna sniffled, sat up, and looked at him with mournful eyes, nodding. "Please." She sniffled again, her body shaking with each breath.

Oh boy, now what? He had to pray something. "Dear God" —he fumbled awkwardly for words—"something terrible has happened, and people are hurting. We need Your help. We pray for peace in Kyiv. We pray that You would comfort Natalia's family, comfort Iryna, and give them all peace. Amen."

He hoped that was okay. He knew God was supposed to love everyone, but why did He let things like this happen? It didn't make sense. That was why his parents had stopped attending church—they couldn't understand why God took their daughter away after they prayed and prayed for her healing. Rick didn't understand, either, but his prayer seemed to calm Iryna, evident by the fact she stopped crying.

"Thank you." She sniffled as she pulled another tissue from the box Rick held out to her.

"Did something happen?" Matt appeared in the doorway in his Sunday robe and slippers, evidently not expecting anyone else to be awake yet, either. Rick summarized what Iryna heard on the news.

Matt's face was drawn and stony, his mouth set in a firm hard line. Rick had seen this expression before—every time they took Cassie to a doctor's appointment. "That's terrible," Matt said, his posture stiff. "I'll make some calls and see if I can find out any more about it. What was her last name?"

"Androshchuk," answered Iryna, her voice as weak and pitiful as the bleat of a newborn lamb.

At the name, Matt jerked to attention. "Androshchuk. I'll look into this right away." He turned to leave but caught himself. "If there's anything we can do, Iryna, please let us know." Without waiting for an answer, he took out his phone and retreated down the hall toward the kitchen.

Rick stared after him. Why had his father reacted that way?

"I must go to the rehearsal," Iryna stated, drawing Rick's attention back to her. She tried to stand, but her legs buckled, and she plopped back onto the couch.

"You're in shock. Maybe you should lie down." He stood to make room for her to put her feet up.

She shook her head. "No, I must go. The others will have heard. I need to be with them." With a bitter laugh, she said, "Viktor will not stop rehearsals for anything."

"Then let me drive you. Did you eat breakfast?" Hunger would only make her more faint.

She nodded. "Yes … I had yogurt and some fruit. I put an apple and some nuts in my bag for later." Her face crumpled, but she fought back a fresh wave of tears as she motioned toward the gym bag sitting next to her on the floor.

"Okay, let me go put on some shoes and grab my keys." After a brief trip up and down the stairs, Rick stuck his head in the kitchen to inform Peters he didn't need to drive Iryna. He quickly ate half a banana and hurried to the foyer.

When he returned, Iryna had risen and washed her face, though she still appeared somber and tense. He ushered her outside, and they walked the short distance to pick up his sedan. He opened the door for her, and as he pulled out of the parking space, he scrambled for something to say to take her mind off the tragedy. Her normally sparkling eyes stared dully ahead.

"I don't have to work today," he offered. "Is it okay if I stay and watch you practice?"

"Sure." She sat quietly for a moment before looking sideways at him. "Maybe we will get you up on the stage. You are not a bad dancer. Have you ever studied the ballet?"

He grinned, glad to see a glimmer of her normal spunk. "No way. I'll be your practice audience."

After a short drive, they arrived at the theater. The other dancers huddled on the stage, but last night's noisy chatter was now replaced by hushed and worried tones. Rick took a seat in the shadows toward the back of the theater and settled in to watch.

The director, Viktor, walked to the center of the stage and addressed the troupe. Only half of the man's words reached Rick's ears. His Ukrainian vocabulary was too limited to understand it all anyway, but he gathered by the man's tone that he was expressing his sorrow over what happened. He switched to a sort of the-show-must-go-on pep talk and told everyone to start their stretches and warm-ups.

The warm-ups lasted for a long time. Rick didn't know anything about what dancers had to do to stay in shape. It was quite rigorous. In addition to the Ukrainian, many French terms were thrown about. "*Plie, i dva, i relive, i chotyry.*" The local dancers followed the strange mishmash of languages with minimal translation.

Eventually, Katherine nodded to Viktor, who clapped for attention and shouted instructions. The dancers moved to take their places for the opening scene, many of them flitting into the wings. Someone in the sound booth queued a recording. Rick supposed the orchestra wouldn't practice with the dancers until later in the week.

Iryna's performance the previous evening was breathtaking, but watching a story unfold with dozens of dancers was completely different. Though she still outshone them all, the rest of the cast acted as extensions of her, like a single organism.

Integrating the American dancers into the program took the bulk of their time. An interpreter aided in communicating Victor's directions to the additional ballerinas, and they soon danced as if they had been working with the Ukrainian company all along. However, in moments between dances, Iryna's shoulders drooped, and she had to shake herself before returning to her place on the stage. Her chin rose in stoic determination, and Rick's heart clenched in sympathy for the pain she was enduring. Masking the ache of loss was a skill he knew all too well.

Though he hated to miss a moment of the rehearsal, when his stomach growled, reminding him he'd missed breakfast, Rick went in search of a vending machine. *I should have grabbed some snacks from the kitchen.* He spotted a custodian and approached him. "Hey, man, is there anywhere nearby I can grab something to eat?"

The man shook his head. "Not much this time of day unless you're up for a walk. Nearest deli is several blocks away."

"What about a vending machine?"

The man replaced the lid on the trash can he was emptying and eyed Rick. "We got one in the employee lunchroom. I suppose I can take you back there. I'm due for a break."

"Thanks."

Rick followed the man through a side door and down a dimly lit hallway to a small dining area with a kitchenette and snack machine. "I'm goin' out for a smoke," the custodian said. "You can find your way back?"

"Sure. Thank you."

The man exited, and Rick shoved some change into the coin slot. He selected a couple snacks and opened one. The fluorescent lights flickered and ticked.

"Needs a new ballast," Rick muttered. As he stood alone in the room munching his snack, the hairs on the back of his neck prickled like someone was watching him. Glancing around for cameras and seeing none, he shook off the feeling, but the paranoia persisted. An urgent need to leave the room seized him.

When he stepped into the hallway, the impression intensified into an almost audible imperative: *Get out of here, now!*

With no good reason to linger, he lengthened his stride and barely restrained himself from running toward the door. He finished his snacks in the lobby and returned to the theater slightly jittery. The dancers resumed their places as he found his seat. The impression of imminent danger receded, but Rick couldn't shake the idea he was being watched. *Get a grip! There's nothing wrong. Hearing the story of Natalia's violent death has me on edge.* Only when Iryna took center stage did he fully focus on the rehearsal again.

At the end of the second act, the director said a few words and dismissed them for the day, perhaps cutting it short because of the sad news. Rick would have stood and applauded if the mood hadn't remained so solemn.

He met Iryna as she descended the stairs from the stage. "Your performance was wonderful. It hardly seems like you need to practice at all."

"Thank you. It looks that way *because* we practice. A lot." She gave him a wry half-smile and wiped the perspiration off her face with a towel. Her cheeks were flushed, and her eyes were bright. Only the tension in her jawline and the hard set to her shoulders gave away her inner turmoil. Even so, she was still beautiful.

"If I hadn't seen everything you did to prepare, I would have thought ballet was easy and fun. I had no idea it took so much work."

"It is very physically demanding. There is much risk of the injury. We have to be careful of ourselves."

Rick noticed she overused her definite articles. It was a common mistake for Slavic language speakers, and he found it endearing. "Well, let's walk to the car and take the drive back to the house and have the dinner," he said.

"Are you teasing me?" she asked with wide eyes.

"A little."

"How mean!" she said with pretended shock. "I have never heard you tease. I remember teasing you and goading—is that the right word? But I never made you mad. One time I even put the pepper in your tea and you just held it quietly and drank it."

"You did that? I thought it was supposed to be that way. I was trying to be polite."

"Hmph."

"You must realize that as the son of an ambassador, my parents drummed into me the importance of representing our nation well. Never offend anyone, eat everything put in front of you, and so on and so on." He paused, the rest of what she said sinking in. "Why were you trying to make me mad?"

"Oh ..." She looked away. "I guess because you were always so nice. It was a challenge." She snuck a glance at him, and he smiled, wondering if that was all there was to it.

"And you like a challenge?"

"Sometimes." She lifted her nose with an air of finality as if that was all she was going to say.

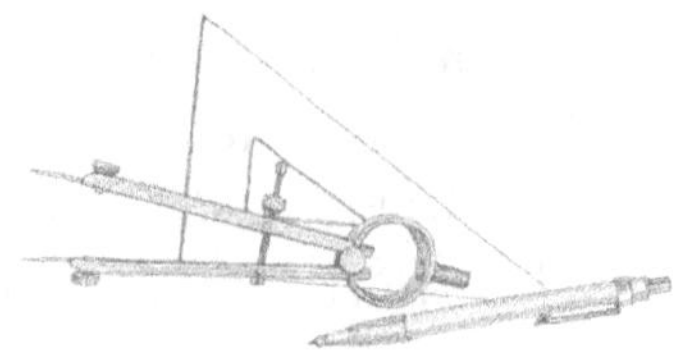

When Iryna met the family in the kitchen for an informal dinner, her hair hung in a damp braid down her back. This was the first time Rick had seen it without it being piled tightly on top of her head or in a bun. It nearly reached her waist.

"You must tell me what you like to eat, Iryna, or if you are on a special diet like an athlete in training. On Sundays, the cook leaves us food to heat up, and we usually eat in here." Beth rushed her words. "We have salad, soup, some salmon I just took out of the oven, and pasta."

"Salad and salmon would be lovely."

Beth served Iryna, and the rest of them helped themselves. Their dinner conversation was polite, and everyone avoided referencing anything upsetting. Beth prattled about local landmarks and suggested sightseeing tours while Iryna picked at her food. Matt contributed an occasional comment, but for most of the meal he stared vacantly into space.

"Mr. Carter ..." Iryna's voice cut through the strained silence. "Did you learn anything else about my friend Natalia?"

Matt shook his head. "Nothing more than the news reported. I'm sorry."

"That's okay." Iryna's posture deflated like a balloon. "Thank you for trying."

She stared at the endive and chopped apples on her plate. Rick shot his dad a question with his eyes. It was unusual for him to come up empty.

Later, he mouthed.

Rick nodded. The best thing he could do was give Iryna a way to occupy her mind for the evening. "So, Iryna, are you up for a challenging game of chess? I believe you owe me a rematch. Or maybe you need to go to bed early?"

"I think I can beat you quickly enough to get to bed on time." She rewarded his offer of distraction with a smile.

"I'll take care of the dishes," Beth said indulgently. "You two go on ahead."

Iryna insisted on helping with the dishes while Rick put away the leftovers. As soon as they finished, everyone adjourned to the living room. A wooden panel hid the television, and Rick set the chess set on the coffee table while his parents settled into comfortable chairs to read and watch their game.

Both players sat on the floor and hunched over the game board. "You can be white since you're younger," Rick said with a hint of a smirk.

Iryna arched an eyebrow and looked down her nose at him. "I will take white, but only because I won the last match."

Rick picked up the black queen and placed the piece on the board. "Don't expect to keep your title."

"Don't expect to win it from me easily." The sparkle in her eyes made him grin.

Iryna began with a classic opening, and Rick shored up his defenses. Despite setting up her pieces for an elaborate attack, Iryna made a few poor moves Rick was certain were errors. A couple of times, he caught her staring vacantly with her lips pressed together and a tightness around her eyes that spoke of hidden pain.

"Would you like to finish later?" Rick asked, his voice soft and sympathetic.

She shook herself. "No, I'm fine." She peered at the gameboard in concentration and caught up with him after a few turns.

The game lasted longer than their previous match, and it wasn't until nearly two hours had passed that Rick finally captured Iryna's last pawn, putting her king in check at the same time. Besides his king, he only had a bishop and a knight, and she managed to elude him for the required fifteen moves to force a stalemate.

"While I have been practicing ballet, you have been practicing your chess." Iryna wagged a finger at him.

"I still haven't beaten you. I'll have to practice more."

Iryna stifled a yawn. "I really must go to bed now. Good night, everyone!"

Rick stood as his parents said their good nights and walked with her to the stairs. "I have to go into the office for a while tomorrow, but I can drop you off at the theater first and then pick you up when you're ready, if that's okay."

"That would be great." She stood on the first step with her hand on the rail. He put his hand over hers and studied her face with concern.

"Are you going to be all right?"

Iryna looked away and shook her head. "Not for a while."

He refrained from saying "everything works out for good," or "it just takes time," or any other empty platitudes. He knew they wouldn't help. Instead, he squeezed her hand and said, "That's okay. I'm here if you need me. You can borrow my phone again or use the house phone if you want to call anyone without roaming charges." He still hadn't seen her with a cell phone, which was odd.

"Thank you." She climbed the stairs slowly, and Rick reentered the living room.

Beth rose. "Poor girl, to be away from her home and her family and have to deal with this loss alone while working herself to death."

"She's not alone, Mom. She has us and the rest of her company. They are grieving as well."

"That's true." Beth bit her lip. "I wish we could do more for her. Maybe you could take her sightseeing to keep her mind off things."

Rick didn't put her off this time. "I'd love to if she's up for it and not too busy."

Beth glanced sideways at him. "She has certainly turned into a beauty."

Rick hid a smile. His mother was incorrigible. "Yes. She was horribly ugly as a child," he said with a straight face. Iryna's teasing was rubbing off on him.

"Oh, you're impossible!"

He grinned and kissed her good night.

After his mom left the room, Rick sat next to his father. "So, what did you find out, really?"

Matt sighed. "It's not good. None of the news crews caught Natalia on camera, but a bystander captured a brief, distant video of her. Turns out the glass wasn't thrown randomly. Someone snuck up behind her and hit her with a full vodka bottle. Deliberately singled her out."

"Really? She was murdered? That's crazy." Rick was incredulous.

"She wasn't even part of the protest, just there to support her boyfriend who was one of the speakers. Someone took advantage of all the activity and shouting to knock her on the head. She might have survived, but it was a while before anyone noticed, and the police had to clear out the mob before they reached her. She died of internal hemorrhaging. It actually happened"—Matt paused as he looked at his watch—"two and a half days ago now, just as Iryna and her troupe were leaving for New York."

"Wow. That's terrible. Any leads on the killer?"

"The video was too blurry, and whoever it was wore a hooded sweatshirt and cap."

"Did they check nearby security cameras?"

"Nothing better than the cell phone footage. The killer didn't enter the metro station, either, at least not without changing clothes." Mr. Carter shook his head. "Vasyl thinks it's better if Iryna doesn't know the details."

Rick wasn't sure about that. If it was his friend, he'd want to know everything. Apparently, Iryna's father had the same habit of sheltering his family from reality as his dad did. Knowing wouldn't change anything, though. Since there was nothing they could do about it, Vasyl was probably right.

As he got ready for bed, an uncomfortable thought struck him. What had his dad hidden from *him*? He knew few details about his father's work prior to his ambassadorship in Ukraine, except that he and Vasyl had both been stationed in Poland in the 1980s. His dad was almost like a spy in those days, secretly undermining the communist regime while working at the embassy. He wasn't sure exactly what Vasyl's role in overthrowing the government had been, if any.

Most of it happened before he was born. His mother had returned to the States for his birth because of the highly volatile political situation, but the two men had become friends during their time in Poland. It was partly due to these political connections that his father had been able to secure the role of ambassador to Ukraine after the fall of the Iron Curtain. What exactly had they done in Poland?

Rick glanced at the matchbook on his nightstand. *Poland.* Did the matchbook mean anything? Had someone placed it there to send some sort of message? He'd have to mention it to his father tomorrow. And, depending on his reaction, maybe push for a little more information.

CHAPTER 5

Rick rose early the next morning to be sure he was ready whenever Iryna needed to leave. Then he messaged his assistant he might be a little late. His office was in the opposite direction as the theater from his parents' house, but it was worth missing work to spend more time with her. And she would need a friend to lean on through the grieving process. Even if he didn't know how to help, he could at least be present.

Peters was in the kitchen making his breakfast when Rick walked in. The chauffer's uniform, by his own choice, consisted of black slacks, a white shirt, a black tie, and whatever jacket he felt like wearing. Today, he wore a charcoal cardigan.

"Hear you're putting me out of a job," Peters said.

Rick felt himself flush. "Well, she is an old family friend. Thought I should drive her."

The corner of Peters's mouth twitched. "I suppose I can find something else to do." Despite his graying hair, Peters was fit and energetic and enjoyed keeping busy. If he didn't drive Iryna, he would have plenty of projects to tinker with.

Rick had just finished pouring himself a cup of coffee when Iryna entered the kitchen. Peters bid her good morning and excused himself to his room.

Iryna walked up to Rick and peered into his mug. A slight

puffiness around her eyes attested to recent tears, flooding him with a desire to hold and comfort her. But not wanting to disrupt her fragile equanimity by reminding her of her grief, he refrained.

"Would you like some coffee?" Rick gestured to the single-serve coffee maker. "We have several varieties." He opened a cupboard with a shelf full of individual coffee pods.

"Do you have any tea?" She stood on her tiptoes to study the contents of the cupboard.

"Umm, yes." He shuffled a couple boxes around. "Green tea, English breakfast, or a selection of herbal teas."

Iryna chose English breakfast, and Rick prepared it for her.

"Did you get any sleep?" he asked as she grabbed a yogurt from the refrigerator.

She sighed. "A little. Considering I've traveled across the world and just lost my good friend, that I slept at all is a miracle. The bed is really comfortable, and I love the room."

She bit her lip as if she wanted to say more but held back. He changed the subject. "What do you have to do to get ready for next weekend's performances?"

"Today and tomorrow are going to be very strenuous practices, working on everything until it is perfect. Wednesday and Thursday will be less so, as we will only go through it once each day with the orchestra before our first performance on Friday."

"I will head to the theater as soon as I'm finished with work, but if you need me earlier, just give me a call." He pulled out his phone. "What's your number? I'll add it to my contacts."

"Oh, I don't have a phone."

Rick stared at her. "What? How can you not have a phone?"

"I have a phone at my apartment in Kyiv, of course. And I wear a watch. I will wait until you pick me up."

While he'd noticed the absence of a phone, it never occurred to him that she had none at all. Rick filed away this strange detail to review later and grabbed his keys to drive her to the theater.

"I do need to call my father," she said as she lowered herself into the car a few minutes later. "I was distracted yesterday and forgot. May I borrow your phone? I know the number."

"Of course." He logged into his device and handed it to her before pulling into the street. He did not deliberately eavesdrop on their conversation, but a few phrases caught his ear. "Did you say 'matchbook'?"

"*Prosto sekundu*," Iryna told her father before glancing at Rick. "*Tak*, I mean, yes. Why?"

"Because I found a matchbook from Poland in my jacket pocket."

Iryna spoke rapidly into the phone. Vasyl raised his voice on the other end. "What did it say inside?" she asked Rick.

"Inside?" He frowned. "I didn't look inside."

Iryna repeated his words in Ukrainian for her father's benefit. She listened for a few more minutes before ending the call. In a low voice, she said, "There was a message inside the matchbook I found. It said, 'Your turn soon.'"

"'Your turn soon,'" Rick repeated, perplexed. "What does it mean?"

Iryna shook her head. "He's not sure, and he's worried. Especially since you got one too. He said to be careful, and he's going to investigate."

"I'll check inside mine to see if it says the same thing."

Despite heavy traffic, they arrived at a reasonable time. Rick pulled over on Sixty-Second street and opened the door for Iryna. As he drove away, he turned back to look at her, and she smiled and waved. His heart warmed. The tragedy in Kyiv had prevented him from inquiring any further into her feelings for him, but his regard for her was increasing by the minute. At the very least, he found her extremely attractive. Mesmerizing. Immensely talented. Comfortable to talk to and be around.

What was her opinion of him? That he was nice? A

challenge? What happened when he failed to be a challenge and became just another starstruck, adoring fan? Women found him good-looking, but that wasn't enough to form a long-lasting relationship. Did he want a long-lasting relationship? He'd never met a woman who made him think about it before. He definitely wished she was staying longer than a week.

When he reached his office in Brooklyn, his assistant Mark met him at the door, bouncing on his toes. Mark was a competent young draftsman still working on his master's degree. As Rick's only employee, he also had to double as secretary. Mark took his job very seriously, sometimes more seriously than Rick, but was jumpy and obsessive when left in charge.

"Sir, several clients called, and the Dore project proposal needs your final approval." Mark waved a notepad in the air.

Rick groaned when he read the first message. A client building apartments in a tiny lot was trying to get the most from the space and called daily with questions about the design and floor plan. "What does Mr. Acosta want now?"

"He wants to know why the hallways have to be so wide."

Rick called Mr. Acosta first to get the worst out of the way. After explaining numerous times about building codes and safety requirements, he ended the call on an amiable note. He rubbed his forehead and tackled the rest of the pile. It took him until lunchtime to catch up on all the calls. He approved Mark's final drafts for the project proposal due the next day and ensured the model and presentation were ready.

While reviewing specifications for a new project, his mind kept wandering to Iryna. Was she able to concentrate? Were the rehearsals going well? He would have to leave earlier than usual to pick her up on time, and Mark wouldn't be happy about that. He hadn't talked to his mom about staying at the house all week, either, though it wasn't really necessary. She would be immensely pleased. He should probably call her now and talk about it in private so she wouldn't say anything embarrassing in front of Iryna.

He dialed the number, feeling somewhat foolish. He might as well be back in high school with his mom hovering over his shoulder every time he talked to a girl on the phone.

"Hello?"

"Hi, Mom. Thought I'd make sure it wouldn't put you out if I stayed the rest of the week."

"You know better than that. I was counting on it. I told Martha to plan on four for dinner. Unless you're taking Iryna out?" she hinted.

"She has a long day today and tomorrow. I was thinking of taking her somewhere Wednesday or Thursday."

"Well, we're flexible, so whatever you want to do is fine!"

Beth's chipper tone conveyed her happiness, but fortunately, she didn't press him further.

"Okay, see you this evening."

He managed to get a little more work done before it was time to leave. Mark frowned at Rick on his way out, but the draftsman could handle the office by himself for an hour. It would do him good to take on the responsibility.

When he arrived, Rick parked in the garage and went inside to wait for the rehearsal to finish. After the director gave everyone some final instructions, gasps of dismay mixed with congratulations and light applause followed. The dancers gathered around Karina, the understudy, and gave her hugs and pats on the back. One male dancer kissed her and twirled her around. The American extras hung back to give them space. Eventually, everyone picked up their things and left. Rick intercepted Iryna as she left the stage, and she filled him in.

"Karina is going back to Kyiv to replace Natalia. We are sad to see her go, especially her husband, Yegor, but it is the good opportunity for her. She will miss seeing the rest of America, but she will play the lead role." Iryna sighed and blinked several times. "Though no one wants to get the lead this way."

"Oh." It would be tough to finally get a promotion only

because the person better than you died. "So who will be your understudy now?"

"They are sending Masha Zherdeva over to take her place."

"Why move everyone around? This Masha couldn't do Natalia's part?" He thought understudies had to memorize all the parts. That was the whole point.

"She could"—Iryna grimaced—"and probably wanted to, but she is not quite as good as Karina. Masha is technically perfect but lacks artistry. That, and she is difficult to work with, so no one wants to put her in a leading role full-time. This isn't a temporary replacement like someone coming down with the flu or twisting an ankle. This is permanent. Which reminds me—a pastor at the nearby Ukrainian Orthodox church agreed to hold a memorial for Natalia on Wednesday evening for the ballet corps to attend. Can we go?"

"Absolutely, if you want to."

"Thank you. I would like to go. I feel badly not being able to attend her official service, but this will help."

The last memorial service Rick had attended was Cassie's. It was also the last time he had been to a church. His jaw tensed. Because of his memories, it would be an emotional service for him too.

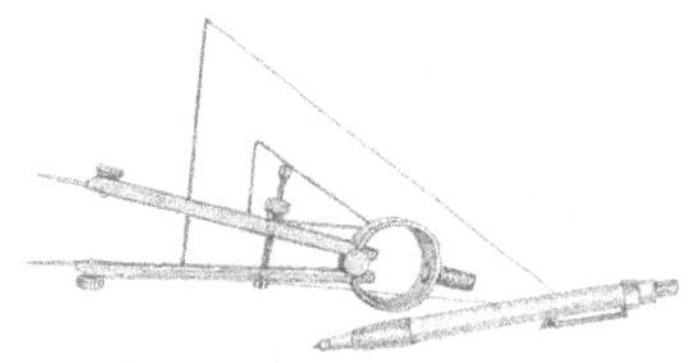

After a more formal dinner in the dining room, Iryna retired early. Matt asked Rick to accompany him to the study while Beth retreated to the exercise room.

Matt closed the door and motioned him into a chair. "I spoke with Vasyl again today."

Rick nodded. He'd expected that. "What did he say?"

"Even though the government over there has their hands full right now, he is concerned about this incident with Natalia Androshchuk," Matt continued. "As am I. Her father is an old friend."

"Natalia's father?" asked Rick in surprise. This was news to him. No wonder his dad had jumped to investigate.

"Yes," Matt answered without elaborating. "It appears someone may have pretended to be one of the protestors simply for the purpose of provoking a clash with the police and working up the crowd. The organization behind the protest denies starting any trouble."

"Do they think it has any connection with the murder?"

"It's going to be difficult to determine. It would take a great number of interviews and footage review, and they don't have the manpower for that right now. He doesn't want to worry Iryna with it yet."

"All right," Rick agreed, though reluctant.

"More worrisome to me are these matchbooks." He tossed one to Rick. "This is the one from your room."

Rick flipped it open. His stomach clenched as he read the words Iryna had quoted. *Your turn soon.* He pointed to the word above it. "What does this word 'sol-o-dars-nick' mean?"

"Solidarity is the name of an independent trade union that helped end communist rule in Poland."

"Did you work with them?" He kept his tone even, but a hint of anger and frustration crept in. Why was he only learning about this now?

"I may have." His dad offered a wry smile, then sighed. "But we have no idea why anyone would bring it up now or what it means. Someone at the party must have slipped them into your pocket and Iryna's bag. Which is disturbing."

Rick agreed. "It isn't … you don't think it could just be a prank?"

"I don't know. The reference to Solidarity is too specific."

Rick leaned forward as Katherine's comment niggled at his brain. "One of the trainers asked about your time in Poland."

Matt's eyes glinted. "Really? What did you say?"

"I said it was before my time."

Matt pursed his lips.

Rick suddenly realized what he'd done. "Oh. I confirmed it, didn't I? Sorry."

"If she was fishing, yes." He scribbled a note on his legal pad.

"So, what do we do now?"

"For now, you and Iryna sit tight. Vasyl and I will do some digging. Just be careful until we know what this is about."

A nagging uneasiness dogged Rick as he left his father working at the computer. Too agitated to sleep, he went for a jog instead of joining his mother in the exercise room. Already hours past dusk, the park across the street was closed, so he turned right and jogged a circuit around the quiet neighborhood. Thoughts whirled around his head—worry about the murder and its implications, the significance of the matchbooks, concern for Iryna, uncertainty about how to proceed with her, or if he should. Getting to know someone who lived on the opposite side of the world would be difficult. He pushed aside his thoughts and tried to enjoy the exercise.

Headlights shone on him from behind, moving slowly. His dad's warning rang in his ears. Rick turned the corner, and so did the car. He ran up the steps of a nearby house as if he planned to knock on the door. The car passed him and continued down the street. Unable to silence the warning bells in his head, he returned to his route and pushed himself faster.

After a couple miles, his tension lessened, and he returned to take a shower. The streaming water relaxed him. *I don't have to decide anything about Iryna right now. We can see how things go the next few days.* There was no reason to rush into anything, especially with vague threats looming over them, and he had nothing to lose if he did choose to pursue a relationship at some point.

Once he'd dried off and dressed for bed, he lay down and stared at the ceiling. His mind mocked his conclusions. *There is something to lose if I pursue a relationship.* Cassie's loss would always hurt. He thought about Natalia's family grieving her loss. Loss was inevitable. *What I really have to decide is if Iryna is worth the risk.* The memory of her face left little doubt. No matter the risk, he lacked the power to resist.

CHAPTER 6

"Good morning." Rick couldn't help but offer a wide grin when Iryna walked into the kitchen. After hearing her coming, he pushed the button to brew her tea.

"Good morning. Will you be driving me today?" she asked as she peered curiously at the coffee maker.

"I can drop you off, but I have to head over to Hempstead in the afternoon to present a project proposal, so I won't be able to pick you up," he said regretfully. He handed her the mug of tea and brewed a medium roast coffee pod for himself.

Iryna breathed in the aroma of her steaming beverage. "Mm. Did you make this just for me?" Her smile melted Rick's insides.

"Of course."

"Thank you." She sat at the table and emptied a packet of sugar into her tea. "It's okay if you can't pick me up. The consulate has arranged for us to tour the city. We will see the Time Square and go to a ball game at Yankee Stadium."

Rick brightened. "I could join you there and bring you home afterward."

Iryna's face lit up at his suggestion. "That sounds perfect. I'll ask if I can leave a ticket for you at the sales box." Her eyes crinkled as she sipped her tea, and his heart did a flip.

Rick set some bowls of yogurt on the table and sat, holding

his coffee. *A lifetime of breakfasts like this would not be too many,* he thought as he gazed across the table at her.

Iryna scooped a spoonful of yogurt into her mouth. "This is good," she remarked. Her eyes darted around the kitchen, a thoughtful expression on her face.

"What is it?"

"Would it be possible … I would like to cook a meal for your family. Maybe breakfast would be best. If I wrote a list of items, could Peters shop them for me?"

"Sure." He fished a pen and notepad out of a drawer and handed them to her. "And we'll pay for them, so don't worry about that."

"Are you sure? I brought some American dollars."

"Of course. You're cooking, so we'll buy."

"Okay." She bit her lip, forming the English letters with care. "I will write the list in English, Ukrainian, and Russian in case he needs to show it to a clerk. I don't know what your labels will look like."

"Good idea."

"Your mother will not mind if I use her kitchen?"

Rick grinned. "She'll try to protest that guests should not be working, but she will love it. If we leave it as a surprise, then you won't have her hovering over you and talking the whole time."

"I would not mind either way." Iryna smiled as she returned the paper. "Peters will be able to join us for the breakfast, yes? I included an invitation with my list."

"Of course. That's very thoughtful. He usually eats with us. He just likes to give us space when we have company." Rick slipped the list into Peters's slot on the hanging organizer by the door before finishing his breakfast.

They washed the few dirty dishes together as naturally as if they'd been doing it for years. Rick stole a glance at Iryna as she wiped a spoon dry. *I wonder what she's like when she's angry. She's exuberant and passionate with her art. Does she have an intense temperament? Would she throw things and yell?* She never snapped at her coworkers. He wished he could watch another practice. Was she still the little girl who put pepper in his tea? There was so much he wanted to find out about her.

On the way to the theater, Rick used all his conversational skills to gather information without prying. "What is it like to have an understudy? Does she have to mimic you, or does she do her own thing?"

"Well"—Iryna pursed her lips in thought—"understudies usually bring their personal style to the dance, but Masha has none, so she studies my movements while I dance and copies me. It will be a little more work for me to have her here because Alexei likes me to repeat steps for her sometimes. She arrived yesterday evening, so we'll have to bring her up to speed today."

"How can she be an understudy if she needs that much help? I thought they were supposed to be the second-best dancers."

"Oh, Masha is good," insisted Iryna. "Her execution is flawless. She has no creative interpretation, so I model that for her."

While humming a few bars of music, Iryna gracefully moved her arm. Rick swerved slightly before fixing his eyes back on the road.

"I suppose that's the difference between being an architect and a foreman."

"Mm, yes, probably. What is it like being an architect?"

Rick appreciated Iryna talking with him rather than playing with a phone. More than one woman he dated had sat texting or even talking to someone on the phone while he drove instead of talking to him. Not that he was vain enough to expect to monopolize a woman's time, but the purpose of a date was to get to know someone, and you couldn't do that if you didn't talk.

"It's an exciting challenge," he said. "Designing or redesigning a building requires creative problem solving. You have to understand the client's needs and the restrictions of the space and find a way to meet them both."

"Can you take me to see something you designed?"

It gratified him that she was interested enough in what he was doing to want to see something in person. "If it wouldn't interfere with your pre-performance routine, I could take you to see something on Saturday morning."

She clapped her hands in delight. "I would enjoy that."

Rick's pulse increased. It was time to broach the subject of dinner on Thursday.

"Would you like to go out to dinner with me on Thursday evening, if it won't keep you up too late?" He held his breath for her reply, but he didn't have to wait very long.

"Oh yes, that would be very nice." Her eyes lit up. "I can sleep in on Friday morning because the curtain call for the performance is later than our rehearsals normally start. I think I can manage to stay up for the dinner."

Rick couldn't help but grin as he pulled up outside the theater. "I'll see you at the game," he said as he opened the door for her.

"Good luck with your presentation." She waved as he drove off.

Mark met him at the door of his office, nursing the air of a martyr. "Mr. Carter, you remember you have an important presentation this afternoon?"

"Yes. Let's get to work."

Suitably chastened, Rick appeased his assistant by going over the presentation several times and practicing what he was going to say. Mark ran the slideshow, and they rehearsed until they knew the timing down to the millisecond. By lunch, they had worked out all the kinks. They loaded the models and other equipment into the car and took off for Hempstead.

They arrived in plenty of time to set up in the company boardroom before the meeting began. Rick placed the model in the center of the table and arranged his brochures while Mark hooked up the computer and projector. At the appointed time, the prospective clients arrived, and the company president introduced Rick to the board members. Then he presented his proposal.

When he finished showing the last slide, the executives exchanged smiles and nods. Several members asked follow-up questions and held side discussions. After satisfying everyone's queries, the president thanked him for his presentation and told him they'd be in touch soon. Rick left them with the model and some pamphlets to talk it over.

Mark let out a long breath as soon as they stepped into the elevator. "I think that went well." He offered a tentative assessment, as if fearing fate might frown on his presumption.

"Couldn't have gone better. Great job with the slideshow. Now it's up to the clients."

They loaded the rest of the gear into the car and headed back to the office. Rick let Mark off early to make up for leaving him in charge. He quickly listened to the phone messages and sent a few emails before grabbing his keys to head to his car.

He debated whether to drive straight to the stadium and arrive a little early or run home to change into something more casual and risk being a little late. He decided to go to his parents' house to throw on a jersey and pick up a baseball glove.

His mom met him in the foyer with raised eyebrows. "I thought you weren't coming home for dinner."

"Just changing real quick, Mom," he explained as he ran upstairs. "Can you ask Peters to drive me?" he called down as an afterthought. He might be tired by the time the game was over, and he wanted to give his full attention to Iryna.

Wasting no time, he changed into a Yankees jersey and jeans, grabbed a cap and glove, and hurried back downstairs.

"Peters is pulling the car around," his mother said.

"Thanks, Mom." He smiled and kissed her on the cheek.

"Have fun, Ricky," she said as he walked out the door. He heard her sigh and remark on how boyish he looked before the latch clicked.

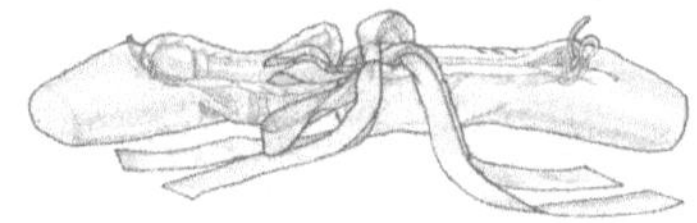

Iryna rubbed the fuzzy wool of her new scarf against her cheeks as she waited with the rest of the company for the train to take them to the baseball stadium. Their afternoon of sightseeing and shopping had been an exciting whirlwind of lights and sounds. The only way she would have enjoyed it more was if Rick had been there.

"This station feels like home, doesn't it?" asked Yegor at her shoulder. "If I closed my eyes, I could imagine I was in the Metro in Kyiv. Except for all the people speaking American, that is."

Iryna laughed. "The New York accent is much different from the British, isn't it?" Their last tour had taken them through Western Europe as far as London.

"Yes, it is. I can hardly understand it." The crowd pressed forward, causing Yegor to shuffle closer to her. "Here comes the train."

Iryna heard the clack of the wheels on the tracks, and time slowed. Her heart pounded in her ears.

Get back!

The impression of impending peril was nearly audible. Iryna glanced at her feet. She was safely behind the yellow line. This mode of transportation was as familiar as a waltz, so why was she scared?

Get back!

The warning rang so loudly in her mind, Iryna whipped around and pushed through the waiting commuters until several rows of people separated her from the edge of the platform. A hand gripped her arm, and she jumped.

"Are you okay?" Katherine asked. "Is something wrong?"

Iryna shook her head. The train rolled into the station and screeched to a halt. Her pulse slowed with it, and she took a deep breath. "I'm fine."

The crowd surged toward the open doors, carrying Iryna and Katherine with it. Katherine found her a seat and stood in front of her. "Breathe. Deep breaths," Katherine urged. "You look like you're having a panic attack."

"I'm okay," Iryna insisted. She'd never had a panic attack and wasn't convinced that's what she was experiencing. Whatever it was, it was over now.

She leaned back and closed her eyes. *I'm fine. It was nothing. I'm fine.* The curtain had fallen on the scene, but she couldn't shake the impression that danger lurked in the wings, waiting for its next cue.

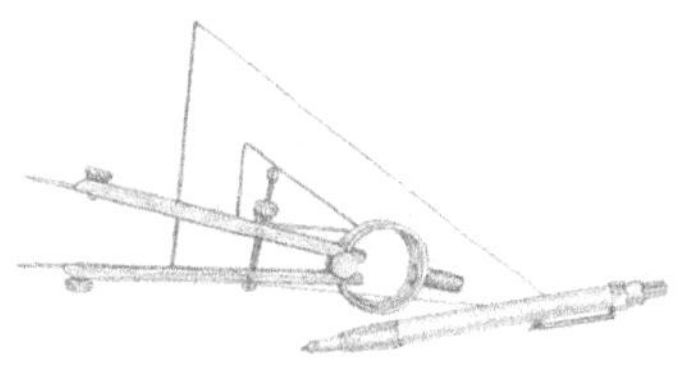

Rick pounded his fist in his glove as he sat in the back of the family limousine. He hummed to himself and tapped his foot impatiently.

"Thanks, Peters. I've got the door," he said when they pulled up to the stadium, opening it before the car stopped moving. "I'll text you when the game is over."

He slammed the door as he headed to will call to pick up the ticket Iryna had left for him. He arrived at the seats reserved for the dancers just as the players took the field.

"Rriiick! Over here!" Iryna squealed and waved. "This is so fun!" She grabbed his arm and shook it with excitement. Luckily, he wasn't carrying any popcorn, or it would have spilled everywhere.

He settled into the seat next to her and noticed her new scarf and NYC sweatshirt. "Did you enjoy your tour? It looks like you did some shopping."

"Yes! It was so much fun. So many interesting things—things I had only heard about, but now I have seen them for myself. New York is so big."

"What was your favorite part? Times Square? Rockefeller Center? Or maybe the subway," he teased. "That should have made you feel at home—" He broke off as Iryna's face fell and she stared at her hands. He leaned toward her. "What's wrong?"

"I … It's nothing. I had a panic attack or something while we were waiting for the train."

"I'm sorry. There are a lot of people—"

"No." She cut him off. "That wasn't why. I felt uneasy. Like I was in danger. I know that sounds silly—"

"Actually, it doesn't. I had a similar feeling at the theater the other day when the janitor let me into the staff area, and again while jogging last night. It was weird." Iryna stared at him intently as he continued. "It was almost like something was telling me to get out of there."

"I felt the same," she exclaimed. "But nothing happened."

"Maybe it was just the power of suggestion after finding those matchbooks with the weird messages."

"Maybe." Iryna didn't sound convinced.

The crowd roared as the home team took the field, bringing Rick's and Iryna's focus back to their surroundings. Fans in one section across the field chanted loudly.

"What are they doing?" asked Iryna.

"That's the Bleacher Creatures taking roll call,'" Rick

explained. "They chant the name of each starting player until they wave back."

During almost every play, one member of the troupe or other tapped him on the shoulder to ask a question.

"What is 'ball'? Isn't it always ball?"

"When can the player steal?"

"Please explain, what is 'error'?" and "What is it—'box seats suck'? Are they empty, like vacuum? Why sit on box?"

"This area we are sitting in is a box," Rick explained.

The dancers found that humorous. "Ha ha! We suck!"

Baseball was compared to European "football." Baseball was not as fast-paced, but everyone agreed it would be hard to hit such a small ball with a stick, and the fans were just as rowdy. The dancers clapped and cheered and booed along with the rest of the fans. They yelled and pointed like excited children when they appeared on the screen and the announcer stated that the Ukrainian National Ballet was in attendance.

Rick enjoyed getting to know the dancers. They were good-natured and open and seemed determined to enjoy themselves. Rick wondered if Masha was there, but he didn't notice anyone new. She must be back at the hotel recovering from jet lag and a long day of rehearsing.

Rick showed Sergei, the male dancer on his left, how to wear the glove and the pocket that helped players catch the ball. "Make sure you close the glove around it so it doesn't fall out, like this." He demonstrated the technique.

"Wow, thanks!" Sergei practiced opening and closing the glove with dizzying rapidity. He had such great balance, flexibility, and extension, Rick was certain if a foul ball popped behind the net in Sergei's vicinity, he would contort himself into a position to catch it.

As soon as Rick had a moment to turn to Iryna, he gave her his baseball cap. "Now you're a real fan." He grinned as she pulled her braid through the back of the hat.

A consular official who shared the burden of answering

questions, especially for those who couldn't speak English well, bought everyone hot dogs and drinks. Rick almost forgot to eat his food because he was so absorbed with watching Iryna.

"What kind of meat is this?" she asked as she eyed the mustard-covered bun.

"I'm not even sure." Rick watched for her reaction as she took her first bite.

Iryna chewed, nodded, and swallowed. "It's good!" When she finished, she licked her fingers, smearing yellow on her cheek.

"Hold still," he said, lifting his napkin. She froze while he gently wiped her cheek. The intimate action caused his fingers to tingle.

"Thank you." She flashed him a brilliant smile. "I'm having a wonderful time. I think everyone else is too."

"There's nothing better than a baseball game to introduce someone to American culture. It's called 'America's Pastime.'" He swallowed as he noticed her enthralled expression. "I've been to plenty of games, but I've never had more fun than I'm having tonight."

A loud crack turned their attention to the field, and the crowd roared as the ball sailed over the wall. The crackle between him and Iryna simmered as the energy around them rose. Rick was glad for the distraction—he needed more time to think before acting on the attraction.

Sergei paid close attention to the batters' swings. When a player came to the plate who had a tendency to get under the ball, Sergei moved around, switching seats when he thought it would give him a better angle. Halfway through the game, his persistence was rewarded. A ball popped high in the air and flew over the net. Iryna squealed and covered her head while Sergei leaped. The ball smacked into his glove.

Shocked, he nearly dropped it. "I caught it!" he cried with delight.

"Well done, Sergei!" Iryna and others congratulated him.

"Look." Rick pointed at the jumbotron. "You're on the big screen." Sergei's catch was replayed with a quip that maybe baseball players should take ballet.

Between innings, Iryna stood and said, "I need to use the toilet."

Rick rose from his seat, but rather than let her pass, he exited before her to lead the way. "I'll go with you." After her experience in the subway, he wasn't going to let her go alone. He held out his hand, and she kept a tight grip on it as he led her to the closest restroom. "I'll wait right here."

"Thanks. I'll just be a minute."

Rick shoved his hands into his jeans pockets and leaned against the wall. The short line at the concession stand tempted him to purchase a snack, but he resisted. His eyes wandered, observing the passersby. In a dark corner by the stairs, he spied one of the dancers—Maxim, he thought—with a stranger. They stood close, facing the wall, so he couldn't see what they were doing. The stranger reached inside his windbreaker and handed something to Maxim, who stuffed it inside the pocket of his hoodie.

I hope that's not what I think it is, Rick thought grimly. Maxim turned and hustled back to the stadium entrance while the stranger sauntered off in the other direction. Rick made a mental note to avoid the man in the future. He didn't want to be near anyone carrying illegal drugs.

By the time Rick and Iryna returned to their seats, there was a player on second with one out. The pitcher struck out the next two batters, to the delight of the crowd. Both teams scored more runs with several exciting plays, but Sergei's catch was the highlight of the night.

Eventually, the Yankees won. Rick texted Peters to bring the limo around, and he and Iryna said goodbye to the rest of the group as they headed back to the subway. When she slipped her hand into his, a pleasant warmth spread from his fingers to the tips of his ears. Her touch repelled the chilly night air better than a steaming mug of coffee. *Does she know how she affects me? Is she holding my hand because she wants to, or is she worried about getting lost in the crowd?*

Before he could pursue this train of thought, Peters pulled up. Rick opened the door for Iryna and himself to save time in the heavy traffic. When they were settled in the car, Iryna blinked and took a deep breath through her nose.

"Don't pretend you're not tired. I know that trick," teased Rick.

"What trick?"

"The yawning without looking like you're yawning trick."

Iryna laughed. "Well, I am very tired. I could probably fall asleep right now."

Rick angled his body in the corner. "Here. You can use me as a pillow and sleep if you want to."

"I think I will," Iryna murmured. She nestled against him with her head on his shoulder. In minutes, she was asleep, breathing slowly and evenly.

Rick bent forward and rested his cheek against her hair to keep her from jostling too much as the car turned. A protectiveness rose up in him. Holding her this way filled a need deep in his soul he didn't know he had. It reminded him of what it felt like to be an older brother. Other than his mother, he hadn't allowed himself to feel protective of anyone since Cassie died. The prospect of opening himself up to being hurt was scary, but his desire to be near Iryna grew stronger every moment. By the time they stopped in front of the house, he hadn't drawn any closer to resolving his inner conflict.

I know one thing for sure. A week is not going to be enough time with her.

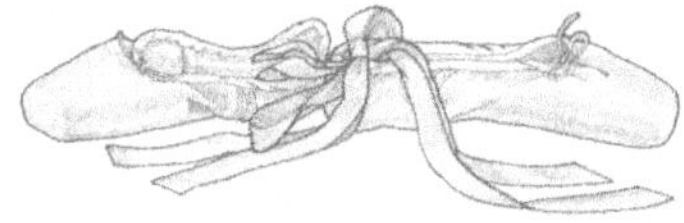

"Hey," Rick whispered in her ear, "We're back."

Iryna woke slowly, stretched, and opened her mouth in an enormous yawn. With a groan, she leaned forward to grab the cap she'd set on the floor. She shivered when she left his warmth.

Rick helped her out of the car and offered her his arm. *He is so kind and thoughtful—walking me to the restroom, being my pillow, comforting me after the news about Natalia. But he is so measured and polite. A week is not going to be enough time for him to make a move,* she determined. *I'm going to have to make one first.*

When Rick stopped in front of her room, she placed a hand on his chest and gazed into his eyes. "Thank you for taking such good care of me." She stood on tiptoes and kissed him tenderly on the cheek. When a look of surprise flashed across his face, she lost her nerve and backed away before he could respond. "Good night."

She'd almost closed her door all the way before she heard him wish her good night in return. She could only hope his delayed reaction meant he enjoyed her surprise kiss.

CHAPTER 7

The next morning, Iryna rose earlier than normal. Though tired, she was used to a rigorous schedule. Checking the refrigerator, she discovered Peters had been successful in acquiring a carton of *kefir*, a type of thin yogurt drink ubiquitous in Eastern Europe. After a short search for the rest of the ingredients, she whipped up a batch of Ukrainian pancakes served with jam and sour cream. She only burned one while she hunted for a spatula. As she flipped the last pancake from the frying pan onto a plate, she heard conversation in the hallway.

Beth burst into the room. "Oh Iryna, what a surprise!" She clasped her hands together. "You didn't have to do this. You already gave us gifts."

Rick entered the kitchen, followed by Mr. Carter and Peters. "I rousted everyone from bed so they could eat while it's hot."

"Smells great." Mr. Carter peered eagerly around Rick's shoulder.

"Come and sit." She waved the spatula toward the table. "I don't always have time to cook, but I enjoy it when I do."

Peters and the Carters crowded around the small table, leaving an empty chair next to Rick. Iryna set the platter of pancakes on the table and slid into her seat. "*Prigoshchaites.* That means you should treat yourself to the food."

They complied with alacrity, devouring every single pancake. Iryna ate only one. The fried bread was outside her normal diet. Instead of filling her plate, she sipped on a small glass of the leftover *kefir*.

"Delicious," declared Mr. Carter, leaning back and patting his belly.

"Is there anything you can't do, my dear?" asked Beth.

"I cannot do the calculus. I failed that miserably," said Iryna with an exaggerated sigh, glad that everyone had enjoyed the meal. She secretly wanted Rick to know she could do more than dance. She risked a glance at him to find his eyes gazing at her with admiration and his chest swelling.

"I'll wash the dishes," Peters offered with the hint of a smirk, "since I'm needed for so little else."

"Remember, you shopped for the groceries, so we would not have had breakfast without you." Iryna offered her most winsome smile.

Peters tapped a finger against his chin. "That is true—"

"But we'll still take you up on your offer to do the dishes," Rick said, cutting him off. He pulled Iryna's chair out as she stood. "I have to take our multitalented guest to her rehearsal."

Iryna wished to make a witty reply, but with Rick beside her, she could only smile with stars in her eyes.

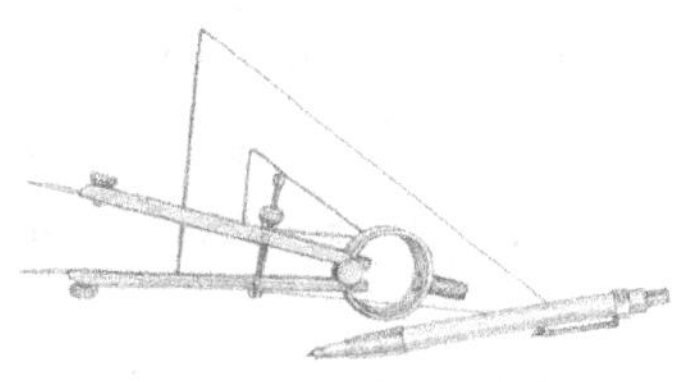

Rick maneuvered his sedan through the morning traffic while navigating his thoughts. The mystery of the matchbooks remained unsolved, as did his uneasiness at the theater. With so few leads, he had no idea what action he could take. While he wished he could dismiss his fears as unfounded, the identical matchbooks made that impossible. Natalia's upcoming memorial kept the idea of death at the fringes of his consciousness when he would rather not think about it.

"How did your presentation go?" Iryna asked, interrupting his unusually morbid reflections. "I didn't get a chance to ask last night."

"Very well. Thanks for asking." Rick focused his eyes on the road and his mind on Iryna, which he was happy to do. She continuously impressed him with her kindness, consideration, and easy playfulness. "I hope to hear from the company soon."

"I'm so glad."

"Was Masha at the game last night? I didn't notice any fresh faces."

"No, she stayed at the hotel to recover so she would be ready for today's rehearsals. Though we will only go through it once, it is our first practice with the symphony, so it's important."

Their pleasant chatter made the time pass swiftly. He wanted to talk to her about the previous evening but wasn't sure how to bring it up. Iryna acted like it was perfectly natural to fall asleep on someone's shoulder, but a bluebird landing on his arm would have affected him less. She'd kissed him on the cheek, but what if that didn't mean anything? She might view him like family. Eastern Europeans greeted each other with kisses all the time.

But what if she *did* still have a crush on him? He wasn't sure if he wanted to know the answer yet. More importantly, he hadn't prepared a response, so he kept to safer topics.

Before he was ready to see her go, they arrived at the theater. Iryna waved goodbye and raced inside. Rick watched until she disappeared, his heart racing to match her footsteps.

On the way to work, he called a florist and arranged for a half dozen Stargazer lilies to be delivered to Gramercy Park. Even-numbered flower arrangements were traditional for funerals, and he thought Iryna would like to take some to the memorial.

He and Mark had an uneventful day. They worked on a couple current projects as well as some advertising ideas. During his lunch, he brushed up on Orthodox liturgy and etiquette so he could respond appropriately during the memorial. Then he picked up the phone to call the cleaners to ask them about the matchbook. Since Iryna received one also, the cleaners was likely uninvolved, but it couldn't hurt.

"Hello," Rick said when a woman answered the phone. "I found a matchbook from a Polish hotel in my jacket pocket after picking it up from the cleaners. Do you have any idea how it got there?"

"A matchbook? Certainly not. Some of our solvents are flammable, so we don't keep anything like that around. We also check each article of clothing thoroughly before cleaning. If you found something in your pocket, it had to have been put there after you picked it up."

"All right. Thank you." He ended the call and set down the phone, tapping a beat his on his desk with a pencil. On a blank sheet of paper, he listed everyone he had spoken to the night of the party. If he included waitstaff or others who had stood near him, it was impossibly long. Realizing he had shaken every guest's hand at least once, he crumpled the paper and threw it in the trash.

With determined effort, he focused on business for the rest of the afternoon. Mark only gave him a slight grimace as Rick headed out early to pick up Iryna.

"How did the first rehearsal with the symphony go?" he asked as she sank into the passenger seat.

"Your symphony is awesome. Everything went smoothly. It will be a wonderful performance."

Rick carefully shut her door, walked back around to the driver's seat, and pulled away from the curb.

"So how does it work for an understudy? You said you have

to repeat your moves for her. Do they have to do the entire performance twice—once with you, and once with her?" he asked.

"Fortunately, no. That would make the practices last forever. The understudies work in the wings—what is the word—miming? No, mimicking what we are doing on the stage. The director had Masha and Sergei, who is our male understudy, dance a couple of the more difficult pieces on the stage to see how they were doing, but the entire company doesn't have to do the whole ballet twice."

"And how did they do?"

"They were fine. Masha already knows this ballet—Olena helped her polish her choreography, so I didn't have to help her much after all, and Sergei is a superb dancer. He will have a leading role someday."

"And how are you?" Rick threw a quick glance her way. "Are you ready for this evening?"

"Can a person be ready for such a thing?" she sighed. "It still does not seem real that she is gone."

"I know what you mean." It was still hard to believe Cassie was gone, although he had gotten used to it.

Iryna must have recognized the emotion in his voice. "I was very sorry to hear about your sister," she said. "When your family left, I was sad, but I didn't know until later that Cassie had cancer. It must have been very hard."

"Yes, it was," he affirmed but didn't add more. He tensed his jaw. Iryna said nothing else. They arrived back at the house shortly, and Iryna went to shower and change for dinner. Rick changed into a fresh shirt and a more subdued tie.

The evening meal was served early to allow for travel time to the church. Iryna entered the dining room wearing a tasteful dark-blue dress with a black scarf.

"We'll have to wolf this down to arrive at the service on time," he said. He wanted to tell her how pretty she looked, but he didn't think it'd be appropriate to compliment mourning attire.

"I'll eat after you leave," said Beth. "The last couple days have been so busy that I haven't seen much of you. I'm so excited to watch the ballet. Martha—that's our cook—has been creative in planning some absolutely mouthwatering meals fit for an athlete's diet. I hope you like the dinner."

"Mm-hmm," Iryna responded with her mouth full. "Delicious."

"Well, I suppose you have to eat whether you feel like it or not, to keep up your energy."

Iryna showed a good appetite, but Rick ate mechanically and pushed his food around on his plate. His stomach tightened as he thought about the service and its necessity. Cassie's funeral had passed by in surreal slow motion. Though she was sick for months, he had been in a state of shock. To the very end, he hoped she would recover. He was not looking forward to attending another memorial.

When it was time to leave, Rick excused himself and Iryna. He went to the kitchen and retrieved the lilies as Peters brought Rick's car around.

Iryna teared up as Rick handed her the bouquet. Her lips trembled. "Thank you," she whispered.

Her gratitude warmed his heart, and he squeezed her shoulder, happy to provide such a simple thing for her.

Rick helped Iryna into the passenger seat and then slid behind the wheel. The drive was short, and Rick found a parking spot on the street across from the church. He offered his hand to Iryna as he opened the car door. He told himself he was comforting her, but he needed it as much as she did. The contact made him feel less alone.

Iryna released his hand briefly as he held the church door for her, and she adjusted her scarf to cover her head, but she took his hand again as he led her inside. She paused to light a candle as they entered before settling into a quiet pew. Rick was relieved the church had pews at all since most in Ukraine had no seating of any kind except along the wall for those unable to stand for the entire service. He feared if he had to stand that he would shift back and forth nervously the whole time.

I can do this, he told himself as his chest tightened. *I can do this for Iryna.* Focusing on her was the only way he'd make it through the service.

The sanctuary was silent, and the rest of the dancers hadn't yet arrived. It was a beautiful church, with elaborate chandeliers, a high ceiling, stained glass, and icons with golden halos. Rick noticed someone had provided a publicity photo of Natalia that stood on an easel in the front. Iryna saw the photo and placed the lilies underneath it before returning to the pew.

Cassie's funeral had been open casket. Instead of a photo, his little sister lay there, holding her favorite doll while looking like a doll herself. *I can't think about that.* Rick bit his cheek to refocus his thoughts elsewhere.

The pastor entered through a side door in his black robes and arranged some papers on the podium. When he walked down the aisle to greet them, they stood. Rick put his right hand over his left and said, "Father, bless" in the proper manner. Iryna did the same and kissed the priest's hand.

The pastor introduced himself in English and welcomed them to the church. Iryna thanked him for holding the service. "I assume Ukrainian is acceptable for the service, but we do have someone who can translate if needed?" He said it like a question, glancing from Iryna to Rick.

"Ukrainian will be fine, Father," answered Iryna. "Most of the dancers speak or understand it. Few of the younger dancers speak fluent Russian, and few of the older staff speak English." She looked at Rick. "You will be okay?"

"Oh yes, it will be a good opportunity for me to brush up on Ukrainian. Don't worry about me." He smiled. It wasn't the language that would make the service difficult for him.

"Then that is settled. We will start shortly." He nodded and moved on.

When they resumed their seats, Iryna gripped his hand, whether for her own comfort or his, he didn't know, but he gripped it back just as tightly.

The rest of the troupe arrived, entering in reverent silence. Most of the women wore headscarves, but a few didn't. Many lit candles, crossed themselves, and bowed before the icons as they entered. Soon they were all seated, and the service began.

Rick went through the motions with everyone else, standing when required, which was often, and listening to the readings and the homily. Since he hadn't specifically studied religious terminology during his time in Ukraine, he didn't comprehend all of it. But he did catch the main idea, which was Christian unity.

God wants unity with humankind, but the two are separated. Separation is due to sin, and death is the consequence. Spiritual death separates people from God, and physical death separates people from each other. For those who trust in Him, separation from loved ones is only temporary. One day, believers will be united again.

Rick hadn't really thought about being reunited with Cassie. He only knew that she had been ripped away. Her loss made him doubt God's love. Once doubt crept in, it affected every aspect of his faith.

If Heaven is real, could Cassie be with God now? His heart lightened at the thought of meeting her again and that she still existed somewhere, in Heaven. The sermons he'd heard in his youth focused more on Christian life on Earth than the afterlife. He wanted to know more about it but doubted this was the right time or place to learn.

The service ended, and everyone was invited into the fellowship hall for *kalach*, a traditional sweet bread, and tea, served by ladies from the church. The dancers filed past Natalia's picture, kissed it, and walked into the hall. Many of the dancers had misty eyes or tearstained cheeks.

When everyone else had moved on, Iryna lingered over the photo, tracing Natalia's features with her fingers before dabbing her tears with a handkerchief. Rick wrapped his arm around her shoulders, and she leaned into him.

"I can't believe she's gone. It hurts so much." With one hand, she clung to his lapel, while pressing her handkerchief to her eyes with the other. Rick hadn't thought anyone even used those anymore.

"I know," he murmured, rubbing her back gently. His eyes stung, and he blinked rapidly.

They stood there until Iryna squared her shoulders and stepped back, sliding her hand into his as they followed the rest of the mourners.

As everyone received their bread and tea, the conversation picked up and people grew more cheerful. They shared memories of Natalia and discussed good times they'd had with her. A couple of the American dancers who had come to show support offered their condolences and left. Iryna nibbled her *kalach*, listening while others spoke and attempting a wobbly smile.

Across the hall, Rick noticed one girl who avoided talking to anyone. Her bleach-blonde hair was pulled back in a severe ponytail, her eyebrows frowned, and her jaw was set. She stood in a corner, glaring at the room's occupants. He wondered if she was angry Natalia was gone and was having difficulty coping, or if something else stirred her ire. He would have asked Iryna about her if she wasn't already talking to someone.

Rick refilled his tea. "Thank you," he told the ladies serving the refreshments. "It is very kind of you." His Ukrainian sounded stiff to his ears, but the ladies smiled as if he'd spoken perfectly.

He drank his tea and caught a sly glance from Iryna. She

rejoined him shortly. "Would you like some pepper?" she said. Her eyes were still red, but Rick admired her attempt at levity.

"If it means you're giving me your attention, then yes," he replied. She wrinkled her nose. "Everyone has good stories about Natalia," he ventured. "It sounds like she was an amazing person, besides being a wonderful dancer."

"She was." Her voice lowered and her eyes turned glassy. "We all loved her. I was going to retire after this season, and she would have taken my place, but now ... I don't know. I may need to stay on another year until Karina is ready."

Rick was incredulous. "Retire? But you're so young! And so talented!"

Iryna gave a half smile. "Exactly—the best time to retire. It's very hard on the body and the joints to keep up this pace for so many years."

Now that he thought about it, many professional athletes had short careers compared to those in other occupations.

"What will you do after you retire?" He was curious.

"I want to open a dance studio for the ... ungifted? No, um, the poor?"

"Underprivileged?"

"Yes, I think that is it. The underprivileged youth in Kyiv. Very few of them have the opportunity to learn the performing arts. It would be a charity, or a no-money business."

"A nonprofit. That's admirable."

"It would be for the fun too." She warmed to the topic, her voice regaining its normal intensity. "I would get to dance what I want, choreograph performances for the dancers, try new techniques."

"Like your ribbon dance at the party?"

"Yes! Things like that."

Rick could sense her enthusiasm for her project. He wanted her to have anything she wished for, but not on the other side of the world. Now that their paths had crossed for a second time, he had to find a way to converge them.

The rest of the group prepared to leave since they'd arrived by charter bus, so Rick ushered Iryna to the door while she bid good night to her fellow artists. As they drove away from the church, Rick's thoughts returned to the service, and he longed to learn what Iryna thought about it.

"The pastor talked about believers being reunited in Heaven. Do you think you will see Natalia again?" Rick said somewhat hesitantly, not knowing how Iryna would react or if she would want to discuss it.

"Of course," she answered, surprising him with her certainty. She cocked her head to look directly at him. "You don't think so?"

"I don't know. What makes you so sure you will?"

Iryna shrugged. "She was a good Orthodox Christian. She went to church. Why wouldn't we see her again?" She seemed to accept the idea without question. Maybe it wasn't something she had put much thought into. Or her faith was so ingrained she took it for granted.

"Do you think that's all it takes?" Rick frowned.

"All it takes for what?"

"To go to Heaven. All you need to do is attend church? And do you have to be Orthodox?"

"Well, no." Iryna wrinkled her brow. "You have to be a good person, but you can't be a good person by yourself," she reasoned. "You need God's help. And other believers to encourage you. You are thinking of Cassie?"

"Yes," he confessed. His tension eased slightly at the prospect of speaking about his sister with someone who had known her. Iryna might be the only one he could share this part of his heart with since his parents were reluctant to talk about Cassie.

Iryna pursed her lips. "I have been with friends to what they called an 'e-van-gel-i-cal' church"—she sounded it out, forming the word on her tongue—"and I believe they are Christians. They believe in the Bible and Jesus like I do, so I don't think you have to be Orthodox, though the church might not agree."

Rick wasn't sure that was exactly comforting. He didn't really know what Cassie had believed, although they had gone to church. It was a small international church in Kyiv that had grown bigger as Westerners flooded into the former Soviet countries.

"Cassie was only eleven." He said her name with difficulty. What level of faith was required in one so young?

"I think you have to have faith that God will do the right thing," Iryna offered. "It's either that or believe in no god at all, which to me would be much sadder."

"That's a bleak prospect," Rick agreed. He had a lot to reflect on. Cassie's loss didn't shred his insides like it did before. His anger had simmered for so long it ran out of fuel. The idea reminded him of the girl at the memorial with the grim expression.

"Was that Masha who stood around scowling the whole time?"

"If you mean the blonde girl who always looks angry, then yes. That is her usual expression. She is the type of person who is never happy but is happy not being happy, if you know what I mean," Iryna explained with a sigh. "That is why no one likes to work with her, even though she's technically very good. I feel guilty saying so, because I'm sorry for her in a way, but I was hoping to have some time without her. Now she's here anyway."

"I'm sorry." Many offices had that one annoying coworker everyone disliked but wasn't bad enough to fire. He squeezed Iryna's hand and boldly left it there while she stared out the window. The contact felt almost natural now, as if their hands belonged together. *Such a silly thought, after so short a time,* he chided himself. He was sure her thoughts had returned to Natalia, and he left her alone with them for the rest of the drive.

When they arrived at the house, he let her in the front door before parking the car. He returned to find she had already retired. After debating between hitting the sack and spending a few moments with his parents, filial duty won out, and he sank into a chair in the living room. His parents smiled at him, and his heart swelled with gratitude. Not everyone was blessed with such a good mother and father.

Neither of them asked how the service went. Instead, they let him sit and relax. He reflected on the pastor's sermon and wished he had more answers, for his peace of mind and his parents' as well. It would be nice to be able to talk to them about it, but they would resist, and he wasn't ready to fight that battle. He closed his eyes while he thought and drifted off to sleep in the chair.

He woke to his mother tucking a blanket around him.

"Thanks, Mom, but I can make it upstairs."

"Okay. Good night, dear." Beth patted him on the shoulder as he rose.

Rick's thoughts switched to his dinner date with Iryna tomorrow evening, and he experienced a moment of panic. Did he have a clean suit?

"Oh, I had Peters take a couple of your suits to be cleaned in case you need one for tomorrow night," Beth said as if she'd read his mind.

"Mom, you're a gem. I love you." Rick grinned as he walked up the stairs, grateful for something to look forward to after a weighty day.

CHAPTER 8

Thursday morning, Rick woke with butterflies in his stomach, knowing he would be taking Iryna out to dinner that evening. He would finally have some time to talk to her—only her—with no other distractions. His nerves buzzed with anticipation as he went down to the kitchen.

Iryna, dressed in her workout clothes, was puzzling over the coffee maker when Rick walked into the kitchen.

"Here, let me help you." Rick walked over and took the pod of herbal tea out of her hand and put it in the coffee maker. In a few short moments, she was sipping the tea and smiling.

"So, what should I wear for dinner this evening?" she asked, her eyes dancing.

Rick's heart thrilled to know she was at least thinking about the event, if not thinking about him specifically. "It's a nice restaurant, but not as fancy as our welcome party. I'll be wearing a suit and tie, not a tuxedo, if that helps." He smiled.

"Mm-hmm." Iryna held her mug against her lips, studying him as if imagining him in his suit. She turned her back and set her mug on the counter as she stirred sugar into it. Over her shoulder she asked, "So is this a dinner as old family friends, or is this an actual date?" She turned again and met his gaze. "Just so I can decide what to wear," she added in a teasing tone.

It took him a second to react. He wanted to have this conversation with her but hadn't expected it to happen now. He sucked in his breath, gazed at her, and answered seriously. "It's an actual date. If you want it to be." He stopped breathing as he waited for her response.

"Okay." She smiled, blinked, and walked to the refrigerator to grab a yogurt.

"So," said Rick, a little unsure, "does that mean you want it to be a date?"

"I guess you'll have to wait and see."

He emptied his lungs with a surprised laugh. "You're going to make me wait all day to find out?"

"Maybe I haven't decided myself."

"Do you want me to convince you?"

"Ooh, that could be very interesting. Unfortunately, we don't have much time, as I must get to the rehearsal." She picked up her gym bag and headed out the door with a grin.

Rick raised his eyebrows and grabbed his car keys. Although she had baited him into admitting he wanted it to be a real date, he was now certain he really wanted it to be. She must want the same thing, or she wouldn't be teasing him so mercilessly.

"You know, I'm really quite a catch," he joked as they walked to the car. "If you want to hear all my good qualities, my mother will be happy to enumerate them to you."

"Enumerate?"

"List. Or in my mother's case, go on and on and on." Rick opened the car door for Iryna.

"You love your mother—that is very obvious," she said as she sat.

"Yes, I do. And you are changing the subject." He walked around and climbed in the driver's seat.

"I am not changing the subject. Loving the mother is a good quality in a man." She opened her mouth as if to say something else but seemed to change her mind.

"Oh, so you're going to list my good qualities and convince yourself?"

Iryna appeared at a loss for once and crossed her arms, pretending to pout. "Maybe you are a better chess player than me after all."

"So, what are you going to wear?"

"Wait and see."

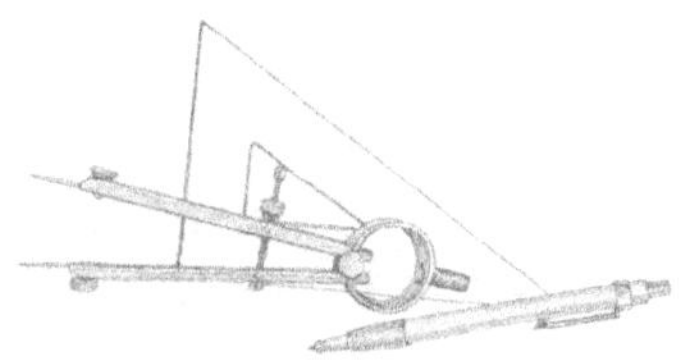

Rick was distracted all day, and Mark repeatedly pointed it out.

"Mr. Carter, I gave you these forms to sign an hour ago. We need to turn them in today." Mark walked up to Rick's desk and nudged the papers toward him.

"Mark, how many times have I told you to call me Rick?"

"Sir, no matter what I call you, we still need the forms turned in."

Rick sighed and focused on the forms while Mark hovered nearby, probably afraid to leave the room lest Rick put down his pen without finishing the paperwork. He filled them out hurriedly and with poor handwriting, shoved them at Mark, and shooed him out of the room. He glanced at the clock, but it wasn't moving fast enough. *Should I buy her flowers?* He debated for a moment. *I'll send her flowers on opening night.* He called and reconfirmed the reservation he'd made earlier in the week. Drumming his fingers on the desk, he reconsidered whether he wanted Peters to drive.

Mark stuck his head in the door and interrupted his thoughts again. "Excuse me, sir. Have you called the printer back yet?"

"For Pete's sake, Mark, who's running this business? You, or me?"

Seeing Mark's downcast expression, guilt immediately hounded him. "I'm sorry, Mark. I'm a little distracted today. I know you're just trying to help. I'll call them now." Rick made the call and let Mark know when to pick up the copies he ordered.

After a half hour of uninterrupted time, Mark entered almost on tiptoe. "Will you be leaving early today, sir?" He put his hands behind his back and pressed his lips together. "I can hold down the fort if you need me to."

Surprised at the offer, Rick glanced up. "You know, I think I will take you up on that." He grabbed his coat but stopped to put a hand on Mark's shoulder. "You're a great assistant. I don't know what I'd do without you."

Mark straightened and a smile tugged at the corners of his mouth. "Thank you."

Rick departed even earlier than he planned. He left Mark in charge and drove to the theater to catch the end of rehearsal. Fortunately, he still had the diplomatic pass Iryna had given him for Sunday's rehearsal so he could enter the theater. The ballet had strict rules about who could watch.

When he arrived, the company was beginning the final act. This was a full dress rehearsal, the last one before opening night, and the orchestra members focused on their music, stage hands juggled props and costumes, and performers lived their roles. The music vibrated through the hall and into Rick's chest, filling his mind as if nothing else existed. Elaborate Ukrainian costumes swirled around the dancers as they moved. A few other observers sat in the audience. Rick assumed they were special patrons or art critics allowed a sneak peek.

Rick paid little attention to anyone but Iryna last time he

was here, but now he noticed all the dancers' high level of skill. As he watched the principal male dancer lift Iryna several times while holding her around her waist, jealousy clouded his mind. *Yegor is married to Karina. It's just part of the job.* Yegor was muscular and agile, performing incredible leaps and spins. Instead of lifting weights in a gym, the male dancers effortlessly and artistically lifted ballerinas. Rick couldn't help feeling inferior.

Iryna wore a fluffy white cloud made of a gauzy material with lots of feathers for her part as the swan princess. She and her partner danced a duet of intricate steps and athletic leaps, concluding with an impressive *grande jete*, during which they appeared to almost fly. When they exited, the remaining dancers briefly stole the spotlight.

Masha, he noticed, danced a supporting role in the *corps de ballet*. She held her poses for a fraction of a second longer than the rest of the girls, and he wondered if that was a deliberate ploy to gain more attention. She couldn't hold anyone's attention for long when Iryna was on the stage.

When she returned for the next scene, Iryna sported a more traditional Ukrainian costume and headdress. She danced almost completely bent backward for part of the piece.

"So, I hear you are takeeng our Irrreena out to deener?" a thickly accented voice beside Rick said. When he turned, Rick recognized the choreographer he had spoken to at the party. Alexei reminded Rick of movie representations of KGB agents rather than a former dancer.

"Yes, sir." He wondered if the man was attempting to stand in as a father figure and if this was going to turn into an interrogation.

"That ees good. She vorks too hard." Alexei sat next to Rick and slouched while observing the dancers.

"Dancing is a much harder job than I imagined," Rick commented, simplifying his vocabulary for the benefit of his listener, who merely nodded in assent. He racked his brain for a tactful way to ask if Iryna had dated much or why she wasn't dating another dancer, but he couldn't think of anything. Fortunately, Alexei threw some hints his way.

"Many een our company would love to be een your shoes this evening, but Irreena has passed them all by."

"Why do you think that is?" Rick bit the inside of his cheek.

Alexei spread his hands, palms up. "Some say only she has passion forrr thee dance." Rick waited, hoping for more. "But I theenk that een every thing, like een her dance, she weell accept only thee best and no thing less."

Rick frowned as he pondered Alexei's words and tried to puzzle out what they meant. What if Iryna had impossibly high expectations for him? Or had she already approved of him and should take it as a compliment that she was going out with him? He guessed he'd just have to wait and find out. *Easier said than done.*

As the performance ended, he and Alexei both stood, and Alexei clapped him on the back before walking toward the stage. Rick was gratified to have Alexei's approval, at least.

He waited while all the costumes and props were put away and the director gave his final instructions to the cast. When the troupe finally dispersed, he spied Iryna looking around for him, and he waved at her. She saw him and smiled, and his doubts melted away as she gathered her things and scampered toward him. A couple of the male dancers looked sideways at him when she approached and put her arm through his.

"You may not want to be too close to me right now. I'm very sweaty!" Iryna said.

"I don't mind." Rick smiled as he took her bag from her. It would be obvious to everyone that he was no longer escorting her as a family friend. As they walked out, he noticed a woman with a press pass scribbling some notes and pointing at him while questioning a member of the troupe. Right now, he was the lucky man walking with the most beautiful, most fascinating woman he had ever met.

Their conversation on the way home was all about the rehearsal. Rick praised every aspect of the performance and asked several questions about the dances, backstage logistics, and the story behind the ballet. Iryna explained everything, gesturing wildly and lapsing into Ukrainian in her excitement.

Even in rush hour traffic, the drive was short, and they soon arrived at the Carter residence. Their private parking space was free. *Mom must have had Peters move their sedan to the garage with the limo so I could have the spot today.* Rick checked his watch as he opened Iryna's door and saw it was just after six o'clock.

"How much time do I have to get ready?" Iryna asked.

"The reservation is for eight o'clock. We'll need to leave by seven-thirty, so that gives you an hour and a half. Is that enough time?" Rick said, slightly worried he hadn't allowed enough.

"Oh, that will be plenty," Iryna replied. She patted his arm as he opened the door of the house, then she rushed up the stairs. "See you at seven-thirty!" she called out.

Rick took less than an hour to get ready, and even though he showered and shaved again, he was back downstairs by six forty-five. He had debated waiting for her upstairs, but it would be weird to have her date right across the hall or waiting outside her bedroom. He was highly aware of her nearness. Staying at his apartment the rest of the week might be wise.

He entered the living room and found his mother reading a magazine.

"Wow, honey, you look great. I love that suit." His mother swept her eyes over him. The suit was newer, tailored and more expensive than his tux, though less formal. Its dark-brown fabric matched his deep-brown eyes and wavy dark hair. He wore a blue tie and a lighter blue shirt for contrast.

His father came in and picked up the newspaper. "Evening, son."

"Hey, Dad."

"You and Iryna going out this evening?"

"Yes, sir." A thought occurred to him. "Should I have asked

her father first? I didn't think about that 'til just now. Diplomatic relations and all. Would he expect me to ask him?"

"No, I don't think that's necessary. Unless you're planning on proposing?" His father arched his eyebrows and peered at Rick over the top of his reading glasses.

"Ha ha." Rick flushed slightly and joked, "I'll save that for the second date."

A door closed upstairs, and Rick rose. "Oh, Mom, I'll be heading back to my apartment tonight after I drop Iryna off, and she doesn't have to be at the theater as early, so can you arrange for Peters to drive her over tomorrow?"

"Sure," Beth said, throwing a puzzled look at her husband as Rick walked out of the room. "What's that about?" she whispered.

Rick didn't hear his father's answer because he was gazing up the stairs at Iryna. She wore a shimmering evening gown of sapphire blue, the same color as her eyes, with hints of sea green. As she walked down the stairs, it flowed like a sparkling river. The neckline had extra fabric arranged in a cowl-like fashion, and she had a shawl of similar material draped over her bare arms. Her long dark hair hung in loose curls, reminding him of a mermaid. Compared to the theatrical makeup, what she wore now was minimal, but the overall effect was stunning.

"So, does this look like a 'date' dress?" she asked softly as she reached the landing.

"I—" Rick's voice was hoarse, and his heart pounded. He could hardly trust himself to speak. "How did I get so lucky?" He offered her his arm, and she took it, smiling.

He led her out the door, completely oblivious to his parents standing and watching from the door of the living room.

Rick helped Iryna into the car and walked to the driver's side. It was most practical for him to drive his car, as he didn't particularly relish Peters or anyone else chaperoning, but it was hard sitting next to Iryna without being able to put his arm around her shoulders, especially when she looked so beautiful.

The drive to the restaurant was quiet. Rick stole a glimpse of Iryna every couple seconds. She glanced sideways at him and caught him staring. They both laughed nervously.

Rick pulled up to the Seagram building, an iconic New York landmark, and tipped the parking attendant as he handed him the keys. He opened the door for Iryna and took her hand. Iryna stared up at the tall, stately building. Rick led her carefully up the steps and through the door.

"Oh, this is lovely," Iryna exclaimed at the floor-to-ceiling windows, soft lighting, and upholstered chairs.

"Dining here is like stepping back in time," Rick agreed. They were a little overdressed for the restaurant, whose dress code was business casual, but this was a special occasion.

The eyes of everyone in the restaurant followed Iryna as they walked in. Iryna was the most beautiful woman in the room, Rick thought, so he couldn't blame people for staring.

The hostess seated them at a cozy little table, and Iryna poured over the menu. "Everything looks delicious, but I have no idea what to get. You order for me."

"Okay. Do you have any allergies, or anything you dislike?"

"I like everything, but I should avoid the fried foods or the heavy creams, things like that."

Rick ordered pumpkin soup, endive and apple salad, and Dover sole with grilled broccoli. The food was delicious, but Rick enjoyed the conversation even more. He discovered Iryna had continued at the diplomatic school while studying ballet, moving on to a special academy for dancers when she was twelve. She joined the ballet company full-time at sixteen and finished high school with a tutor. She'd had a special tutor for English since she was five. In turn, he told her about attending college and earning a master's degree in architecture.

"So," he said, strategically waiting until she had a mouthful of fish so she would have time to think, "tell me why you're not dating another dancer? It must be hard to meet other people with your rigorous schedule, and you would have so much in common already."

"Why are you not dating another architect?" Iryna responded as soon as she swallowed.

"Ha. Good point. But really, why aren't you? It can't be because they haven't asked."

Iryna lowered her gaze and pushed her fork around. "I have dated a dancer." Rick waited as she paused and took a deep breath. "When I was beginning to be noticed and earn larger roles, I dated another young dancer in the company. He was very nice, and I liked him a lot. We would go to the football games—I think you call it soccer—and hockey games, and he would always make sure we were on the big TV screen. We went to the children's ward at the hospital to read to the patients and would get our pictures in the paper.

"Because we were always together, whenever anyone talked about what a great dancer I was, they talked about him too. When I won my first leading role, he was also given a big part. Then one day, he told me he had been offered a lead in the Moscow Ballet, and he was going to take it. He had a starring role and he didn't need me anymore, so that was that. He was my first serious boyfriend, and I couldn't bring myself to date another dancer after that. "

"You mean he took advantage of your talent so he'd get noticed?"

"Yes, something like that."

"I'm sorry. That must have been difficult." He grew incensed at this unnamed dancer but was glad she was no longer with him.

"It was. Most upsetting was the betrayal, the being used, not the loss of him specifically, because I soon realized I was not in love with him. I dated a couple famous people of my own after that, a soccer player and a businessman, but it felt … empty. Then I went to the international church with a friend I had known at school, and the pastor spoke about the will of God.

He said that if you are doing what God wants you to do, only then you will be content. So I decided to focus on expressing myself through dance and enjoying that, and letting God fill the empty space how He wants."

"So how do you feel now? Did it work? Are you content? Happy?"

Iryna smiled. "Yes, I am content with doing what I was meant to do and being who I was meant to be. Happy is not quite the same thing. In English, you know, it is from the same root as 'happening,' which has to do with what is going on, not who you are. Happiness comes and goes."

As Rick took a bite of his food, he chewed on the idea.

"What about you? Why is a handsome, successful man like you not dating anyone?"

"I have had some similar experiences to yours, though not as extreme. Most girls hang around me because of my social pedigree and financial stability. I've never been the exciting playboy type. I've always thought I was a little boring."

"You are not boring!" Iryna exclaimed. "What is it—the social pedigree?"

"It just means you come from an important or wealthy family. Your name is established in society. People invite you to parties because your parents have a big house instead of inviting you because they enjoy your company."

"Oh, that's terrible!" Iryna said, and Rick smiled at her outrage on his behalf.

"I've gotten used to it." His heart beat faster as he followed up on her earlier comment. "You don't think someone who just gets up every day and goes to work and back home is boring?"

"If a person is doing what they love, and it is interesting for them, then it cannot be boring when they talk about it to other people. Enthusiasm is con-ta-gious." She stumbled over the word but continued. "The movies think all women like what they call the 'bad boy,' but I think all anyone longs for is security and someone trustworthy they can rely on no matter what.

There is enough excitement to be found in the world without being in doubt of whether you are loved."

Her eyes grew unfocused for a moment, but then she rested an elbow on the table, propped her chin in her hand, and gazed at him with a smile that made his heart melt. Not a wide smile or a laughing smile, but a smile perfectly relaxed and content. One that stopped time, letting them savor this moment forever. She was here with him now, and that was what mattered.

"Besides," she teased, "you play the chess, you dance the ballroom, and you like the pepper in your tea. What could be more interesting than that?"

Rick was unable to reply, as the waiter arrived with their dessert, cherries flambé. Iryna clapped and laughed as the waiter set the warm dessert on fire then poured it over ice cream. Iryna's obvious enjoyment pleased the waiter, and the display attracted attention since not many diners indulged in dessert. Some nearby ladies grew more animated as they attempted to re-secure the attention of their dates. Rick felt proud that he was here with the loveliest woman in the city and able to treat her to anything she wanted. Iryna, focused on the delicious fruit dish, remained oblivious to the other diners.

"Thank you for the wonderful dinner, Rrrick," Iryna said after the waiter took their plates. "It is so nice to be here with you."

Rick was touched that she truly wanted to be with him regardless of where they ate. He reached over and grasped her hand across the table. No one he'd dated had shown interest in him as a person, only a means to an end because he had invitations to all the right parties. How could he show her he was not like the other guys she'd dated? He wanted to tell her he cared about her, but he struggled to find the words.

He also feared letting himself fall in love only to lose her like he'd lost Cassie. If he were honest with himself, he knew it was too late to turn back now. He was already in deep.

Rick met Iryna's gaze. "I would be happy to be with you anywhere."

They stared into each other's eyes until the check was delivered, then he silently offered her his arm and they walked out of the restaurant. The valet brought the car around, and Rick helped Iryna into her seat. Her gaze wrapped him in warmth as he walked around to the driver's side and started the engine. He risked driving one-handed so he could wrap his free hand around hers. The energy between them was so thick he could hardly breathe.

They drove in silence for a while before Rick forced himself to speak. He wanted to clarify a few things, and he needed to explain about transportation the next day.

"I'll be heading to my apartment after I drop you off instead of staying at the house, so Peters will drive you to the theater tomorrow. If it's okay, though, I'll drive you back after the performance?"

Iryna looked sideways at him. "Sure, that's fine."

Rick was relieved she didn't question him, because he wasn't sure how he would explain his feelings on the subject. There was one more area he wanted to investigate further. Depending on how she answered ... well, he planned to kiss her.

"So, have you really had a crush on me since we were kids?" He swallowed.

Iryna frowned. "A crush? What is it, 'a crush'?"

"Um ..." He paused. Of course she wouldn't know this American slang. "A crush is when you really like someone, but they don't know it. It's not quite as strong a feeling as being in love."

"Oh ... well ..." She shrugged, adopting a lighthearted tone as she declared, "Of course I had a crush on you. You were such a handsome, polite, and dis-tin-guished young man. How could I help it?" She tossed her head, avoiding his eyes.

"And now that you've seen me again," he persisted, "after such a long time, do you feel the same way?"

Iryna gaped in mock indignation. "I don't think it's fair that I should have to answer all the questions! What about you? What did you think of me? Or did you think of me at all when we were children?"

"Very well," said Rick, releasing her hand as he maneuvered into the parking space in front of his parents' house and turned off the engine. He unbuckled his seat belt and looked at her with a twitch in the corner of his mouth. "I will admit that I did *not* have a crush on you back then. Being a mature three years older than you, I thought you were a pretty, funny, but smart-alecky little girl, and I haven't thought about you since."

"Oh!" exclaimed Iryna, putting a hand on her chest.

"But now," he said quickly as he slid closer to her on the sedan's bench seat, "now I have a *huge* crush on you. You are a beautiful, intelligent, highly talented, graceful woman with an amazing sense of humor, and all I can think about all day is when I will see you again."

"Oh," she said again, her voice airy and inviting.

Rick slipped his arm around her waist. Her breath quickened as he drew her closer and repeated, "So, do you still feel the same way about me?"

With a strangled little cry, as if the word hurt her pride to say but was a relief to have in the open, she whispered, "Yes."

No sooner had she said it than his lips were on hers, and the energy around them exploded like a thousand firecrackers. Rick kissed her again, and Iryna wrapped her arms around his neck and returned his kiss with passion, trembling in his embrace yet devouring his mouth with hers. No one had ever kissed him this way, reveling in his caresses as if he were the fulfillment of a lifelong dream. Someone who truly liked him for him.

Intoxicated by the supple pressure of her body against his, Rick kissed her mouth, her cheeks, her neck. She moaned softly and tangled her fingers in his hair while he struggled to keep his hands in appropriate places. It would be easy to get carried away if he wasn't careful. Kissing Iryna could become an addiction.

He wanted to do things the right way with her, even if he wasn't sure what that would look like, without taking advantage of her childhood affection for him. *I have to slow this down. I must make sure this is real for both of us.*

He brushed his lips against her cheek and whispered her name. "Iryna." He put his hands on her shoulders and made her look into his eyes. "Iryna, I've never felt this attracted to anyone before. It's—you're different." His voice was hoarse and heavy with desire as he groped for words to explain the battle in his mind. "You said you are trusting God for your future. I want you to trust me too and know that I would never do anything to hurt you. Will you allow me to take you back to the house now and say good night before I take things too far?"

Iryna's eyes widened, but she nodded slowly. Rick cupped his hands around her face and kissed her once more, deeply and fervently. Then he exited the car and walked around to open her door. The night had grown chilly, and he feared her shawl would not be enough, so he took off his jacket and placed it carefully around her shoulders after helping her out of the car. She took his arm as they walked up the steps.

Rick unlocked the front door and held it open for her, but Iryna remained standing on the top step.

"Rick, I—"

She broke off and threw her arms around him, burying her face in his chest. He wrapped his arms around her, surprised at her sudden display of emotion. Her vulnerability, however, confirmed to him that he had done the right thing. She needed to know he would take care of her and protect her, even from himself. He wanted to exercise self-control and put her first.

It had been a difficult week for Iryna with the death of her friend, and he wanted to give her what strength he could, so he held her tightly. A jogger passed by, then someone walking a dog, but he didn't care.

Eventually, Iryna let go of him and stepped through the door. She reached out and let her fingers touch his one more time as she simply said, "Thank you, Rick" and silently closed the door.

Rick let out his breath as their separation produced an immediate pain in his heart. He leaned forward and rested his palm on one of the wooden panels as if trying to stay as close to her as possible.

How did I fall so hard so fast? he wondered. *I need to be careful, because her heart is involved, too, not just mine.*

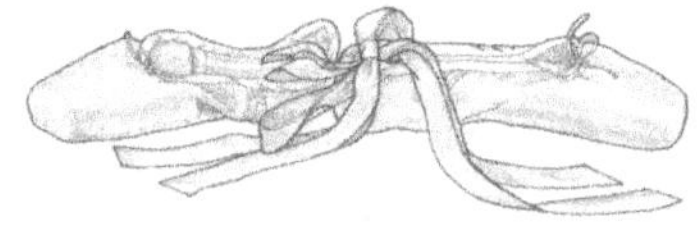

Iryna climbed the stairs slowly. She had indeed trusted God with her future, and He brought her back to Rick after she thought she would never see him again. She was sure she would be disappointed and he would not live up to her imaginary version of him as an adult, but he had surpassed it. He was everything she had ever hoped and dreamed of.

And his kiss! Hungry, but gentle and respectful at the same time—almost reverent. She'd been kissed before, but never like that. After months of anticipation, every nerve in her body had tingled with pleasure so intense she had grown lightheaded. Rick had ruined her for a kiss from anyone else.

After only five days with him, I am a hopeless mess. But he is learning to care for me. Even to the point of setting aside his desires for my sake. No man has ever done that for me.

She hadn't told Rick everything about her past. The soccer player she had dated after her breakup with the dancer wanted more than she was willing to give, and he was nasty about it. He didn't force her, but he hurt her. She was unable to dance for a week after he twisted her arm. He didn't bother her after that, but she suspected it was because her father found out about it and warned him off.

Iryna smiled as she thought of her father, the old bear. Soft and cuddly to her, but all snarls and claws to everyone else.

He would like Rick. Her heart swelled as she thought of reintroducing Rick to her father. If things went that far.

Afraid of disappointment, she pushed the future from her mind, entering her room without turning on the light. She paused and breathed in the scent of Rick's cologne on the jacket she still wore, then walked to the window where the moonlight streamed in and glanced down to the street. Rick's car was still parked at the curb. *Why is he still here? Didn't he say he was going back to his apartment?*

Out of the corner of her eye, she noticed movement in front of the door. It was Rick! She watched, fascinated, as he slowly descended the steps. When he reached the sidewalk, he turned and glanced up toward her room, and she shrank back quickly so he wouldn't see her.

After she heard the car door close, she returned to the window and watched him drive away. Her knees weakened, and she sank onto a chair. She hardly dared dream of where their budding relationship would go from here. Instead, her fingers touched her lips, reliving the kiss of a lifetime.

CHAPTER 9

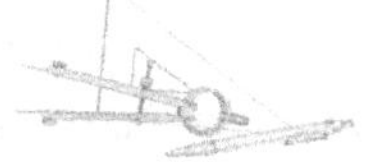

Rick was worthless at work the next morning. He had lain awake most of the night thinking about Iryna, his lips burning with the memory of her silky skin, while anticipating watching her perform that evening and driving her home again. Was she having as much trouble concentrating as he was?

Mark apparently gave up trying to get him to focus on work and took all the calls himself. "I'm sorry, sir. He's unavailable at the moment. Can I take a message?"

At lunch, Rick drove back into town to order flowers for Iryna.

"I would like to buy a bouquet of roses and have them delivered," he said to the smiling woman behind the counter.

"Certainly," she replied. "Would you like to choose one of our premade arrangements?" She gestured toward a cooler like a game show hostess. "We have either one dozen, eighteen, or twenty-four."

Rick glanced at the roses and shook his head. "I need an odd number of flowers."

"What number?" the florist asked, brow furrowed.

"An odd number, not an even number. I'm giving them to someone whose culture views even numbered flowers as unlucky." The larger bouquets looked rather unwieldy. "Could I get a dozen plus one?"

She leaned back, eyes wide. "I'm not making a bouquet of thirteen roses! Why don't you just take one out?"

Rick considered. "That seems kind of stingy."

"You can add three to make fifteen," she suggested, "but I have to charge a premium on single flowers."

"That's fine."

While she worked on the arrangement, Rick labored over the card. How should he sign it? He debated for a while and finally wrote simply, "To Iryna, From Rick." He'd let the red roses speak for themselves.

After he finished at the florist, Rick stopped at an electronics store and bought a smartphone with video calling capabilities. He activated it and added the number to his account. Hopefully, he could convince Iryna of its benefits. When he took her to see one of his projects tomorrow morning, he would surprise her with it. He already had in mind the building he would show her.

Rick returned to the office with only a couple hours left in the business day, and now that he had settled a few of the things knocking around in his head, he was able to devote a couple hours to catching up. Time would go faster if he was working. He threw himself into work like a shark on a feeding frenzy, but when he finished, he wasn't sure if he could explain to anyone what he'd accomplished.

Mark cleaned up after him, putting memos, permit applications, and other paperwork in their proper places. "You'll need to stop by the Henderson project next week to ensure the work matches your specifications, sir."

"Thanks. Please add it to my calendar. Also, the Colby renovation."

At closing time, Rick flew out the door, barely registering Mark's sigh of relief as he locked the office after him. He briefly wondered if Mark had a girlfriend. His staid assistant rarely volunteered personal information. He probably considered it improper to discuss at work.

When Rick arrived at the Carter mansion to pick up another suit, his parents had just sat down for dinner. He joined them for a quick bite.

"I'll be driving my car to the theater," he said.

"Oh, you're not going to ride with us?" Beth exclaimed.

"If I ride with you, I have to ride back with you."

"And?"

Rick's father came to his rescue. "He knows I'm dying to spend some quality time with my wife. Leave the boy alone, dear."

"I'll see you in the theater, Mom." He shoveled another bite of food into his mouth and rushed upstairs to change as Beth shook her head.

"Why doesn't he want to ride with us, Matt?" His mother's words reached his ears as he bounded up the steps.

"For someone who's spent so much time trying to set her son up with a girl, you're awfully slow to recognize when you've been successful."

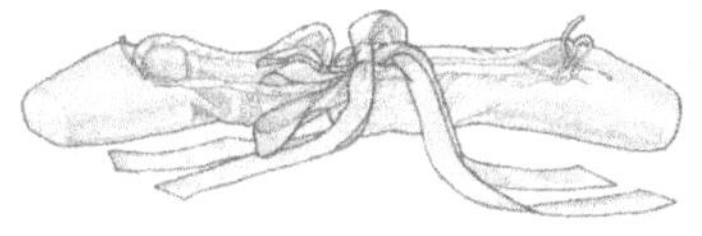

Iryna limbered up with the other dancers and completed her stretching routine like she was in a dream. Rick was falling for her. It was the only explanation for his behavior. He was not one to take things lightly. She just had to give him time, and his attraction might grow into love. She smiled at Masha across the room, her euphoria expansive enough to include everyone in her happiness. Masha frowned, but Iryna didn't care.

Two nearby dancers smirked at each other. "Iryna the great has fallen," whispered one, and the girls giggled.

Except for bittersweet memories of Natalia intruding, Iryna's soaring spirits remained undaunted. She had fallen, hard, and she wouldn't have it any other way.

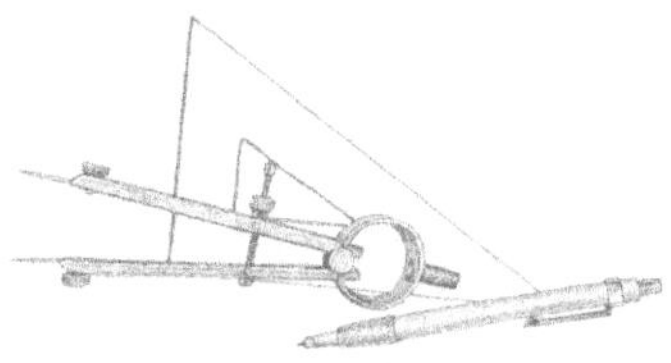

Rick arrived at the theater early. He hadn't been to a performance in a while, but he thought he remembered bringing a date here a few years ago. The theater was beautiful, with plush red seats, a golden curtain, and a gigantic spherical chandelier hanging from the center of the ceiling. The Carters had purchased tickets in the middle of the floor. They would have some of the best seats in the house. Some people preferred the view from the first ring, but his parents liked to be closer. His mother had bought tickets for all three performances, "just in case." Even if they didn't attend every performance, he certainly would.

Rick wished he could have gone backstage to wish Iryna luck, but he wasn't sure if his diplomatic pass would admit him, and security was tight. He also didn't want to throw off any pre-performance rituals the dancers might have. He was nervous for Iryna. Did she get anxious before performances?

Mr. and Mrs. Carter arrived shortly, and the theater filled up. His mother chattered about the drive and how glad she was that she didn't have to park the car. After she exhausted nearly every subject under the sun, Rick interrupted her.

"Just ask, Mom."

"So, how was the date? You're driving her home tonight?"

"Good, and yes."

"What are you, fifteen?" She pouted. "That's all I get, when it was my idea in the first place?"

"I love you, Mom," Rick said, his tone both teasing and truthful, and he kissed her cheek as an oboe played a long note. Other instruments harmonized as the players tuned them. "I'll catch you up later," he promised.

The lights dimmed, and the symphony played the first notes of the prelude. The audience conversation level lowered to a murmur and then fell silent as the curtain rose on act one of *Swan Lake*. The first scene opened at the palace of the prince, played by Yegor. As the theater patrons settled in to enjoy themselves, the dance company spun a magical tale reinforced by the amazing music of Tchaikovsky, dazzling scenery, exotic Ukrainian costumes, and, of course, that moving art form called dance. Along with the *Nutcracker*, *Swan Lake* was considered one of the penultimate Russian ballets, performed by every noteworthy company with former Russian or Soviet connections.

Rick sat in tense anticipation since Iryna wouldn't make her debut until the second act. As the short first act ended and the audience stretched their legs for a brief intermission, the buzz of conversation was overwhelmingly positive. Everyone was impressed with the mix of tradition and innovation in the set design, costumes, and choreography. "I always thought *Swan Lake* was one of the most boring ballets, but this interpretation is incredible!" a lady said nearby.

They haven't seen anything yet, thought Rick.

"It certainly is a lovely ballet," said his mom, leaning toward him. "When does Iryna come in?"

Rick explained what he had been able to gather from the

rehearsals. It seemed strange that the star performer wasn't in the first act, but she had so much to dance in the rest of the ballet, it made up for it. Iryna played two characters, the swan princess and an evil clone who tried to steal the prince. Rick's retelling of the plot was a little thin, since he had kept his focus solely on Iryna.

The warning bell rang, and people returned to their seats.

The curtain rose on a scene by a lake, and a flock of white "swans" alighted on the water, revealing Iryna in the center. From her first steps, the audience applauded with murmurs of approval. Each of her moves were graceful and conveyed deep emotion. When the scene changed and Iryna played the character of the sorcerer's daughter, the transformation was so complete, Rick hardly believed his eyes. Iryna performed with her entire soul, and he imagined her real-life experience of betrayal helped her to portray both the motives of the sorceress and the feelings of the swan princess in a way that tugged the heartstrings of every viewer.

When act two ended, the theater immediately filled with enthusiastic praise for the talented Ukrainian prima ballerina.

"She's the most amazing dancer I've ever seen!"

"Best interpretation of Odette performed in this theater!"

The success of Iryna's American debut was assured.

Matt and Beth were also profuse in their compliments, gushing about how they were honored to have such a star as their guest.

"Even after her performance at the party, I was not prepared to see her dance ballet!" said Beth. "Wow!"

"Quite impressive." Matt nodded.

The bell rang again, and everyone resumed their seats. For the entire third act, the audience held its breath as if afraid to break the performers' spell. Once the final scene was over, the theater erupted with applause. When Iryna stepped onto the stage for her curtain call, the clapping of thousands of hands shook the building like an earthquake. Dozens of flowers were brought up to the stage, but Rick observed his red roses were put directly into Iryna's hands, as promised. He had given lavish tips to ensure she received them onstage. After everyone took their final bows and the curtain closed, the applause rumbled for several minutes. Iryna emerged again, waved, and kissed her hands at everyone. A long time passed before the noise subsided and she was able to duck back behind the curtain.

When everyone finally left their seats and moved toward the exits, Rick said good night to his parents. After his mom gave him a quick hug, his dad put a hand on his shoulder and spoke in a low voice, "Be careful. We still don't have any leads on whoever is behind the matchbooks."

"I will." Rick had almost forgotten about them amid the busyness of the last two days. "Let me know if anything comes up."

He wove his way through the crowd, unsure where to wait for Iryna. Eventually, he made it around to the stage entrance and asked if his pass allowed him backstage. An attendant waved him through, and he entered a chaotic but jubilant scene of costumes being collected and hung on racks, scenery being moved, people walking by, and dancers standing around in groups talking and stretching. Though a lot was going on, Rick recognized the organization behind it all.

One of the dancers noticed him and motioned for him to follow.

"*Pryvit*, Rick, *tsym shlyakhom.*"

"Thanks," he replied without knowing whether he'd spoken in English or Ukrainian. It was getting easier and easier to switch between the two.

Rick congratulated the dancers as he passed, who smiled and waved at him. When they reached Iryna's dressing room, several reporters and a TV crew were interviewing her and taking pictures. The Ukrainian National Ballet had scored some publicity. His guide slipped away with a nod, and Rick stood in the shadows, watching.

Iryna was great with the press. She posed, smiled, and gushed about how much she enjoyed New York, offering just the right amount of personal information without really saying anything of substance. One of the reporters, who Rick recognized from the rehearsal the other evening, asked her about the "handsome, mysterious stranger" she left with.

"He is an old family friend," replied Iryna with a smile.

"You're sure he's not more than that?" the reporter persisted.

"Not at all."

The reporter appeared momentarily at a loss, probably unsure if she was understanding what Iryna said or if the foreign dancer was having trouble expressing herself in English. Iryna took the opportunity to end the interviews, saying it had been a long day and she needed to rest before tomorrow's performance.

As the reporters packed up and moved to leave, Iryna turned and saw Rick. Her face radiated sunshine. She stepped into her dressing room and waved him over. He reached her in a few short strides, and she pulled him in quickly and shut the door.

She kept hold of him and let him encircle her with his arms as she said, "Sorry. I didn't want the reporters to see you. Not that I would mind them knowing anything, but I didn't know what you thought about it."

"It's not something I've really considered. I suppose it's impossible to avoid the media. What exactly did you say to that reporter back there?"

"I said I was *not* sure you were *not* more than a friend." Iryna spoke softly, her lips tantalizingly close to his.

"Mm-hmm. Well, I'm sure you are more than that to me," Rick replied. Then he kissed her. He had been eagerly anticipating this moment ever since the door closed between them last night. His desire was, if possible, even more intense during their second kiss than the first. He drank in the sweetness of her lips, the warmth of her body against his, her stiff tulle skirt crinkling between them. They were interrupted by a knock at the door.

"Miss Shevchenko, we need your costume."

Iryna turned her head toward the door without letting go of Rick. "Okay, just a minute."

Rick let his eyes roam the tiny room that was little more than a closet. On the vanity, amongst all the hair and makeup paraphernalia, sat his roses, carefully placed in a vase of water. Since he didn't see a screen or anything to change behind like in the movies, he released her reluctantly. "I'll be right outside."

"It'll only take a minute, then I'll be ready to go."

Rick smiled sheepishly at the costume attendant as he stepped into the hall. The attendant nodded at him with an air that said, "You can't shock me. I've seen everything."

In moments, Iryna opened the door, dressed in a sweater and jeans with her duffel bag over her shoulder. A fringed shawl draped over her shoulders made the outfit a little less casual. "Sorry to make you wait," she said as she handed the gown to the attendant.

"No problem," the attendant replied over her shoulder as she pushed the cart down the hall.

"The company is getting together to celebrate at the hotel. I don't want to stay up late, but I should make an appearance, if that's okay?" Iryna beseeched him with her blue eyes.

"Sure, that's no problem, as long as I get to go with you," he replied.

"Absolutely. I cannot go anywhere without my mysterious, handsome stranger!"

"Do you want to walk with me to the car, or wait while I bring it around? It's in the garage."

"Oh, I'll walk with you. I'm not that tired." She linked her arm through his.

As they strolled arm-in-arm to the car, Rick looked down at Iryna, his heart brimming with emotion. He didn't want to name it. It was too soon, and he was afraid of what it would mean. On the other hand, he wanted to learn more about her. He wanted to dig deeper and find out what drove her.

"You were amazing tonight! The city is at your feet. Congratulations!"

"Thank you!"

"Tell me how you feel after something like that. How do you get through such a grueling performance?"

"It feels wonderful! It is so much work, and I empty myself of everything I have until I am nothing but a shell at the end, but when everything goes well, it's worth it. It seems kind of proud-ful to say, but the applause fills me up again."

"Wow, I don't know if I've ever experienced anything like that."

"You also asked how I get through it." Iryna lifted her eyes to him shyly as he opened the car door for her. "This week was especially hard, after what happened to Natalia. Today I was thinking of you."

Rick caught his breath. "Really?" What a strange notion, to be someone's inspiration.

"Really. I could not have gotten through it without you," she said, then kissed him.

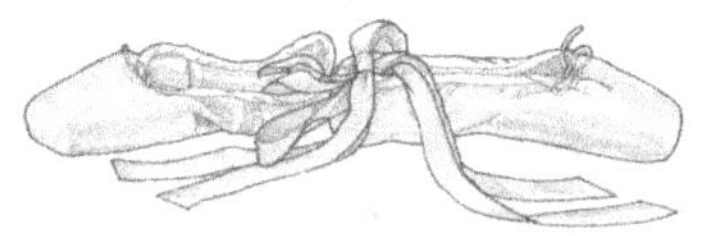

As they walked into the hotel bar, Iryna soared on an emotional high. She had just completed the greatest performance of her life, and she was on the arm of ... of a miracle. She could view it no other way. Her fellow dancers cheered and offered toasts as she entered. Many of them, like Iryna, had not bothered to remove their makeup, and it gave the gathering a surreal quality. Yegor caught her and twirled her around, setting her up for a bow, at which the company gave her an enthusiastic ovation.

After being handed around the room to receive her accolades, Rick guided Iryna to a table next to Katherine. As Maxim, the dancer who played the sorcerer, took the last empty seat, a brief frown of annoyance crossed Rick's face. It was gone so quickly she wondered if she'd imagined it.

Iryna opened her mouth to reintroduce them all, but he surprised her by greeting each of them by name. *It must be part of his diplomatic upbringing.* She smiled to herself at the thought.

"Can I get you something?" Rick offered as he pulled out a chair for her.

"Just a tonic water. I don't drink the alcohol. It dehydrates."

"Sure—be right back."

Iryna followed him with her eyes as he wove his way to the bar. Rick conversed casually and comfortably with everyone he ran into. She was proud to have a friend (could she call him her boyfriend?) who was comfortable in any social situation and who made an effort to be pleasant to all her friends. Iryna could have watched him all evening, but her coworkers soon called for her attention. Masha was noticeably absent. Not that most people would mind. Iryna chastened herself at the thought. She would have to make a point of trying to include Masha. It was not right for her to miss things like this.

Viktor, the director, came by to congratulate her, kissing her on both cheeks. "You were the empress of the evening, *Irynka,* my *tsarina.*"

Rick arrived with her tonic and one for himself, so she had something to toast with. Since Katherine spoke cultured English and Maxim had a lively sense of humor, their conversation was animated.

"I brought you a toneeck, but I see you already have one," observed Alexei as he approached their table.

"Oh, thank you, Alexei. You always take care of me."

"Congratulations on a magneeficent performance, my dear. Can I get anything forrr you?" He turned to Rick and tapped himself on the chest. "On me?"

"Thank you, but I'll have to take a rain check. I'm driving." Rick smiled, relaxing into his chair with his arm around Iryna as if implying her safety was his greatest consideration. Her heart warmed.

"No problem, no problem." Alexei patted Rick's shoulder. "But what ees eet, a rain check?"

"It means we will do it another time."

As Alexei nodded in comprehension, they were interrupted by an indignant Sergei.

"Excuse me, Rick, what is this about no drinks for me? Almost any country in world I can drink at eighteen, but America must be twenty-one? Is no sense at all! You do something? I can drink with 'adult' maybe?"

Rick laughed. "Sorry, friend, but I'm afraid I can't do anything about that. It's even illegal here to buy it for someone else, though I know that's not the case in most European countries."

"You know it's not good for you anyway," Iryna chided, trying not to sound too matronly.

He reached for the extra tonic on the table. "What is this?"

"It's a tonic. No alcohol, but very refreshing. Try it!" Iryna encouraged.

"That is no good! How I am to have fun?" he complained as he languished against the edge of Katherine's chair and dramatically threw his arm over his eyes.

"What—our delightful company and intelligent conversation is not enough for you?" Katherine teased as she playfully shoved him away.

At that moment, a few of the young American dancers entered the room, and Sergei's eyes strayed in their direction. He switched briefly to Ukrainian. "Iryna, my idol, you were amazing tonight, but if you will excuse me, I will try some conversation with those *unattached* lovely ladies over there." He strutted off in their direction like a bantam rooster. Iryna made an exaggerated sigh and rolled her eyes, but she smiled, not truly annoyed.

"I take it we should pity those poor girls who just arrived?" Rick grinned.

"Only eef they are wanting a drink, because he can't buy for them." Alexei chuckled.

Iryna shook her head at the banter.

Rick turned to Katherine. "You were curious about my father's time in Poland. How did you know he worked there?" Iryna sensed Rick had a serious motive for asking, despite his casual tone.

Katherine scrunched her nose in thought. "I heard it mentioned. I don't remember by whom. Does it matter?"

"No, I was just wondering."

Iryna turned to Rick as she finished her tonic. "I think I am ready to go, if you don't mind."

"Certainly. You had a big day today, and you have another performance tomorrow. Good night, Alexei, Katherine, Maxim."

"Take care of our Iryna!" Alexei said.

"Yes, sir. I will."

Iryna stood to leave and wrapped her scarf around her shoulders. "Good night, everyone! Bravo!" The company cheered and congratulated her again while they made their way out of the room.

Iryna looped her arm through Rick's as they walked through the lobby. Her eyes drooped, but as they passed the elevator, her attention was drawn by someone stepping into it as the doors closed.

She clicked her tongue. *That looked like Masha. What is she doing?*

She shrugged off the thought without mentioning it. They walked out the door and down the block to where Rick had parked the car. Rick opened the door and circled to the driver's side. Iryna slid over and buckled herself in the middle seat so she could lean on his shoulder. He kissed the top of her head and pulled away from the curb. Iryna closed her eyes and soon fell asleep.

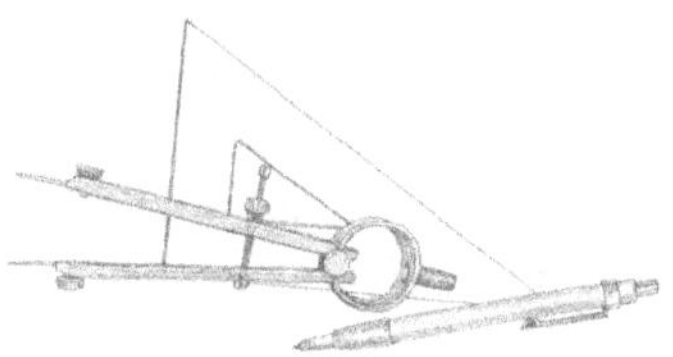

Rick marveled at how easily Iryna was able to fall asleep. It must have something to do with her physically demanding occupation. Having her next to him sent warm and contented feelings through him.

Suddenly a loud pop sounded, and the car jumped first to the right, narrowly missing a streetlight, then lurched hard to the left, causing the car in the next lane to brake hard while its driver blared the horn. A truck pulled out in front of them from a side street, and Rick jerked the steering wheel to the right.

As adrenaline pumped through his system, he barely had time to blurt a short plea for help. "God!" His sedan responded at the last second, and they escaped, losing only a mirror as the truck swerved to avoid them. Rick regained control of the car and brought it to a stop in an empty parking space in the far-right lane. He let out the breath he had been holding. Iryna had been jostled awake and was blinking.

"Are you okay?" Rick looked her over with concern.

"I think so." She sat up a little straighter and rolled her neck and shoulders around. "What happened?"

"I'm not sure. Stay here while I get out and check."

There were fortunately far fewer vehicles on the road than

normal at this time of night, so Rick only had to wait a few moments for the road to clear. The truck that had clipped their mirror didn't even bother to stop. Rick opened the door and stepped out, immediately seeing the problem. The front driver's side tire was completely shredded. The big pop must have been the tire blowing. *What in the world could have popped the tire?* They hadn't passed any construction or other debris. The tires were all fairly new and in good condition. He took his car in for routine maintenance as needed or had Peters check the car over whenever he visited his parents.

Oh, well. He sighed, briefly informed Iryna of the situation, then headed for the trunk and the spare tire.

The driver's side was not the best place to change a tire, even at this time of day. With shaking hands, he rummaged in the toolbox to see if Peters happened to stock it with any flares. No such luck. Rick made a mental note to pick some up, though he hoped he wouldn't be in a position to need them again anytime soon. He took a few more deep breaths to try to calm his heart rate. He considered calling a tow truck, but that meant Iryna would be up even later.

As he hefted out the tire, blue-and-red lights reflected off the black paint of his sedan. A police car pulled into the space behind them. Rick turned and waved with relief.

"You need some help?" the officer asked as he exited his cruiser.

"I just need to change a tire, but if you have a couple of flares, I'd appreciate it."

The officer glanced at the blown tire and nodded. "I can do better than that." He climbed back in his car, shifted into reverse, and angled the car halfway into the adjacent lane, effectively diverting the flow of cars and blocking Rick from traffic.

"I'll stand back there with my flashlight and wave people around you," he said, stepping out of the cruiser.

"Thank you. That'd be great." Rick jacked up the car and

removed the bad tire as quickly as possible with his limited experience. He hated taking the officer's time, but he was thankful he was here.

The spare fit into place easily. Rick made sure the lug nuts were tight. Once he was satisfied everything was done correctly, he put the wheel, the loose chunks of rubber, and the tools back in the trunk. He stepped up on the sidewalk and walked back to thank the officer.

"Anytime. Glad to be of service." The officer hesitated for a moment as if trying to decide whether to say something else. "You know, I don't usually drive this way, but I had a feeling I needed to tonight. I guess you were the reason. Take care." He waved and returned to his vehicle.

Rick shook his head and waved his thanks again. The officer waited until Rick climbed back in the car and drove away to make sure they were okay. Rick saw him turn down a side street as he glanced in the rearview mirror. Had God answered his brief cry and intervened on their behalf? Things definitely could have been worse.

"Are you sure you're okay?" he asked Iryna as he turned to her.

"Yes, I am fine. Don't worry." She patted his arm. "I've never watched anyone change the tire before."

"Well, anything for you." Rick smiled. In a more serious tone, he added, "I'm sorry to be getting you home so late. Do you want to skip going out in the morning?"

"Oh, no," she exclaimed, "I want to see your work!"

"All right. Let's get you home, then." Out of the corner of his eye, he saw her try to suppress a yawn, but she didn't fall asleep again.

They reached the house in Gramercy Park after only a few more minutes. Rick let Iryna in, gave her a quick kiss, and said good night. After she retired, weariness overtook Rick, and he knew it would be unwise to drive back to his apartment. Even if he wasn't concerned about keeping a respectable distance from

Iryna, he doubted he could make it up the stairs. His legs wobbled from the relief of getting home alive and safe.

Now that all the adrenaline had left his system, he replayed the events of the evening in his mind. If any of those other cars had been in a slightly different place … it didn't bear thinking about. He stumbled into the living room, sprawled out on the couch with a pillow over his head, and soon fell asleep.

CHAPTER 10

Vasyl Schevchenko was not a morning person. Late night stakeouts were more his thing. As a cabinet minister, he kept a more routine schedule, but he still liked to sleep in whenever he had an opportunity. So when his phone buzzed at six, he ignored it. It was Saturday, for pity's sake. It stopped after a minute, and he fell back asleep. Then it buzzed again. Remembering Iryna was in New York, he reached for the phone in case it might be her. It was past the time for her first US performance to end. He knocked the phone off the nightstand and muttered a curse as he bent to pick it up.

"Vasyl …" his wife chastened, her voice drowsy.

He sighed. "Allo?" No reply. The phone kept buzzing. *Blasted smartphones,* he thought as he swiped the screen. After half a lifetime in surveillance, he'd resisted carrying anything so traceable. At the insistence of his colleagues, he finally broke down and bought one. He was still figuring it out. "Allo?"

A deep Ukrainian voice with a Polish accent came through the speaker. "Vasyl? This is Bogdan Androshchuk."

"Bogdan." Vasyl's mind snapped fully awake. Bogdan was one of the few people who knew he'd been a double agent, and he would trust him with his life. If he was calling, there was a good reason.

He got up, walked into the bathroom, and turned on the faucet so his wife wouldn't be disturbed. His former KGB instincts kicked in, and he suspected this conversation was one he might not want her to hear. "What can I do for you?"

"I heard you've done some digging into Natalia's death." Bogdan's voice was heavy with grief but steady with deliberate control. Vasyl knew better than to wonder how Bogdan discovered he had made inquiries. Even retired, Bogdan possessed innumerable resources.

"I cannot tell you how sorry I am, Bogdan. She and Iryna were friends, but even so, I would have looked into the case for old time's sake." He paused. He had put off calling Bogdan to tell him about the video footage, hoping to get a lead on the perpetrator first. "Unfortunately, the police don't have much to go on."

"I'm at her apartment. I have something you need to see." The tone of Bogdan's pronouncement filled Vasyl with a sense of dread. Whatever it was, did it have implications beyond Natalia's murder? It had to be bad for Bogdan to call him personally.

"Give me the directions." As Bogdan spoke, he wrote some brief notations on a pad of paper. "I'll be there in an hour."

Vasyl dressed quickly, poured some chai in a thermos, grabbed a pastry, and walked to his car. He would have gotten there much faster by taking the Metro, but he'd be vulnerable and exposed in the dense commuter crowd. Better to suffer through the terrible city traffic under his own power than relinquish control.

As he drove across town, he fell back on his training protocols and reviewed Bogdan's current situation dispassionately, like he would a case file. Bogdan had had an easier time than he had during the transition from Soviet control to independence in Poland. As a friend of Solidarity, he was treated like a hero rather than a traitor for working against the government. He helped reform the government and held a cabinet post for many years before his retirement. At nearly eighty, Bogdan still possessed a formidable intellect, and Vasyl occasionally bounced ideas off him. It was always nice to have someone around he could count on to be discreet.

Bogdan's beloved wife, who he had met in Poland, had recently died, and Bogdan moved to Kyiv to be closer to his relatives on his father's side as well as a couple of his children. Natalia was here already, and one of his sons was here studying at the university. Bogdan had been devastated by his wife Cela's death. She was much younger than he, and he had never considered that she would go first, but at least the brain tumor took her quickly. After that, Bogdan needed to be around family. And now Natalia was taken before her time. Few men could handle that much sorrow, even a hardened government official like Bogdan.

In just under an hour, Vasyl pulled into a parking garage near Natalia's apartment. He glanced warily at the other vehicles. Anyone who worked for the government wore a target on their back, and this was no time to let his guard down. He walked around the corner to the tall apartment complex. It was an older, Soviet-era building, but one that had been remodeled and updated for a younger generation. Vasyl pressed the buzzer for Natalia's number.

"Allo?" Bogdan's voice came through the speaker.

"*Tse ya, Vasyl.*"

A click sounded as the magnetic lock on the door released, allowing him to enter. Since the apartment was only on the second floor, he took the stairs instead of the lift. No telling how reliable the elevator was. These old buildings were notorious for leaving people stuck between floors, and it looked like the remodel was only superficial. Bogdan must have been listening for his approach, because he opened the door before Vasyl raised a hand to knock.

"I apologize for waking you up so early." Normally he would have followed this up with some snarky comment about Vasyl's sleeping habits, but the old man's face appeared haggard, and his shoulders drooped. It would take some time for Bogdan to recover from this latest loss. Maybe he never would.

"No problem, old friend." Bogdan stepped aside, allowing Vasyl to enter the apartment. "What did you find?"

"Come and see."

Bogdan walked over to Natalia's kitchen table, where it appeared he had been sorting through the mail. He held up a yellowed poster with several creases. The image on the poster was well known to Vasyl, a picture of Gary Cooper from *High Noon* with the caption "Solidarity" in Polish. What made his chest tighten were the ominous words written in marker across the front: "One down, two to go." His mind also registered that the date on the original poster, a call to vote for the anti-communist, pro-union party, had been cut off.

"My God," he whispered and stared at it for several moments without speaking. Bogdan also remained silent. What was there to say, after all? After a minute, Vasyl asked curtly, "The envelope?"

Though Bogdan was wearing rubber gloves, Vasyl was not, so Bogdan picked it up from the table using a tissue and handed it to him.

"What made you think to wear those?" He nodded toward the gloves. "Did you already have an idea it was not a random attack?"

Bogdan shrugged. "You never know" was his only reply. Vasyl turned his attention to the envelope.

"Posted in Kyiv the day she was killed," he said aloud to himself. "That's not much help, as the sender was most likely the same person who ..." He trailed off. "No return address. Standard envelope." He threw it back on the table. "If he was smart, no DNA or fingerprints, either, but we can check anyway."

Bogdan found a plastic bag in the kitchen and placed the envelope carefully inside.

"What do you make of the removal of the date?" Vasyl asked.

"Perhaps the date is not relevant, and he wants us to focus on something else. He knows we would notice it missing, so he is pointing out that the date is unimportant?"

"Hmm. But there is nothing to go on!" Vasyl reigned in his growing frustration and anxiety. "There were three of us working together, but who else was aware of it? And why would they even care? And why now, after so long? Why Natalia?" Bogdan shrugged again, and Vasyl paced up and down the small kitchen. "You have four children, so that can't be what he's referring to. It must be related to Poland. You and Carter and I were all there. It has to be some sort of revenge, but for what?"

"People died, on several occasions, due to the action or inaction of our various governments. But it is a long time to wait for vengeance," conceded Bogdan. "And there were many others involved, not only us. It is inexplicable."

"There must be some twisted reason here somewhere. We have to dig it up." A vague theory formed in his mind, but he wanted more information before divulging it. Vasyl considered Bogdan and hesitated before asking his next question. "A bystander caught it on video. Have you seen it?"

Bogdan glanced down and nodded slowly. Then he looked at Vasyl and gave a wry smile. "I still have resources. It is all right that you did not show me yourself. I would not have wanted to show me."

Vasyl stared at the wall, sorry that he had been too afraid to come to his friend earlier. He added, "We say 'he,' but it could easily have been a 'her.' The video quality is poor." Bogdan grimaced in acknowledgement.

The poster followed the envelope into the bag, and Vasyl took it. "You will also need this." Bogdan handed him a thick folder, and Vasyl raised his eyebrows. "To help you eliminate suspects. This is information on Natalia's boyfriend and all the protesters in his political action group." With a twitch at the corner of his mouth, Vasyl tucked it under his arm. Of course Bogdan would have a file on his daughter's boyfriend. The amusing thought was chased away almost immediately by present circumstances.

"We will get to the bottom of this," he promised his friend through clenched teeth. He didn't ask Bogdan to pass on anything else he came up with, because he knew he would.

Vasyl cast a last glance around the apartment. His eyes focused on a jumble of items lying on a side table. "Bogdan!" He pointed to a matchbook. "Matt told me Iryna and Rick each found one of these in their belongings!"

Bogdan clicked his tongue. "I had not noticed that." He picked up the book and studied it. "*Gdansk.* Well, there is no doubt what the note means, then."

They walked in unspoken agreement to the door and parted with determined eyes and grim faces.

When he returned to his car, Vasyl took the time to perform a thorough inspection of the vehicle. Once he was certain the car had not been tampered with, he climbed inside and typed a series of numbers into his phone. At least he could take some sadistic pleasure in the fact that he was not the only one who would have to wake up early.

CHAPTER 11

It was barely three o'clock in the morning when the phone on Matt Carter's nightstand vibrated. It had nearly buzzed itself onto the floor by the time he picked it up. He stared at the screen for a few minutes while the sleep cleared from his eyes and his brain processed the information he was seeing. Vasyl was calling. Matt knew implicitly that it had to be something important. Nevertheless, as he answered the phone, he said, "Vasyl, it's three in the morning."

As Matt listened to the voice on the other end, his eyes widened, and he sat bolt upright. He threw the covers off the bed, jumped to his feet, and made his way to his study. He shuffled papers on his desk and opened his laptop. "The reference to three is a little thin, isn't it? It might mean anything," he suggested without conviction. Vasyl had to be right. It was the only thing that made sense, and yet it made no sense at all. He sighed and ran his fingers through his hair as he listened to his friend make his case again. A chill gripped his heart when Vasyl mentioned the matchbook.

"You're right. One child from each family. This must be someone who lost a child, then?" he mused. "If it was a parent of one of the miners, they must be very old by now, and that can hardly be seen as our fault."

He was silent for a few moments as Vasyl spoke.

"Yes, I know, murderers are not rational," Matt agreed. "Yes. It has to be something that we were directly involved in, but we did our best to keep our movements discrete. Who could have known? And what other collateral damage was there?"

He listened again for several minutes.

"All right. I'll dig around and see what I can come up with. The Warsaw paper has online archives. I'll start with that. But first, we must put some protective measures in place."

They spoke for some time, deciding the best way to keep their families safe. When the call ended, Matt immediately made another phone call while typing frantically on his computer. Because he was so focused on his research, the time flew by. Shortly after six, he woke Rick up.

He was relieved when he heard Rick's sleepy voice on the other end. "Hey, Dad, what's up?"

"Son, we have a bit of a situation here. I'm going to be sending Peters to pick you up. Can you—"

"Dad, I'm downstairs on the couch. We got in late last night, so I didn't bother going back to my apartment."

Matt closed his eyes and ran a hand over his face as the tension drained out of him. "Okay, great. Can you wake Peters for me and brew some coffee? I'll wake up Iryna and your mom and we'll meet you downstairs."

"Dad, what's going on?"

"Let me tell everyone at the same time. That will be easier."

"Okay, but Iryna really needs to rest. She has another performance tonight."

Matt sighed. "All right. We'll give her and your mother another hour to sleep. You and Peters and I can hash some things out together first so we can present them with a more complete plan. Get Peters up and make the coffee. I'll be right down."

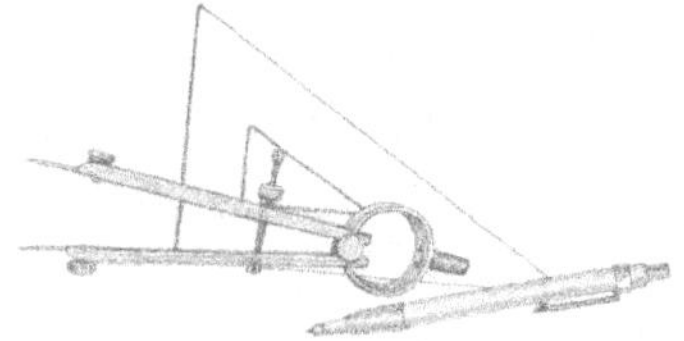

Rick stared at his phone for a moment, bewildered, before shaking the drowsiness out of his head and making himself move toward the kitchen. He left his belt, tie, and jacket where they were on the back of the chair, rolled up the sleeves of his untucked shirt, and walked to the kitchen in stocking feet. He turned on the coffee maker so the water would heat, then woke Peters up.

While Peters got dressed, Rick splashed some water on his face and ignored the dark stains on his clothes acquired from changing the tire. By the time his father came downstairs, Rick was filling up a third cup of coffee and Peters was dressed and sipping from a mug at the table. They both watched Mr. Carter when he entered the room.

Matt sat heavily and took a gulp of his coffee. "I just got off the phone with Vasyl." He gave the two men a brief summary of the call.

"So you're saying Iryna and I are in danger? For something that happened before we were born? That's crazy. Why now?" Rick's questions came out rapidly as he processed the information.

"It's possible that it took the person this long to track us down. We covered our actions pretty well."

"What did you do that someone would take revenge for?" Rick asked, his tone angry, though he was pretty sure his dad would never have done anything morally questionable.

Matt put his hands up. "We don't even know at this point. Everything we did was to help the Polish people and end the Cold War. Without more information to go on, we have to act as if our assumptions are correct. Regardless of the cause, our immediate concern is to keep you and Iryna safe."

"I can drive Rick everywhere, including work, so he won't be alone," Peters suggested.

"Yes, I was going to say the same thing. Thank you, Cecil." A small part of Rick's brain was surprised his dad used Peters's first name. He wasn't sure if he'd ever heard it before. But once Peters mentioned driving, Rick's chest tightened, and his stomach churned. The tire blowout the previous night took on sinister possibilities.

"Dad," he said hoarsely, "could someone sabotage a car by causing a delayed tire blowout?"

"Uh …"

Rick continued before allowing the others to respond. "That's why we were late last night. One of my tires blew on Lexington Avenue and I had to change it. I thought it was strange, because the tires were in good condition and I didn't run over anything."

His dad stiffened, and Peters pressed his lips together. "What do you think?" Matt asked Peters.

Peters responded slowly. "It might be possible to weaken the integrity of the tire by making a small slice or nick in the wall without completely puncturing it. Then, as the car heats up and the tire expands, the additional pressure could cause it to blow. Not guaranteed when or where."

"Could you tell by looking at the tire afterward? I kept all the pieces."

"I can look," said Peters, "but probably can't tell anything. It would have been small, and the subsequent damage might obscure it entirely."

"Is that something"—Rick leaned against the counter while

trying to put his thoughts into words—"that someone would even bother doing if the outcome was so uncertain?" Rick was really hoping it was a worthless idea. The danger would feel way too real if someone had deliberately caused the accident.

"There's nothing lost if it doesn't work and everything to gain if it does, from his perspective," Matt said. "The only risk would be if someone saw him do it."

"A deft hand would only need a second," offered Peters. "Might have been done at the theater or the hotel and not blown 'til enough pressure built up."

"Can we question the parking attendants and get surveillance from the hotel and theater?" Rick wondered.

"Without a police report, nobody's going to let you look at security footage, and we can't file a report without knowing if a crime even happened," Matt replied. "I'll ask anyway. The theater might cooperate since the ballet is performing there and they're guests at the hotel. I could ask the ballet's publicist to investigate it, though we don't want too many people involved in the questioning at this point."

"Wouldn't it be best to make everyone aware of what's going on so they can help look out for Iryna? How are we going to keep her safe when she leaves? Should she continue the tour with all this going on?"

"We don't have enough information to make a decision yet. Someone had to put that matchbook in your pocket, but they might not be working alone. We might be sending her into greater danger if she returns to Kyiv," Matt answered, addressing Rick's last question first. "As to informing everyone, what do we say without causing widespread alarm? Very few people know Vasyl was a double agent, and he'd like to keep it that way. We can't exactly say there's a mad killer on the loose targeting ballerinas. That would be a last resort. And Vasyl already has someone positioned in the troupe to keep an eye on her."

"He does? Who?"

"He wouldn't say. He doesn't entirely trust his own spies, and he wants us to keep an open mind. Plus, he's going to ask the consulate to assign additional security to travel with the group."

"I still think it would be beneficial for us to know who it is. What if Iryna needs their help? Or what if we waste a bunch of time looking at the wrong person?"

"He sent this person before we learned about the Polish connection, so no one can be cleared of motive yet."

The three men fell silent, and Rick stared at his empty mug as he considered the morning's revelations. "If we discount the past and only look at the immediate results, the people who benefit are Karina and Masha. Karina got the lead role in Kyiv, and Masha might have thought she would get it. Plus, Masha had opportunity. She was there at the time Natalia was killed, and now she's here in the States. Everything else might be a smoke screen."

Matt nodded. "That's the kind of open-minded thinking we need. Don't take anything for granted."

"Only the timing of the matchbooks doesn't work for that theory," Rick mused. "Oh, and I asked Katherine where she'd heard you'd been in Poland."

Matt clicked his tongue. "That was risky. I'd rather you hadn't tried to interrogate anyone."

"I kept it casual. She said someone had mentioned it, but she didn't remember who."

"I'll keep that in mind. But before we can focus on solving the case, we have to make sure everyone is safe," declared Matt. "So don't go anywhere alone. Peters will be glued to your side. We will escort Iryna everywhere while she is here, and someone from the consulate will accompany her on the rest of the tour. I'll go wake up Iryna and your mom. Take Peters out to your car and show him your tire, then we'll meet back here when the ladies are ready."

Matt and Peters stood, but Rick tapped dad's shoulder as they left the kitchen and whispered in a low voice, "Dad, I'm sure you didn't do anything, but is it possible Vasyl or Bogdan did something you don't know about, something you could get blamed for? Do you really trust them?"

"In my heart, I do, yes." Matt sighed, his eyes focused far away. "My mind can think of all kinds of scenarios. I can't say it's impossible for them to do wrong, but I have no reason to doubt their word or intentions."

"Vasyl's not the type of person who would put his daughter in danger to save his reputation?"

"Vasyl is a person who can be very passionate for a cause, but after the fall of the Soviet Union, his family became his focus. He poured everything into Iryna. I think defending her would be his priority now. I'm sure if he thought letting his past become public would protect her, he would do it, even if Russian-Ukrainian relations suffered as a result."

Rick nodded. He wasn't sure if he wanted to trust anyone right now, even Vasyl, but it seemed they would have to.

As he and Peters walked to the car, Rick gathered his scattered thoughts. He glanced up and down the street, searching for suspicious strangers. *I'm already becoming paranoid.*

His brain wanted to separate himself from Iryna so he wouldn't be hurt if something happened to her, but his heart wanted to wrap her in his arms and never let her out of his sight. There was no question as to which would win, but he hated that a battle existed at all. *How is a person supposed to function when their life is in danger? This is insane!* It might be better not to think.

His parents had left their spot in front of the mansion free again, so Rick had parked there. He opened the trunk and showed Peters the remains of the blown tire. The tread had completely separated from the rest, and the edges were mangled.

"Not much hope of finding anything," Peters mused. They took each piece out and laid them on the sidewalk, inspecting them carefully. Eventually, they decided it was impossible to discern if any of the edges had been cut by a tool. However, there did appear to be a definite point of origin. The tire wall had some fissures that were longer than the others and seemed to radiate from a central point. "You're lucky it was on a one-way street, though."

"Why's that?"

"No oncoming traffic. That's the highest probability for a fatality. Most of the streets downtown are one-way. I would have picked the front passenger side to pull you toward a lamppost or building."

"Hmm. So if it was sabotage, whoever did it is not familiar with the city. That makes it unlikely there's an American accomplice, at least." Rick paused, thinking. "I was a little apprehensive about changing the tire on that side in the middle of the road. If the cop hadn't shown up, I might have called a tow truck."

"If there were no injuries from the blowout, that would be another way to put you in danger. If he thought you were the type of person to change his own tire. Many people aren't."

They surveyed the wreckage of the tire again. "Looks like the wheel is useable," observed Peters. "Scratched, but useable. I'll get a new tire as soon as I can. Probably Monday. But unless you ran over something, the tire should not have blown. This car is what, two years old?"

"Yeah, about that."

"And your mileage"—Peters hopped in the car, turned the key—"is only seventy-eight hundred. Have you had the tires rotated?"

Rick nodded. "Last time I had the oil changed."

"What about tire pressure?"

"The car has sensors that let me know if it gets low, and then I air them up. It happens sometimes when the weather changes."

"And that didn't go off yesterday?"

"No."

"So somebody didn't just let air out of the tire. Well, you

should have another twenty to thirty thousand miles left with this brand of tire."

They put everything back in the trunk of the car and headed inside. Rick's spine stiffened. As chilling as the morning's revelations were, they would be a worse shock for Iryna. At least he'd been kept in the loop. *I have to be strong for her.* It would be easier to be strong for her sake than for himself alone.

CHAPTER 12

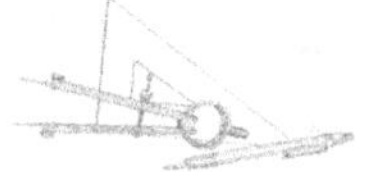

When the men reentered the kitchen, Iryna leaned against the counter, rubbing the sleep out of her eyes and sipping a cup of tea. Beth looked up from her seat at the table, and her mouth tightened as they walked in. Rick worried about how they would react to the news, but he expected his dad, ever the diplomat, would find a way to break it to them gently.

"As I told Rick and Peters already, I got a call from Vasyl early this morning." Iryna straightened at the mention of her father. "I am sorry to have to tell you this, but video has surfaced showing that Natalia was killed intentionally."

The ladies gasped in surprise. So much for diplomacy.

"In addition," Matt continued, "Natalia's father was going through her mail and found a note that indicated there are two more targets. A matchbook identical to the two you found"—he nodded at Rick and Iryna—"was among her belongings. This, unfortunately, indicates that you two are in danger as well."

"What? Why?" exclaimed Iryna. "I don't understand!" Tea sloshed from her mug as she threw her arms wide in protest.

"This is crazy! There must be some mistake," Beth protested.

Matt shook his head. "There is no mistake. The motive is unknown, but the threat is clear."

"What are we going to do?" Beth's voice was strained.

Matt sat next to her and patted her knee. "We have a plan. Don't worry."

Rick walked quietly over to Iryna, rescued the mug of tea, and took her hand. She clutched his with a death grip. When Matt finished explaining the safety and security measures they were putting in place, he asked if anyone had any further thoughts or questions.

"Iryna?" Rick cradled her name with concern.

Iryna had gone pale and was trembling, but she spoke vehemently. "I am so much in the rage right now, I cannot even think."

"I know it is a huge shock …" Mr. Carter began.

"It is more than a shock, it is the impossible thing! That someone has killed my Natalia on purpose, when she did nothing to them!" Upset, her accent became more pronounced. She balled her free hand into a fist.

Her other hand squeezed Rick's tightly, and he squeezed it back. He cared too much for her to step away now. They would face whatever came together. He would have to deal with the fear gripping his heart at the thought of something happening to her.

Beth spoke up, her voice timid. "It seems like, dear, there must be something more we can do. Other than hiring a bunch of security guards and barricading ourselves in the house, which is what I feel like doing."

"I know. The problem is that we have so little to go on. Vasyl has the police and his personal contacts all working overtime to find anything on Natalia's killer. On our side, we have no evidence of any crime for US authorities to work with."

"We could upgrade our burglar alarm system to include cameras," suggested Peters. "That way we can keep an eye out for suspicious activity in front of the house and our parking spaces. Right now, it only notifies us if a door or window is opening."

"Good idea. Can you contact the security company about that?"

Peters nodded and made a note on his phone.

Rick's mind melted, rendering him unable to concentrate. Like his mom, he wanted to take action, but there was no action to take. Next to him, Iryna radiated tension. He released her hand and put his arm protectively around her shoulders. Hopefully the contact would comfort her as much as it comforted him.

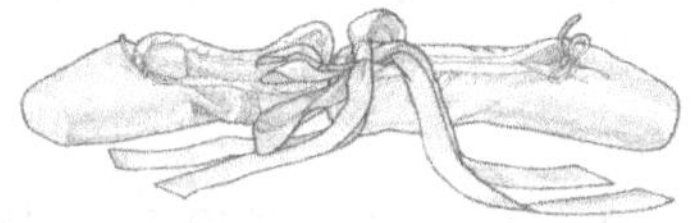

Iryna stood in silence with clenched teeth. She was so mad, she wanted to punch something. She wanted to blame somebody—maybe her father—for being involved in something that put her in this situation. Blaming him wouldn't be fair, but nothing about this situation was fair. When tears pricked the corners of her eyes, she furiously blinked them back.

Calm down! You can't do any good if you can't think clearly! Breathe. Slow, deep breaths.

The gentle pressure of Rick's arm around her shoulders grounded her. Gradually, her muscles relaxed.

Iryna was only mildly perturbed at the thought that her father was keeping tabs on her. He had always done that. It was nothing new, and she knew it was because he cared about her. She put those thoughts aside. This was a problem to be solved, like a chess game, so she needed to be emotionally detached. The solution must lie in the past.

When a moment of clarity found her, a question popped into her head. "What language was the note on the poster written in?"

Matt frowned. "Let me check. Vasyl sent me a picture. Hold on." He jabbed the phone with his finger until he found it. "Ah. Russian." He held up the phone for her to see.

"Why Russian instead of Ukrainian or Polish? That would seem to point that the writer's first language is Russian." Iryna answered her own question. "That is his or her most comfortable or most natural language to write." Everyone leaned in, studying the poster.

"It does appear more natural than the wording on the matchbooks," agreed Matt. "This would eliminate most families connected to the miners or other victims of state violence in Poland during that time."

"Unless Russian was used on purpose to throw us off," Rick suggested.

"I'm not sure our perpetrator is that sophisticated. His attempts so far are blundering at best. We may be looking at someone working from emotion more than cold intellect," Matt said.

"The letters formed are like the fluent writer also, not like someone copying the—what is it?—font from the online translator. The letters would look differently if the person did not know the language. It has to be written by someone who at least speaks Russian," Iryna insisted.

"That's an astute observation. We should call your father and see if he noticed. Maybe you should call." Matt held the phone toward Iryna. "Just to reassure him with your voice."

"Thank you." Iryna took the phone and dialed his number. "*Tato.*" She stepped out into the hallway for some privacy.

"*Irynka.*"

At the sound of her father's deep voice, Iryna broke down and cried.

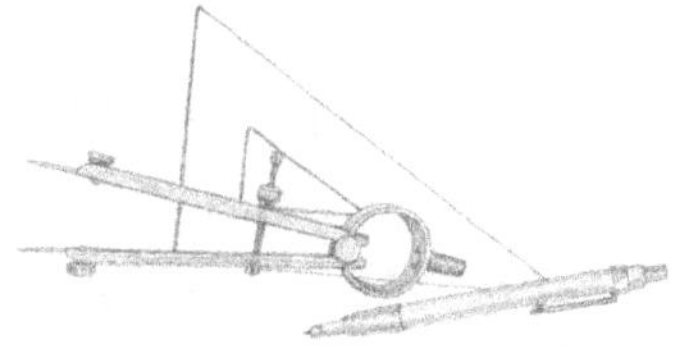

"Well, while Iryna's on the phone, I'll fix some breakfast. We can't live on coffee," Beth said.

Everyone rose from their seats, eager to do something proactive. Peters retired to his room to call the security company. Matt climbed the stairs to retrieve his laptop and begin searching Polish news articles from the eighties for victims of violence with connections to Russia.

Unsure what else to do, Rick helped his mother make breakfast. He needed help dealing with his fears, but he wasn't sure how to bring the subject up. They still weren't able to talk about Cassie, after all.

"How are you doing with all this, Mom?" he asked, broaching the subject.

"Whew. It's a lot to process." She pulled the milk and eggs out of the fridge and set them on the counter. "You know, I came back to the States to give birth to you while your father was still in Poland. I worried about him every day. I worried about myself, about delivering you without him. I kept busy so I wouldn't think about it."

She was doing the same thing now by fixing breakfast, he noticed. Not that there was anything wrong with keeping busy. But holding things in and not talking about them wasn't going to work for him.

"I'm sure they will catch whoever did this very soon," Beth said brightly, as if she could force her will on the future with sheer optimism. The dishes clattering on the counter hinted at her internal distress.

Though wishing didn't alter reality, Rick followed his mother's cue and behaved normally. In a short time, scrambled eggs, toast, and microwaved bacon were on the table.

"The security company can come this afternoon to install the cameras," Peters announced as he walked back into the kitchen. "They were going to make us wait two weeks, but I convinced them it was urgent."

"Excellent!" said Matt.

"Dad, are you and Mom going to be home today? I was going to show Iryna one of my renovations and then drop her at the theater, and if Peters is driving me, someone will need to be at the house."

"I think I can do everything that needs to be done today from here." Matt typed on his laptop while chewing a slice of bacon. "These library archives should keep me busy for a while."

Iryna came back in and returned the phone to Matt. "My father says he will get on the Russian angle right away."

Beth handed her a plate and she sat, chewing her eggs mechanically. Rick watched Iryna surreptitiously and noticed her eyes were red. Shortly, she rose and excused herself.

"Thank you for the breakfast. I will go and shower." She looked at Rick. "I will be ready to go whenever you are."

He nodded, and she turned and left the kitchen. After what she'd just learned, he longed to hold her against his chest and never let go. He admired how she'd responded. Iryna had taken a punch to the gut and held herself together like a champ, but would she fall apart as soon as she was alone? He couldn't be at her side every hour of the day, but he would do everything he could to keep her safe until this mystery was solved.

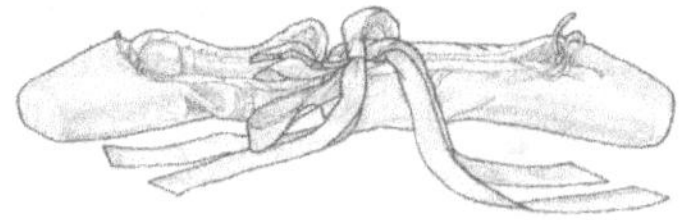

Iryna climbed the stairs, shut the door of her room, and stared at the wall. Why? Why did things like this happen? People could be so evil! When she thought it was unintentional, she was angry and sorrowful. She mourned the loss of her friend. But now she was incensed. She wanted to hurt whoever hurt Natalia. She grabbed a pillow off the bed and screamed into it, then punched it a few times for good measure.

With her equilibrium partially restored, she entered the bathroom and turned on the shower. The hot, steaming water soothed her as it ran over her body. She practiced her breathing again and imagined the anger going down the drain.

Natalia is with me. She was always in my hands. Vengeance is mine. I will repay.

Iryna heard the words clearly in her mind. *But God, why didn't you* do *something?*

Natalia is with me.

Was God really speaking to her, or was her subconscious bringing things to mind that she had heard before? Did it matter if it was true, anyway? Though it didn't exactly soothe her tortured spirit, it was still truth. Natalia was in Heaven. What did any of this matter to her anymore? If Natalia was given a choice to still be on Earth, is that what she would choose? Iryna exhaled a long, slow breath and released whatever anger remained. Questioning God would do no good. She must focus on the present.

Rick. Rick was in the present. His life was in danger too, if their conjectures were correct. No matter what the future held for them, she wanted to be with him today. That was all she could handle—today. That was enough.

CHAPTER 13

By the time Rick had showered, changed clothes, and headed downstairs, it was nearly ten o'clock. His mother sat in the living room reading the paper. When he came in, she held up the entertainment section. "The ballet received rave reviews! They're predicting that the entire tour will be sold out by tonight." Beth's pitch rose in an unnatural manner. Though she pretended everything was all right, the danger that threatened them had obviously shaken her.

"Wow, that's awesome." He took the paper to humor his mother and glanced at the review. High praise was given to the entire cast, but especially to Iryna. The critic compared her to Anna Pavlova and Margot Fonteyn. Rick wondered if Iryna would be able to dance well this evening, or if the thought of her life being in danger would visibly affect her performance. Who would be able to perform under such circumstances?

Beth appeared to be absorbed in another section of the paper. Rick set his down and paced around the room. How could he help Iryna? He didn't even know how to help himself. Praying comforted her before. Maybe they should pray again. If God really helped them last night, would He continue to help them? What if he had crashed into a car, or been run over while changing the tire? Would he have gone to Heaven? The question felt more urgent than ever.

Peters popped his head into the living room. "Hey, Rick, walk with me to get your folks' car? We won't take yours until I can get a new spare."

"Sure." Rick was already wearing a sweatshirt and jeans, and the sunny morning meant he didn't need a heavy jacket.

As they strode around the corner to the parking structure, Peters explained, "Your dad doesn't even want me walking around by myself right now. We also gotta check the car out and make sure it hasn't been tampered with."

When they arrived at the parking space, everything seemed in order. The car alarm still worked, there was no evidence of anyone trying to break in, and all the tires appeared to be inflated properly. Peters even crawled under the car with a flashlight to make sure no one had planted a bomb or loosened any cables. No brake fluid dripped, and everything under the hood looked as it should.

"Just to be safe, you stand over there behind that pillar while I start it," Peters directed.

Rick obliged reluctantly and let out a sigh of relief as the engine turned over and Peters backed the car out of the space. They drove back to the house, and Rick bounded up the steps. Iryna waited just inside, sitting at the bottom of the stairs.

"Ready to go?" He smiled when he saw her. Her brow cleared as she stood. "If you'd rather stay—"

"I'm ready. I've been looking forward to it." The corners of her mouth curved up into a smile. That was a good sign. Peters kept the car running, so Rick took Iryna's hand and led her to the car. They both slid into the back seat, and Peters drove the car across town.

"I thought it might be a good idea if we prayed again."

Iryna nodded her agreement. Rick realized he didn't know Peters's views on prayer.

"God ..." *What exactly is the proper form of address?* "Thank you for keeping us safe last night. Please keep us safe today. Help my dad and Vasyl to track down whoever is responsible for Natalia's death. We pray that you comfort Natalia's father and the rest of her family. Show us what to do today. Thank you. Amen."

"Amen," said Peters from the front seat.

Rick worried his prayer was extremely inadequate given the circumstances, but Iryna squeezed his hand in approval.

"So where are we going?" she asked.

"We are going to tour an urban housing renovation project I designed. In the city, there isn't much space, and it's very expensive. Developers are always trying to get the most they can for their money, so I create plans to maximize usage for the available space while still trying to make it look nice."

"Beauty and function. I understand. We have the same to consider with costumes and set designs."

"Exactly. The one we're visiting this morning is one of my favorites. We won a grant to create family-friendly spaces that still meet the minimum occupancy requirements."

"You mean you had to include a certain number of apartments in the plan?"

"Yes. It was quite a challenge, like a puzzle, but I really enjoyed it."

Iryna grinned widely at him, and her eyes sparkled with humor.

"What?"

"Your face lights up when you talk about your work. I can sense your enthusiasm. It's cute. It makes me even more excited to see it."

A pleasant warmth crept up Rick's neck. Though unused to the attention, it heartened rather than embarrassed him when it came from her.

The car pulled up to the building, and Peters dropped them off in front. The parking on the street was all full, so he said he'd circle the block 'til he found a spot. "Just call me when you're ready to go," he said as Rick helped Iryna out of the car.

From the outside, the building didn't appear too different from the others on the block. The main difference was the glass door with glass side-panels and a large picture window above it.

"Bullet-proof glass," Rick explained. "It provides plenty of light in the foyer but maintains the safety of the entry without bars or anything like that. The two-level entry cost me an apartment, but it was what sold them on the design. Come on." He held a thick key card to the door, and it buzzed as the magnetic lock disengaged. With a bit of pride, he held the door open for Iryna and ushered her inside.

"Oooh!" Iryna gasped as she stepped through the doorway.

They were met by a gorgeous built-in planter packed with flowering shrubs, decorated with artistic tiles, and surrounded by wooden benches. There was even a large rubber tree in the middle with branches stretching toward the high ceiling. What was ingenious, though, were the walls. The outside of the manager's office, laundry, and mail room had been turned into a playground. Thick plexiglass panels studded with "rocks" formed a climbing wall on the outside of the mail room. Climbing ropes were anchored in place outside the manager's office. Various spinning toys and mazes adorned the wall of the laundry room.

Two women sat at a bench sipping coffee, watching their young ones play. The entry was made of tile, but a composite playground material covered the floor around the planter and play area. Little paths of colored circles meandered across a green background. Two toddlers jumped from one circle to the next playing an imaginary game, and a father typed on a laptop while his son climbed the rock wall.

Rick walked around to the manager's office and stuck his head in. An elderly, white-haired man with a mustache sat at a desk checking the security monitor. He jumped up quickly when Rick entered and came around to shake his hand.

"Mr. Carter, how nice to see you!"

"How's everything going, Sidney?"

"Great! Happiest apartment building I've ever managed." Sidney grinned. "Who's this lovely lady?" he asked as Iryna walked up.

Rick put his arm around her waist and introduced her. "This is my girlfriend, Iryna. She's a world-famous ballerina," Rick said proudly. Iryna blushed when he said "girlfriend." "I'm trying to impress her," he added shamelessly.

"Well, this is the place to do it! Big, expensive buildings are all very fine, but this is the kind of thing that makes a difference to everyday people. Hard to raise kids in the city. No place to play, crowded into a tiny room worth half what you're paying for it. This guy here"—he patted Rick's shoulder—"has some really good ideas on how to help people out."

"Thanks, Sidney. We're just going to walk around for a few minutes, and then we'll be out of your hair."

"Take your time. Wonderful to meet you, Miss Iryna." Sidney took her hand and patted it. "I've been wondering when this young fella might decide to work on a family of his own." He winked.

Iryna's blush deepened, but Rick grinned again. He showed Iryna around the rest of the downstairs. There was a counter in the laundry room for folding clothes that also housed the coffee maker. Though small, the room fit several stacking front loaders—enough to meet the needs of the families living in the building. He led her past the elevators to the stairwell, and they walked up the first flight to the small opening on the second floor that overlooked the foyer. Iryna reached out and touched one of the uppermost leaves of the rubber plant.

"I can't show you any of the apartments because they're all full, but I knew you'd appreciate the indoor play area. Parents like having a safe place for their kids to play that's close by, no matter the weather."

"It's wonderful. You are so creative and thoughtful! I love it!"

"I'm glad you think so. I hope you don't mind that I called you my girlfriend." He encircled her with his arms.

"Yes, I'm happy you did." She raised shining eyes to his and rested her hands against his chest.

"Now there's one other thing I'm curious about."

"Oh?"

"Why don't you have a cell phone? I'm not sure I fully understand the reason."

Iryna laughed. "Is that such an important question?"

"It is. Really. I want to know." He put his forehead to hers.

"Well, uh, because I don't need it."

Rick kissed her nose and her forehead gently, keeping it tame since Sidney might be watching on the camera. "Why not?"

"Why not what? What is the question?" she asked, a little breathless.

Rick chuckled. "Why don't you need a cell phone?"

"Oh, uh, well, I have the phone at my apartment, it has an answering machine, and I have a laptop for the internet and the email."

"What about directions while you're out and about, or finding someone you're meeting?"

Iryna scoffed. "When I go out, I know where I am going, and if someone can't be where they say they're going to be, then they're not very reliable, are they?" She gave him a sly, sideways glance. "You have been able to find me without a cell phone."

"Yes, I have." He smiled, but it faded quickly. "But you're going to be leaving tomorrow evening, and I won't be able to see you every day. With everything else that's going on, I'd like to be able to get a hold of you quickly and know where you are. I'm going to worry about you." His throat tightened, and he paused for a moment, unable to continue. While they'd explored the building, the danger threatening them had receded. Now, it returned to center stage.

Iryna raised a hand to his cheek. "Rick …"

He closed his eyes briefly, savoring her touch. Then he

focused again on what he wanted to say. "If it's okay with you, I'd like to give you this cell phone." He let go of her and pulled a new phone with a sparkly case out of his pocket. "So you can call or text me anytime. We can FaceTime with it, too, so it won't seem like we're so far away. It will show me your location, unless you don't want it to," he added quickly, "and I've already programmed in my number and both our parents' numbers. What do you think?" He searched her expression for a clue to her thoughts, but she was staring at the phone.

Iryna took it and looked up at him. "Thank you." Her voice squeaked a little. "My father distrusts them, but I don't mind you knowing where I am." She wiped an escaped tear away. "It will make me feel better too." She squeezed him tightly and nestled her head against his chest.

They stood for a moment, holding each other. "We'd probably better go, so you're not late for your warm-ups." Reluctantly, they headed downstairs as Rick texted Peters that they were ready.

"You know, Father only recently bought a cell phone because all the cabinet ministers and the government officials were complaining that he was too hard to find. He says technology makes it much easier to spy on people, but also for them to spy on you."

"I don't know if I should look forward to or be afraid of meeting your father. He sounds like a formidable man. Intriguing, but formidable."

"He can be scary when he wants to be, but even though he is overprotective, he is a wonderful father."

Peters pulled the car around, and they climbed in.

"Do you need to eat lunch before we go to the theater?"

"No, that's okay. They are having food catered since we are all from out of the town. Our trainer has special nutrition drinks made too." Iryna bent over her new phone and explored the apps. Rick's phone vibrated.

"Excuse me a moment. My girlfriend is calling," he deadpanned. "Hello?"

Iryna giggled, and soon they were both laughing. "Your picture shows up when I call you. You did that?"

"Yup. Now let me take one of you with my phone so I have a more personal one and don't have to use a promotional photo." Iryna gave him a radiant smile, one that would remind him of her sweet, vibrant personality. More and more, he appreciated how she was different from any other girl. All their social media pictures were fake poses with puckered lips, and that was not the way he would want his girlfriend to present herself to the world. Iryna's social media accounts were more career-oriented sites, and she didn't update them often. They might have been set up by the ballet's publicist.

"What are you going to do this afternoon?" Iryna asked while he saved the photo to his contacts.

"I'm going to hang out at the theater and snoop around. Maybe I can talk them into letting me see the security footage from last night."

Iryna's face became serious again. "What should I do? Just act normal?"

"Yeah, at this point we're not sure if the person is connected with the ballet at all. Just be careful, and don't go anywhere alone. Be suspicious of anything out of the ordinary. If Dad's right, and this is a single person with no prior experience in … this"—he waved a hand—"you know, out for revenge, but not a professional—then he might try any number of methods until something works. If I'm not right there, call me if you don't feel right about *anything*."

"And I'm staying with you, Rick," said Peters firmly from the front.

"Thanks, Peters." Rick accepted his company without argument. Peters's presence would be a comfort. He was like family. Peters was the one who had taught him to drive and maintain a vehicle. Practical knowledge flowed from him like a fountain.

They dropped Iryna off at the stage entrance, and Rick climbed out to open her door and give her a quick kiss. His stomach twisted as he watched her disappear through the door. Would she be all right? *God, please keep her safe.*

They parked the car in the garage and walked to the front of the theater. Rick fought his fears with each step. *Everything's going to be okay. We've been warned. It's going to be okay. It has to be.*

CHAPTER 14

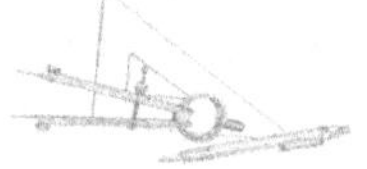

After making inquiries and receiving instructions, Rick and Peters made their way to the security office. Rick knocked, and a young woman wearing glasses and a Bluetooth earpiece opened the door. Behind her on a desk sat several computer monitors. She snapped gum between her jaws as she spoke. "Hey there. Brad texted to tell me someone was coming back. Lucky you caught me. Just finished a software upgrade, and I'm about to head out. What can I do for you?"

Rick put on his most charming smile, and Peters instinctively retreated down the hallway to let Rick handle this on his own. "Hi. I think someone might have messed with my car last night in the parking garage. Would it be possible to check the video and see if it shows anything?"

"Well …" She appraised him. "I guess we could take a quick look. Come on in."

Rick was surprised how easy that was. He had expected to be told it was against policy, or that he needed a warrant. Since only one chair sat in the small room, he stood behind her as she clicked on the keyboard.

"I'm Amy, by the way," she said over her shoulder.

"Rick. Nice to meet you. I appreciate you doing this."

"No problem. Okay, do you know what section you parked in?"

He told her and gave her the make and model of his vehicle. "There it is!" Rick pointed to his car.

Amy backed up the video to when he pulled in and noted the time, then fast-forwarded to when he left, fortunately too fast to see Iryna kiss him.

"If you're just looking for someone keying your car, you're going to need to watch it in real time or you'll miss it, and I haven't got time for that." She extracted the selected video and saved it in a file. "Give me your email, and I'll send a link to a read-only file with temporary access, then you can look at it later. If there's something there, send me an official request from your insurance company or the PD, and I can give you a hard copy."

"Wow, that's awesome. Thanks so much." He gave her his email, and she typed it in and hit *send*.

"Or you can email me if you want anything else." She winked.

"Thanks, but I have a girlfriend."

"Ooooof course you do. Well, hope the video helps."

Rick thanked her again and left her as she gathered her gear. Peters stood right outside with raised eyebrows.

"Got it! Just have to download it on my phone and we can play it."

They made their way backstage, where the dancers were warming up. Iryna met them with an extra pass for Peters and rushed back to practice. They found a couple chairs in a corner out of the way and settled in to watch the security video. It was incredibly boring. An attempt to sabotage his tires could take less than a minute, though, so they had to watch the whole thing.

Rick's thoughts wandered while he stared at the screen. Having Peters along was reassuring, for the man was unflappable. He wondered what Peters thought about God. It might be easier to talk to him about it than to his parents.

"Did you ever go to church, Peters?"

"Every Sunday. Still do."

Surprised, Rick glanced away from the screen but quickly directed his attention back to his task. "Really? I didn't know that." He felt guilty for never noticing.

"Yep. I eat breakfast with your parents, and then I go out—as long as they don't need me."

"So …" He paused. He had so many questions, he didn't know which ones to ask, or how. "So, I've started praying again. I remember a little bit from church when I was a kid, but I don't really know how to do it by myself. Like, how do you start?"

"Well, you can always use 'The Disciple's Prayer,' or 'The Lord's Prayer' as most call it, for an outline. That's how Jesus taught his disciples to pray." Peters recited it. "It starts out 'Our Father,' so we are addressing God the Father. Then you confess your sins and ask for His provision and His will in your daily life. Many other New Testament prayers end 'through our Lord Jesus Christ' since He's the One who made it possible for us to communicate with God. Pretty simple."

They fell silent for a moment while Rick thought about that, then Peters added, "It's not like He's going to ignore you if you don't follow some exact prayer formula, though. He looks at your heart."

Rick watched the video. No one had come near his car yet, and quite a bit of time remained. "Did my parents ever talk to you about why they stopped going to church?"

"Nope. When they came back to New York for Cassie's treatment, I asked if they'd be needing me to drive them anywhere on Sunday mornings, and they said no. Figured it wasn't my place to say anything if they didn't bring it up."

"But they went to church before that, right?"

"Yeah, before that, your mom stayed here for a while when

you were born, when your grandparents were still alive. They all attended church."

The dancers finished their warm-up routine and gathered around Katherine as she wheeled a cart in. Iryna picked up a cup with her name on it and exchanged a few words with Katherine. The trainer poured liquid from a blender into two more cups. Iryna carried them over to Rick and Peters. "Katherine makes these. They're very healthy but still taste good."

Rick paused the video and took a cautious sip of the green smoothie. "Not bad."

"How's it going?" Iryna nodded toward his phone.

"Nothing yet. There's still a long way to go."

Peters stood, walked over to Katherine, and struck up a conversation about the smoothie ingredients. Iryna took his chair. The other dancers stretched on the floor or walked around.

Iryna finished her drink and leaned against Rick. He took her hand and squeezed it. "It's going to be okay."

"As long as you are here, it is." She sighed and squeezed his arm with her other hand. He closed his eyes and savored her closeness, memorizing the way her slender curves nestled against his frame.

Alexei came in and called some dancers to another room to work on the choreography for the swans. Iryna gave Rick a peck on the cheek, grabbed her duffel, and skittered off with Alexei's group. Rick signaled for Peters to join him as he followed Iryna, wanting to keep her in view.

They spent the next hour watching the rest of the security video. A woman climbed into the passenger side of the car next to his, but she didn't bend over or even turn to face his car. The vehicles on either side of Rick's car pulled out, but no one approached the driver's-side tire.

"Well," Rick sighed, "if anything happened, it wasn't at the theater."

"I'll head over to the hotel, put on my sternest expression

and chauffeur's cap, and maybe they'll let me see their video. If you're good here until I get back?"

"Sure, I'll be fine. I'm staying backstage tonight. Do you want me to walk with you back to the car?"

"No, better not. I wouldn't want you walking back by yourself. If I don't text you in five minutes, send security to check on me. I'll be back by the time the ballet's over. I'll be praying for you."

"Thanks, Peters. Be careful. And thanks, you know, for talking with me."

Peters put his hand on Rick's shoulder. "Anytime."

Rick watched him leave then stared at his phone until he received Peters's text. Assured of Peters's safety, he settled in to observe Iryna and the "swans" practice the lake scene under Alexei's supervision. Watching her dance was like being in a dream. She moved her limbs so fluidly he almost believed she was a bird.

Alexei's barked directions broke the spell. Gone was the congenial sage, replaced by a stern drill sergeant. Rick couldn't imagine how the performance could improve, yet they repeated the movements over and over, striving for perfection.

"Enough for now," Alexei said after rehearsing the same series of steps a dozen times. "*Pyty i roztyazhka.*"

The dancers scattered like pigeons released from a box, leaving Rick and Iryna in the practice studio alone. Iryna fluttered toward Rick and fell into his arms.

"Oh, Rick, I am so glad you are here today. I don't think I could face this alone. As a ballerina, I am used to acting, but this is reality." She gazed up at him with teary eyes and spoke in a whisper. "I'm afraid. I shouldn't be. I should trust in God, but I am."

"Hey." He hugged her and held her head against his chest. "You're safe. I'm not going to let anything happen to you." The soothing words belied the anxiety gripping his heart. Experience proved it was impossible to prevent bad things from happening to those he loved. It also proved God didn't stop people from dying.

Iryna leaned against him, and he rubbed his hands up and down her back. Worried as he was, her presence overrode his other thoughts.

"How are you not afraid?" she murmured.

Rick expelled a quick breath akin to a laugh. "I'm scared to death." Saying it out loud brought relief. "But we've been warned. Our dads are on the case. I'm sure they'll find and eliminate the threat. Though"—his voice deepened—"there's more than one thing that scares me."

"What else scares you?" Iryna asked.

"You."

"Me?" She jerked her head up to meet his eyes. "I am not scary!"

"No," he whispered, "but I'm afraid I'm falling in love with you, and I don't want to mess that up. I don't want to lose you."

"Oh."

As he leaned in to kiss her, the lights went out, plunging the windowless studio into darkness.

CHAPTER 15

Evidently, the room didn't meet the criteria for installing exit signs.

Iryna gasped and clung to him.

"Get behind me," Rick said as he pulled out his cell phone to turn on the flashlight. Under any other circumstances, he might take advantage of being alone in the dark with Iryna, but with someone possibly trying to kill them …

"What should we do?" Iryna gripped his arm.

"I'm thinking." If the power was cut on purpose, how would he know whether it was a ploy to lure them out or to keep them in the room?

Exclamations and warnings to watch out filtered under the door leading to the dressing rooms, along with faint beams of light. The outline of the door to the wings remained black and silent.

"Sounds like there are plenty of people in the hall—it should be safe to exit that way." Keeping Iryna close, Rick strode to the hall door and pressed the handle. It wouldn't turn. With rising panic, he threw himself against the door. "Hey, let us out! Help! Open the door!"

Someone jiggled the handle on the outside. "It's locked with a key. There's nothing to turn or press," answered Sergei in rapid

Ukrainian. Rick had a hard time catching all his words. "Who is in there?"

"Rick and Iryna."

"You are rehearsing in the dark, yes?"

Rick ignored the innuendo. "Get us out of here! Do you see a key anywhere?" He checked the inside handle again, finding no way to release the lock.

"It is dark. I can see nothing."

"Sheesh. Why do so few of you have cell phones?" Rick muttered.

"Tights don't have pockets. Where do you think I'm going to put it, *chuvak*? Isn't there a door on the other side?"

In a duffel bag next to the door, something fizzled and popped. Rick swung the light around and saw smoke billowing from the bag. He gripped Iryna's hand. "There's no way we're going out the other door," he told her under his breath.

"The other door is blocked," Iryna shouted. "Find someone to get us out!"

"I'll see what I can do."

By now, plumes of smoke filled the room, and Rick's flashlight illuminated only dense clouds.

"It's a smoke bomb. We use them for effect," Iryna said, coughing. "It will stop in a few seconds."

Rick switched his light off and led Iryna to the side of the room, equidistant from both doors. Breathing through his shirt, he whispered, "Keep quiet." The bare room contained no furnishings of any kind—nothing he could use as a weapon. The mirrors on the opposite wall reflected occasional flashes of light from under the hall door, further unnerving him. His heart nearly stopped when he heard creaking outside the door to the wings.

A moment later, he heard voices in the hallway.

"Fyodor said he left the key in the door."

"I don't see it."

"Look around." The faint light from the hall grew brighter.

"There it is!"

Finally, a key grated in the lock, and the first door burst open. Rick braced himself, unsure what to expect. Light momentarily blinded him, and he shielded his eyes with his hand.

"Is all well in here?" Masha lowered her light, allowing the glow from Rick's phone to reflect off her features. As he listened to her speak for the first time, her native Ukrainian revealed an unexpectedly airy and feminine quality.

"Yes. What is happening?" Rick asked.

"I don't know. I was going to check the breaker box when Sergei stopped me. The key was on the floor." She held it aloft. "Fyodor said he left it in the door when he unlocked it this morning. It must have fallen. The box is through this way." Masha strode across the polished wood floor to the opposite door and yanked it open.

Rick took Iryna's hand and followed Masha, Sergei on their heels. Numbers held safety, and curiosity overcame his fear. "Has anyone called maintenance?"

"Viktor has contacted them, but I thought I'd check the breakers anyway."

"Since when is Masha an expert on electricity?" Sergei muttered. "And I thought you said the door was locked?" Rick didn't bother to answer.

A figure stepped from the darkness ahead of them.

"Alexei, what are you doing here?" asked Masha, her tone unexpectedly authoritative.

"I heard Rick and Iryna yelling in the studio and headed around to check the other door. Then my phone died, leaving me in the dark. I did not want to trip, so I stood still. Why are you *shnyryayesh'* back here?" Alexei supplemented his Ukrainian vocabulary with Russian.

"I am going to check the circuit breaker," Masha replied as she forged ahead.

"Did you see … one person?" Rick asked Alexei as they passed.

"No. Was this door locked too?"

"No, it wasn't." Rick sucked in a breath. *How did Masha know that? She yanked it open as if she knew it wasn't locked.*

He bumped his thigh on the corner of a shelf and switched his attention back to the path in front of him. The faint red glow of an emergency exit sign shone ahead. Alexei joined Sergei as they forged onward.

"Don't large buildings like this have backup power?" Iryna asked.

Rick shook his head, though he knew she wouldn't see it in the dark. "The generator is attached to the line before the main cutoff. It only kicks in if the power is out elsewhere," he replied in English, wondering how many people would understand how the generator worked.

Ahead of him, Masha stopped, shining her light on the circuit breaker. Before Rick could point out the main switch, she flipped it, and immediately the lights came back on. Everyone breathed a sigh of relief.

Rick stepped forward to investigate the latch. Instead of a lock, a zip tie lay in pieces on the floor.

"Ah, you found it," said a new voice with a New York accent. The name tag on his khaki shirt read "Tomas". "How did it get turned off? No one should be messing with this."

"Why isn't it locked?" Rick asked.

Tomas flipped up the cover, replaced the hasp partway, and threaded a new zip tie through the staple. "Old lock seized up. Told the management I could oil it, but they ordered a new one, and it's not here yet. Shoulda just done it."

As Tomas grumbled, Rick turned to Iryna and whispered in her ear. "I don't think we can learn any more here. Let's hurry back to the studio before anyone takes the bag."

"Can I help?" asked Sergei, who stood close enough to overhear. Alexei was already heading toward the stage.

"Go guard the hall door and make sure no one takes anything from the room."

The young man nodded and scurried away while Rick and Iryna retraced their steps.

"For how long it was off?" Masha's voice floated after them.

Rick barely heard Tomas's reply. "Just a couple o' days."

Navigating past the props proved considerably easier with the lights on. Just before they reached the door, Iryna gasped and tugged on his sleeve.

"What is it?" Rick turned around and followed her shaky finger pointing to a nearby shelf. Among an assortment of plastic bottles and vases meant to resemble glass sat an unopened bottle of premium Polish vodka. A chill ran up his spine, and the hairs on the back of his neck rose as he realized the implications of the bottle. "That isn't a prop, is it?"

Iryna shook her head. "It's a real bottle. It's full. Could it be the same kind as ..." Her voice tapered off.

Rick swallowed. Natalia had been killed with a vodka bottle, but he didn't know what brand. "If we hadn't been warned, we would have run out this door—in the dark—" He couldn't finish the thought aloud. If the killer was quick enough, they might have both died.

But why warn us with the matchbooks? Did the killer expect them to be obscure enough of a warning that we would ignore the threat? Or be stupid enough to panic? He supposed that if Iryna had not found and opened hers, he might never have bothered to mention his to anyone.

"God warned us too!" Iryna tugged on his arm, diverting his thoughts. "That feeling of danger I had in the Metro, and you had the same. If we hadn't listened ..."

Rick caught his breath. Was the killer stalking them then? Had God truly warned him that day backstage? Such a clear pattern of divine intervention would require some serious readjusting of his views of God's character and plans. He patted Iryna's arm, not wanting to examine the implications of this possibility right now. Instead, he switched his attention back to the present and studied the bottle.

The clear, heavy vessel had a long neck, easy to grasp. Rick reached to pick it up, then withdrew his hand, opting to take photos instead. An idea struck him. He pulled off his sweatshirt, wrapped the bottle in it, and tucked it under his arm before reentering the studio.

The bright lights rendered the bare room innocuous. Now that the smoke had cleared and only a faint odor remained, it appeared almost normal. However, a sense of dread settled over Rick as he stepped into the room. Only one navy-blue duffel bag lay on the floor.

"Oh!" Iryna exclaimed as she rushed forward.

Rick sprinted after her just in time to prevent her from touching it, barely keeping the vodka from slipping to the floor. "You recognize it?"

"It's mine! It's my bag!" Her pitch rose, almost hysterical. She turned toward him and sobbed against his chest. "I mean, I knew they were after us, but somehow … this seems so … personal!"

He wrapped his free arm around her, his heart in his throat. "Do you … do you remember whose bag was next to yours?"

"No!" She sucked in a shuddering breath.

The door opened, and Sergei held it for Viktor, who stomped into the room, his bushy black eyebrows in a deep *V*.

"What is going on here?" he demanded with the authority of a tsar.

A nervous-looking man with a gold badge that read "manager" tailed him. He pushed wire-rimmed glasses farther up his nose as he glanced around, his other hand on his hip.

Rick summarized the events without explaining the backstory or mentioning the vodka bottle. Iryna's head remained buried in his chest as Sergei translated the story for Viktor.

Viktor's face grew red, quickly darkening to purple until he exploded. "What is this foolishness? There is no time for such pranks! Get everyone on the stage, now!"

"Do you think we should call the police?" Rick braved before the ballet director stormed away.

"The police? Certainly not!" Viktor bellowed. "That is the last thing we need. We are an international company. Attention from the police is always a bad thing. I will take care of this!"

The theater manager, likewise aghast at the suggestion of calling the authorities, echoed him, "Oh, no, no! Such publicity would detract from our patrons' confidence in our security." He hustled after Viktor, shaking his head.

"Let's go, everyone," Katherine said from the hallway. "You heard the boss. On the stage." She popped her head into the studio. "You too, Iryna."

Katherine disappeared before Rick could protest. Iryna straightened and took a shuddering breath. He grabbed her arm as she turned away. "Iryna—"

"I'm fine," she said, shaking him off, but as soon as she did, she sobbed again.

He set down the bottle and pulled her against him. "Hey, babe, you're all right. We're all right. It's going to be okay."

"How can you keep saying that? Nothing is okay right now! The killer is here, in New York, in this theater! How?"

"I don't know, but we will find out." He kissed her forehead and gently stroked her sleek hair, which was pulled into a tight bun. "Everything will be okay," he repeated, more to convince himself than Iryna.

Viktor's booming voice reached them from the stage as he yelled her name.

"I have to go." Iryna glanced at the door with red-rimmed eyes.

"I'm coming with you." Rick stuffed his sweater and the bottle into Iryna's duffel bag with the remains of the smoke bomb and walked with her to the stage.

Viktor paced like a caged lion, his veins bulging and face

florid as he berated the cast. "… and there is no excuse for this type of behavior. I expect more from you. Your government expects more from you. Your people expect more from you. You are the best we have. Now act like it! There must be no more of this. Who turns the lights out on their coworkers? Only someone who wants to be sent home. What a childish thing to do! Well, I will ensure there will be no more of this." He gestured to a pair of stern men in dark suits. "The consulate has sent over security, and they will keep a close eye on all of you. No visitors will be allowed, and that includes you, pretty boy." He pointed at Rick.

Rick jerked his head up. He had no idea Viktor resented his presence. He opened his mouth to protest, but the director continued, "And you, Iryna Vasylvna, you will focus on what you are here for." Iryna straightened her shoulders as Viktor took a step forward and intensified his glare. "You will give the performance of your life."

"Yes, Viktor Petrovych." The use of the patronymic name indicated respect and conveyed her determination to uphold her national pride.

"All of you will give me your best, or you will practice all night!" he barked. "Find your mark! We have one hour. We will rehearse!" Viktor punctuated his order with an emphatic flourish.

Iryna slipped away from Rick to wait in the wings.

"Iryna," he called.

"I will be fine," she answered, her face set like concrete and her mouth grim. "I needed a slap in the face. I will see you after the show."

"Don't go anywhere alone. Have a security guard walk you out. Call me afterward, and I'll meet you outside."

Nodding, she disappeared behind the curtain, leaving Rick paralyzed.

CHAPTER 16

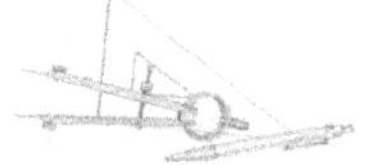

Shock and fear prevented Rick from moving.

"This way." Alexei motioned toward the stairs, and Rick walked forward.

Every movie he'd ever watched where scenery, lights, or sandbags fell on someone came to mind. Every nerve in his body screamed at him not to leave Iryna's side. He turned back to see Viktor's eyes boring holes through him. The consular security guards faded into the wings, one on each side of the stage. *God, please protect her!*

When he reached the floor beside the orchestra pit, his feet wobbled as if he'd disembarked from a ship. Glancing toward the exit, he saw Peters waving at him.

"You're back earlier than expected. Did you find anything?" Rick asked urgently as they stepped into the lobby, where a security guard paced.

"Yes and no."

Rick wanted to scream with impatience.

"The video was grainy, but it showed a hooded figure bending over your tire, right after you arrived. Hooded, with a baseball cap. That's what the attacker in the video from Kyiv looked like."

"So we have confirmation my tires were tampered with, but nothing to go on." Rick sighed in frustration.

"Well, consulate personnel are searching the company's rooms as we speak. The police in Kyiv are running extensive background checks on everyone. They'll turn up something."

Peters's presence was reassuring. Rick relaxed a little.

"What's been going on here? You look like someone took one of those new-fangled defibrillators to you."

"Huh, I feel like it!" Rick recapped the events of the afternoon and showed him the contents of the duffel bag.

Peters gave a low whistle. "We better get this stuff to your dad ASAP. He'll know what to do with it if they're not calling the police."

"Yeah, the director viewed it as a prank. Can you run the bag over? I don't want to leave Iryna here alone, even if they won't let me backstage."

"Sure. You'd better call him and tell him your story yourself, though."

After retrieving his sweatshirt, Rick handed the duffel to Peters and dug his phone from his back pocket.

Matt answered on the first ring. "Hey, Dad." His dad's reassuring voice almost made him break down. He knew he was under stress, but now it caught up with him. "Dad," he repeated, sinking onto a padded bench.

Eventually, he got the story out. Matt expressed appropriate shock and concern. "I'll lift the prints from the bottle and smoke bomb myself, if there are any, and send them to Vasyl. He can run them through their system."

"But how could it be anyone with the company? They had all just left for New York when Natalia was killed."

"There might be more than one person involved."

"You mean an accomplice?" Rick's heart sank. Catching the killer was now more impossible than it was before. The idea of a murderer, or multiple murderers, shadowing him and Iryna left him chilled.

"It's a distinct possibility."

Rick ran his fingers through his hair. "Are you and Mom coming tonight?"

"Not now. I'll need to analyze the evidence you collected. If you took any pictures, I can get started on those."

"I have one of the bottle." Rick sent a text with the photo.

"It's loading. Now I see it. Wait a minute." There was a thunk as Mr. Carter set the phone down. "Yes, it's the same vodka. The same type of bottle the killer used in Kyiv."

Yet another confirmation that he and Iryna were being targeted by the same person. Or organization.

"Dad, what are we going to do? I feel like we're just waiting around to be killed."

"Now, there's no need to get morbid." Matt sounded perturbed. "If we wait long enough, they'll make a mistake. Then we'll catch them. And we will catch them, you can be sure of that."

Rick was surprised by the vehemence in his dad's voice. He'd never heard him talk this way. He knew very little of what his dad had actually done in Poland, and the possibility that he employed questionable ethics entered his head for the first time. However, he refused to entertain the thought. *No, I can't doubt Dad now. I won't!*

"So what do I do?"

"Be alert. Stay in a public space with other people, like you've been doing. I'll send Peters back as soon as he passes me the evidence."

"Okay."

"Is that Rick?" his mom asked in the background.

"Your mom wants to talk."

"Ricky. Rick, honey, are you all right?" Her pitch rose like she was squeezing him through the phone. Rick spent several minutes reassuring her before she let him go. In an unspoken agreement, he and his father made light of the afternoon's events and kept the worst from her. He emphasized the arrival of extra security from the consulate—sent by Vasyl, or they never could have arrived so quickly. His mind snapped back to Iryna, and his anxiety returned twice as strong.

"It's almost like a detective mystery," his mom was saying.

"What do you mean?" Rick asked.

"Like, who was there who should have been somewhere else, who was missing that should have been there? What was in the wrong place? You know. Here's your dad."

Mr. Carter spoke again, but Rick tuned him out. His mother's words stirred something in his mind. He just needed to grab hold of it.

"Dad!" He stood as the realization hit him. "She wasn't there!"

"Who wasn't where?"

"When Viktor was yelling at everyone. Masha wasn't there!"

"Hmm. Well, nothing happened right then, did it? She could have been—I don't know—in the restroom or something."

"Everyone was supposed to be there. She might have gone back to fetch the bottle, not knowing I already had it."

"I suppose. I'll pass it on to Vasyl. He can take a closer look at her."

"She's also the only dancer who was still in Kyiv at the time of the murder."

"Right. She's really the only suspect we have at this point."

"Could it have been her in the video?"

"I haven't seen it myself. Peters has it on a thumb drive. I'll run it through a body scan program and see what it says. In the meantime, be careful."

"I will." Rick ended the call.

The minutes dragged by. As soon as the theater opened for the performance, he scanned his ticket on his phone and found his seat, wearing his jeans and sweatshirt. At least he wouldn't be cold.

The performance ran surprisingly smooth. Iryna's dancing was impressive, almost reckless. Her sweeping movements were more dramatic than graceful, conveying strong emotion. The villain, in particular, had a commanding presence, as if Iryna used the role to work out her angst. As soon as it was over, Rick called Peters and rushed from the theater to wait for her.

As they pulled up to the stage door, Rick opened the door of the sedan.

"Stay in the car!" hissed Peters. "Don't make yourself an easy target."

Rick sat back and closed the car door, fuming at their circumstances. He marveled at how easily Peters adapted to the situation. "How can you keep so calm?"

"I'm worried, same as the rest of you. I'm doing everything I can think of to help, but there's only so much under my control. It's all in God's hands, regardless. I have to trust His plan is a good one."

Based on experience, Rick doubted the goodness of God's plan, if He really had one. He was trying to trust, but his doubts kept getting in the way. A memory of a past conversation flitted through his consciousness. "You served in Lebanon, didn't you? Around the time my dad was in Poland?"

"Yeah. Couple of years in the early eighties," Peters replied gruffly.

Since earning his driver's license, Rick had driven himself or taken the subway, so he'd spent little time in the car with Peters. Only the first two years of their initial return to the US, which were a blur. Peters had always been around, especially on Sunday mornings, but he never talked about his past.

"How come you never got married?"

"Who says I didn't?"

Rick opened his mouth, then closed it, too stunned for words. If Peters had been married, how had it ended? Death or divorce? Had he always believed God's plan was good?

Iryna emerged from the building, clearing his mind of all else as he sprang from the car to meet her. A security guard scanned the street as she exited, but before she'd taken ten steps, Viktor stormed after her.

"Where do you think you are going?" He grabbed her arm.

Iryna gaped at him. "Back to the Carters'. It's been a long day."

The weariness in her words settled on Rick's shoulders like lead weights. "Leave her alone," he growled at Viktor.

The director ignored him and wagged a finger in Iryna's face. "You will come to the hotel. Your focus is off. Too much partying and playing around. You are here for work, for the honor of our country, not for pleasure. Don't think just because your father is a cabinet minister you should be treated differently. You belong at the hotel with everyone else."

"She is coming with us," Rick said firmly.

Peters appeared at Rick's shoulder, cracking his knuckles. Viktor glanced at the consular security guard, who remained impassive in the doorway as if it was not his place to interfere. Rick briefly considered reading Viktor in, but the man might give everything away. There was also no way to assure he was not involved somehow.

"Fine." Viktor released Iryna and held up his hands in surrender. "Masha is billed to dance the matinee tomorrow, but you must still make the curtain call. Then you'd better be ready for the evening performance, or I'll give her the lead in the next town."

Viktor stalked back inside, and the guard closed the door. Only then did Iryna turn to Rick. She sagged against him, her knees buckling. Her legs wobbled, and Rick scooped her up in his arms before she collapsed. For such a strong personality and athletic dancer, her petite frame was light and fragile. He hugged her to his chest and eased her into the back seat of the sedan while Peters held the door open. He walked around and climbed in on the other side.

"Oh, Rick," Iryna said as he slid next to her, "I don't know if

I can do this. I'm so scared and tired. Sorry for making the scene."

"It wasn't you; it was that bully Viktor." The man reminded him of his high school football coach. Demanding and unrealistic.

Iryna leaned against the seat and closed her eyes, shaking her head. "He is a good director, always pushing us to do our best. He just doesn't know everything that's going on." The shudder that ran through her body belied her words.

Rick sighed and intertwined his fingers with hers. "That's for sure."

Iryna opened her eyes and offered a faint smile. "Thank you for standing up to him. There's no way I could go to the hotel tonight after what happened. I wouldn't feel safe."

"If you went to the hotel, I would go with you. I'm not letting you out of my sight."

Iryna kissed his cheek and laid her head on his shoulder. Rick closed his eyes, more exhausted than he'd realized, and shoved thoughts of tomorrow from his mind.

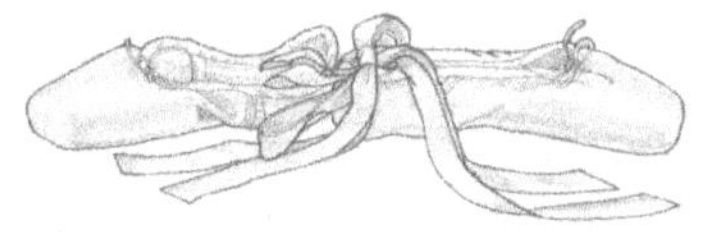

Iryna tossed and turned, twirling her sheets as if she was on the dance floor. When she closed her eyes, she saw only shadowy figures chasing her. *Oh God, why would anyone want to kill us?* No answer came. Iryna wished she had packed a Bible. She grabbed her new phone and, after a few frustrated minutes of searching and trying to type in English, she found a Bible website but did not know what to search. The verse of the day appeared at the top of the screen, so she read it.

The Lord shall preserve thee from all evil: he shall preserve thy soul. Psalm 121:7

But He doesn't! her mind shouted. *He didn't preserve Natalia!*

Natalia is with me. I preserved her soul, came the same quiet answer.

Despite this comforting assurance, Iryna's fears remained. She didn't want to die. Most of all, she wanted Rick.

Rick had been so wonderful. He put himself between her and possible danger. He lavished praise, encouragement, and affection on her at every opportunity. When Viktor grabbed her arm, she'd flashed back to the time Fedir, the soccer player, had done the same, which momentarily paralyzed her. But Rick faced Viktor and defended her.

Iryna hopped out of bed, pulled on her blue flannel robe, and tiptoed across the hall to knock on Rick's door. She raised her hand and hesitated, thinking maybe she shouldn't wake him. Before she changed her mind, she tapped her knuckles lightly on the door, her heartbeat louder than the hollow sound. The door opened almost immediately, and Rick stood before her.

Her Rick.

After all those years of dreaming about him, he was really here. She still couldn't believe it. His hair was disheveled. He wore a thin white T-shirt and baggy blue pajama bottoms. Tall, but not too tall. Fit, but not bulky, he was unutterably handsome.

"I couldn't sleep," she said simply, nearly melting into a puddle as he gazed at her with soft brown eyes that warmed her to her soul.

He reached out, ran his hand down her arm, and nodded. "Me either. Just a minute."

He closed the door halfway and returned with a blanket and a pillow under one arm. Wordlessly, he held out his hand and led her downstairs to the living room, where he settled onto the couch and pulled her down next to him. Iryna snuggled into him, and he wrapped his arms securely around her. Her chest ached with happiness as the terror of the day dissipated like mist in the sunrise.

When he'd emerged from his room with a pillow and blanket, she was surprised. She had expected him to pull her into his room, but he hadn't.

Was this God's way of preserving her from herself? Or was He blessing her with such a wonderful man, a man who cared for her without expectation of anything in return? *I expect things from God in exchange for my love. Is that wrong?*

Iryna didn't know what to make of her question. Along with many others, it would not be answered today. As she settled in beside him, Rick's heartbeat lulled her gently to sleep.

Vasyl stared at the image on his screen. Every time that vodka bottle crossed his path, it was associated with death. At first, he'd written its use by Natalia's killer off as coincidence. It was a popular brand—easy to procure. After Bogdan found the poster, he feared the worst. Now, his gut told him this was all connected to Fadeyushka, but his brain still denied it.

After all these years ... It can't be. An old journal lay open on the desk next to his laptop. He reread the newspaper clipping taped to the page.

January 21, 1982

Up and coming Soviet financier, Fadeyushka Tarnovskyy, was found dead this morning in an alley in Warsaw, Poland. Death was ruled as an accident. The heel on the banker's shoe was broken, and the coroner speculates she fell and hit her head. Glass shards in the scalp match litter on the street. The autopsy shows Tarnovskyy was three months pregnant. There are rumors Tarnovskyy was offering financial advice to the Solidarity movement. Solidarity Radio asserts the Secret Service was implicated in her death, but there is no evidence to support these claims.

This had to be the inciting incident. But he'd studied the evidence meticulously and followed every lead. The killing had all the earmarks of a professional Soviet hitman. The clues led nowhere. His failure in this endeavor still haunted him.

Before he told Matt, he needed more to go on. He could call in a favor, but it might take a couple days. His contact in Moscow might turn up something new. With Iryna in danger, he would call in every favor he was owed and more. Fadeyushka's killer had eluded him. Whoever was stalking Iryna would not.

CHAPTER 17

"Hey."

Iryna woke slowly as Rick's breath tickled her ear. She had a kink in her neck. She twisted around to smile up at him, squinting at the light. "Hey."

"Did you sleep well?" He stroked her cheek, sending a shiver of pleasure down her spine.

"I slept wonderfully." She reached up and traced his jawline, wondering what it would be like to wake up like this every day. She noticed the circles under his eyes. "How about you?"

"I slept with my arms around you. Best night of my life."

"Oh." She closed her eyes again as he kissed her tenderly. His touch rendered her incapable of thought, except for the brief observation that he needed to shave.

Rick's phone beeped, and he grunted as he reached across her to grab it from the coffee table. "Time to get up if you want to make today's early curtain call."

"Ah yes, the matinee." The realization that this was her last day in New York hit her. It was also her last day with Rick. What would they do when she left for Pittsburgh?

"There you are!" Mrs. Carter greeted them with her vibrant alto.

Iryna startled and sat up, wondering what Beth thought of

finding them in such an intimate position, but she breezed in as if nothing was amiss.

"Oh, my dears, are you all right? I was so upset when I heard about the fireworks in the studio. How frightening that must have been!"

"Smoke bomb, Mom."

"Still. The place could have burned down!"

Iryna glanced at Rick, confused, but he frowned and shook his head. Evidently, his mother didn't know the whole story, and he wanted to keep it that way.

"I feel much better this morning, Mrs. Carter."

"Beth, please, darling. I'll fix breakfast." She nodded at Rick. "Your father will join us shortly. He wants to talk to you."

Reluctantly, Iryna rose from her comfortable nest. The sunshine peeking through the blinds threw a cheerful glow over the room. Maybe their circumstances weren't so bleak after all.

She stretched her back and rolled her neck. "Should we go directly to breakfast, or should I shower and dress first?"

Rick rose from the couch. "Better get ready first. No telling how long this conference with my dad will take."

Rather than let her go, he slid his hands around her waist and bent to kiss her again. Her pulse accelerated as she leaned into him. *Now* he was kissing her—when they had no time—instead of last night?

Footsteps sounded on the stairs, and Rick pulled away.

"I'll, uh, be right back," she stammered, flustered. *How does he make me so off balance?*

She greeted Mr. Carter, hurried upstairs, and rushed through her morning routine. By the time she returned to the kitchen, Beth had breakfast on the table. Rick and Peters were already seated, while Mr. Carter stood sipping a mug of coffee.

Iryna sat next to Rick, and he pushed a cup of steaming tea toward her. She took it with a smile, touched by his thoughtfulness. His eyes met hers with a mixture of tenderness and resolve. He had cleaned up as well, and she almost kissed him, forgetting they had an audience.

"I'll take my coffee into the living room so you all can chat," Beth said with a strained smile. Iryna was surprised at Beth's departure. There was no way *she* was leaving the room. She wanted to know everything. Perhaps Beth and unpleasantness did not get on well together.

As soon as Beth left, Mr. Carter got straight to business. "While you're all here, I'd like to catch everyone up to speed," he began, taking the bottle of vodka from the counter and setting it on the table. Iryna's stomach clenched, and the anxiety of the previous day came flooding back. "There were no prints on the bottle or the smoke cannister. Our enemy is careful. However, the vodka is another tie to Poland. It is being used for a reason. Vasyl and Bogdan are combing through their files to find anything that might point to the killer."

Mr. Carter sank into a chair and set his mug on the table, holding it with both hands. "The body scan software shows the killer's profile as approximately five foot five, one hundred twenty to one hundred forty pounds."

Iryna tried to mentally convert the measurements but gave up and opened the search engine on her phone. This, at least, was something that appeared the same as it did on a computer.

"These measurements have a wide margin of error," Mr. Carter added.

"What about the gender?" asked Rick.

"Sixty-eight percent chance it's a male, based on shoulder width and a myriad of other factors."

"Given the weight, that is more likely if we're looking for someone in the dance company," said Peters. "They're slimmer than the average population. That's pretty good that it can get that much from a grainy video clip."

Rick met Iryna's eyes. "How much do you weigh, if you don't mind my asking?"

Iryna stuck her nose in the air. "Fifty-three kilos." She

enjoyed Rick's expression as he typed the information into his phone. "At one hundred sixty-five centimeters, I am on the taller side for ballerinas," she said defensively. "It's all muscle."

"What is Masha? She looked about your height."

"We are almost exactly the same. Any heavier and we could not dance partner routines. Even so, I can only dance with tall men like Yegor."

"Hmm." Rick had never considered weight requirements for ballerinas. "So she's within the range given by the computer. We can't eliminate her as a suspect yet." He turned to his father. "Did Vasyl have any information on her?"

"He did not consider her a viable suspect, but he said he would look further into her background."

"What about the clothes worn in the video?" asked Peters.

"A similar sweatshirt and cap were found in the lobby restroom," answered Matt. "He—or she—ditched it."

"Great." Rick leaned back in his chair. "Now what do we do?"

"First, we need to study the list of items found in each performer's possession to see if there is anything suspicious." He handed them each a set of stapled papers. "I know you may not have time right now, Iryna, but as soon as you get a chance.

"Second, both Vasyl and I agree we will not use anyone as bait, so don't suggest it. We also agree that having the two of you together makes things too easy, as we saw yesterday. When Iryna leaves after tonight's performance, you will stay here, Rick."

Rick leapt to his feet. "What? I'm not letting her go to Pittsburgh alone now. I was awake all night figuring out how I could go with her."

"She won't be going alone. The consulate couldn't send anyone, so Vasyl has hired a bodyguard for her. A bodyguard who isn't also a target. Having one person to protect will be easier than two."

Rick paced the kitchen, fists clenched. Fear imprisoned Iryna in a bleak gray cell with little hope of escape. *This is how Soviet dancers must have felt when they left the USSR during the Cold War—on a leash, constantly watched.* A weight settled on her chest as if it had found its forever home. But though she wanted Rick beside her, she also did not want him in danger.

"This makes the sense, Rick. It is not what I want, but I think your father is right. And it is only until we catch him." She imbued her voice with false optimism, hoping to fool herself as much as everyone else.

"Is there any way we can get the dancers to use a buddy system?" Peters interjected. "Then they could keep tabs on each other for us."

Mr. Carter rubbed his chin. "That's an idea. Perhaps I can get the consulate to suggest it. Vasyl has also had the hotel under surveillance since last night."

"That must be costing a bundle," muttered Rick. "Private contractors are expensive."

"Does the consulate know everything? What has Vasyl told them?" Peters wondered aloud.

"He told them there is reason to believe Natalia's murder was not an isolated incident, and he encouraged caution." Matt looked at Iryna. "He would like you to call him before you board the plane."

"I will. I need to give him my new number." She waved the phone at Rick and smiled at him. He gave her a wan smile in return.

"Though the killer seems to want to use the same weapon, the bottle, sabotaging the car shows a willingness to adapt. I am not an expert in criminal profiling, but I would guess that this person would rather alter their methods than abandon the goal now that we've identified their MO. So just … be wary." Mr. Carter stood. "That's all for now. I'll spend the morning digging into the US theater staff and cast, just in case."

"I'll go warm up the car," said Peters.

When the door closed behind the two men, Iryna rose and walked to Rick. He hugged her fiercely, tucking her head protectively under his chin. "I don't care what anyone says. If you want me there, I will come with you."

"Oh, I want you there so badly! But not like this. Not when it would put you in danger. Let's do as they say, for now."

"Okay, but you say the word and I'm there."

"Thank you." She squeezed him tightly.

"We only have a few minutes until you have to leave for the theater. I need to teach you how to FaceTime."

CHAPTER 18

Iryna studied her fellow cast members carefully as they rehearsed. Rick and Peters sat in the shadows of the floor seats, and it comforted her to know they were close by. Her new bodyguard, Dar, waited in the wings—to Viktor's chagrin—with instructions that "she'd better not get in the crew's way." He didn't seem to mind the consular security who roamed around backstage.

Iryna had warmed up with the rest of the dancers, but she was allowed to relax during the matinee. Giving the understudies one show a week ensured they stayed sharp. It was better than none.

Masha appeared no more enthused than normal. In fact, Iryna thought her frown was even deeper, possibly due to increased concentration. Katherine approached with a cart, collecting empty smoothie cups and handing out water bottles. Iryna slurped down the rest of hers and set it on the cart. "*Dyakuyu*, Kat," she said as the trainer handed her a water.

"*Bez problem.*"

As Katherine wheeled the cart away, Iryna noted she was too short to fit the computer profile. Estimating their heights and weights compared to herself, Iryna studied each of her coworkers in turn. Yegor was too tall. Maxim and most of the girls weren't tall enough. The rest of the men, however, almost uniformly matched the description. Iryna stifled a sigh, trying to remain positive. *We can eliminate over half the cast. That's something.* The majority of the dancers were female, and two-thirds of the swans were Americans from the local ballet company.

Masha chugged down a water bottle and threw it away, stopping to speak to Dar as she passed. They spoke in low tones, but Iryna thought she heard the word *zakhystyty*—protect. Was Masha making a threat? Or was she merely curious as to why Iryna needed protection?

Iryna shrugged it off as useless speculation. She would ask Dar about it later. She wished she could do something productive, like study the list Rick's father had given them, but bringing that out within sight of others would be unwise. *Hopefully Rick and Peters will find something useful.*

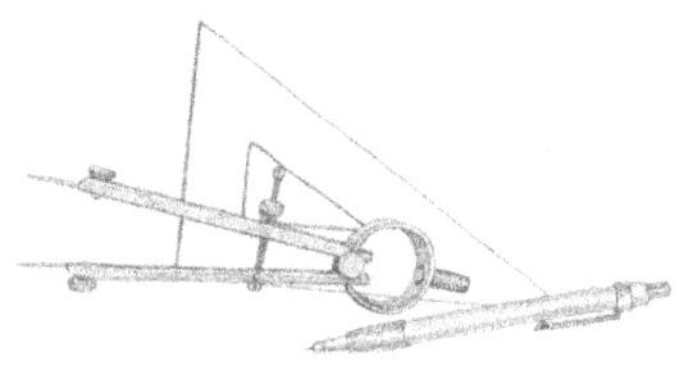

Rick scrolled slowly through the lists of items found in the performer's rooms, searching for anything unusual or out of place. Rather than carry around a physical copy that could be lost or stolen, he had his dad forward the digital version. At least his phone had a passcode. Beside him, Peters peered at his phone, scrolling through the same list.

Pretty much everyone had the same items: clothes, phone charger, toiletries. Viktor had some racy magazines. Sergei had a portable gaming system. When he got to Masha, he scrutinized the list carefully. However, the only unusual item she had was a copy of Lermontov's *Maskarad*. Masha didn't strike him as a reader of classic drama, but who knew?

Rick scanned the lists again, and he scrolled past one before the words registered. *Item redacted. What in the world does that mean?* He took a screenshot and sent it to his dad with a question mark. Then he elbowed Peters and tilted the screen toward him. "What do you think this is?"

Peters leaned forward and read the list. "Hmm. My guess is something illegal that they aren't going to deal with for publicity reasons."

Rick's phone buzzed as a reply from his dad came in.

Tell you later. Don't worry about it.

"You're probably right," Rick said after he read the text. "Who was it?"

"Maxim." Considering what he'd observed at the stadium, he was not surprised. "He's below the height range, anyway." Rick finished reading the lists and handed the phone to Peters. Neither of them found anything remarkable.

"Iryna knows them better than we do," Peters said. "If someone has something they shouldn't have, she'll be the one to spot it."

Wishing for a solid clue, Rick drummed his fingers to the frenetic beat of Tchaikovsky's hunting scene. As if his heart rate wasn't already high enough, the intense music only served to increase his tension. *At least Iryna has an outlet.*

He opened a new page in his notes app and typed in the things they knew so far.

- *Natalia's death is tied to Poland. Evidence: Solidarity poster; Polish Vodka bottle; matchbook*
- *The threat to Iryna and me is tied to Natalia/Poland. Evidence: matchbooks, Polish vodka bottle*

- *Someone about 5'5" and 120 –140lbs tampered with my tire. Evidence: video*
- *Masha was in Kyiv during attack on Natalia. Evidence: flight manifest? Multiple witnesses*
- *The attacker has backstage access. Evidence: breaker switch; smoke bomb; bottle*

Rick studied his list and realized they knew very little. His and Iryna's fathers were working on the vodka bottle connection. With everything happening so close together, he wondered if the murderer had only recently joined the ballet.

He sent his dad a quick text and received an almost immediate reply with a link to a document containing the dates each member of the company joined, whether part of the troupe currently traveling or the Kyiv ballet. He opened the link and perused it. Unable to put faces to all the names, he highlighted the ones he knew:

- *Katherine 15.3.2005 (trainer)*
- *Viktor 20.2.2007 (director)*
- *Iryna 28.6.2009 (prima)*
- *Masha 29.6.2009 (understudy)*
- *Yegor 4.5.2010 (principal)*
- *Natalia 1.12.2012 (prima)*
- *Vlodymyr 26.5.2012 (jester)*
- *Olena 14.4.2012 (choreographer)*
- *Karina 10.5.2013 (understudy to prima)*
- *Sergei 22.6.2017 (courtier, understudy)*
- *Fyodor 31.3.2017 (trainer)*
- *Alexei 7.5.2017 (choreographer)*
- *Maxim 30.5.2017 (sorcerer)*

Most of the dancers joined the corps during the offseason, with a few exceptions. It was interesting that Natalia joined in December. As he read, Rick had to keep reminding himself that

Ukraine and most of Europe listed the day before the month. At first, he was disappointed to discover Masha had been with the company for so many years. Then he saw that she had joined within a day of Iryna. *That can't be a coincidence. But what does it mean?*

Several new members had joined within the last year, and Rick determined to monitor them closely. He cross-referenced the names with a list of those who had been to Poland. Everyone who joined prior to 2017 was in Poland with the company when they toured in 2016, so that didn't help much. Sergei had taken a vacation there with some friends. Another dead end.

With a sigh, he sank back into his chair. All he had left to do was wait and hope, as his dad said, that either he or Vasyl would uncover the truth, or the killer would make a mistake.

During the matinee, Rick and Peters joined the audience and watched the performance. He hoped the bodyguard Vasyl hired was a good one. According to his dad, she had some ties to the Russian mafia but was born to Ukrainian immigrants. With a serious expression, utility belt, and a bulletproof vest, she exuded toughness and competence. The production ran smoothly, and though Masha's performance was solid, it failed to rise to Iryna's level.

After running out to grab some food, Rick and Peters returned for the evening show. Watching Iryna thrilled him as much as it had the first time. His heart ached as he watched her, not only because of her beauty and talent, but also because of the terrible strain they were under. *I can't believe she's leaving tonight. It's been what—eight, nine days since she arrived?* It felt like a lot longer. It had only been three days since he first kissed her, but it might have been an eternity. *How can I be such a mess after such a short time?* Maybe the separation would be a good thing. He needed time to slow down so he could think about the future.

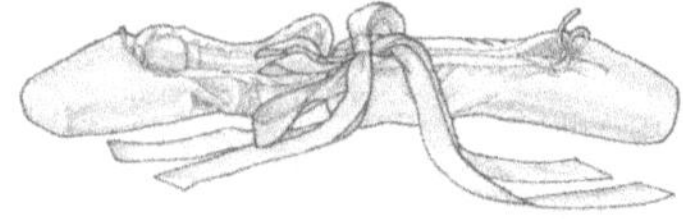

During the evening show, Iryna danced her part purely from muscle memory, too drained to put as much passion into her performance as she usually did. However, the audience applauded as if nothing was lacking, and Viktor gave her neither praise nor remonstrance.

When the ballet finished, the dancers changed into travel clothes and filed onto a tour bus to ride straight to the airport.

"Sit behind the driver." Dar nodded toward the first row of seats.

Iryna sat by the window, and Dar sat next to her where she could monitor the driver's interior mirror. No one had asked Iryna directly about her new bodyguard. When anyone raised an eyebrow, she merely shrugged. Everyone knew who her father was, so surely they assumed he was being overprotective after the smoke bomb incident.

Iryna glanced out the window, but only street lamps and headlights glared back at her through the darkened glass. Though Rick had told her he and Peters would follow them, she could not expect to catch a glimpse of him until they reached the airport.

"Pull the curtain across the window," Dar said.

Stifling a sigh, Iryna tugged the thick fabric into place, settled back into her seat, and closed her eyes. She must have dozed off, because next thing she knew, Dar was nudging her awake. She threw her carry-on over her shoulder and followed

Dar off the bus, exiting only after everyone else had reached the sidewalk in front of the terminal.

Rick stood at the bottom of the steps, waiting for her with anxious eyes. She fell into his arms, and he tucked her head under his chin. They stood there silently holding each other while the noise and bustle of the airport swirled around them.

Rick moved his head to whisper in her ear. "Whenever I see you again won't be soon enough."

"I know. Be careful." She squeezed him tighter, not wanting to let go.

"*Irynochko!*"

Viktor's voice cut through her thoughts, and she loosened her grip on Rick, easing away. As she let her hands slide off his waist, he traced her arms and caught her fingers in his. "Keep your phone with you. It will make me feel better to know where you are. And text me when you get to your hotel. You remember how to text?"

Iryna nodded, her throat tight. "I remember." She licked her lips. "If I have trouble, I can get Sergei to show me." Sergei always had a screen in his hands when they traveled.

Rick groaned. "Don't let that idiot have your phone. I'll get nothing but memes."

Iryna wasn't sure what memes were, but from his attempt at humor, she surmised they were funny but annoying. She offered a wobbly smile. "What if I send you the meme?"

He released a low laugh. "I guess that depends on what it is."

She caught her breath as his eyes burned into hers, and she forgot what they were talking about. "I have to go."

"I know," he said hoarsely. He leaned forward and gave her a sweet, tender kiss that wasn't nearly long enough until Dar wrapped a protective hand around her bicep, leading her away.

The expedited security line checked their identifications and waved the group through. It wasn't until she sat in a bucket seat at the end of a long row at their assigned gate that she stared out the window at the airplanes taxiing by and realized she was crying. She wiped her eyes with the back of her hand, smearing it with black streaks of mascara that she hadn't fully removed. Surreptitiously, she dabbed at her eyes with a corner of her scarf, but her tears only flowed more freely.

Why am I such a mess? I need to pull myself together!

A white tissue dangled in front of her face. Iryna blinked, and Masha came into focus. She grabbed the tissue with a grateful sigh and blew her nose. Masha retreated without speaking. Iryna wondered at the woman she had known for so long but knew so little about. She understood why Rick suspected Masha, but she couldn't bring herself to believe Masha was behind everything. True, some people would do anything to rise above the crowd, even pushing others down, but Masha never made snide comments or gave dirty looks. She merely had a perpetual frown. Maybe it was concentration? Dedication?

Maxim sidled up to her and held out a plain paper packet containing chewy candy. "You look like you need something to help you relax. Try one of these."

Iryna shook her head. "No thanks. I'm fine." She didn't need Dar pressing a foot against hers to know not to take whatever Maxim was offering. Illegal drugs could get you into big trouble in an airport, not to mention the physical effects.

"Your loss." He shrugged and strolled away.

The interaction served to distract Iryna from her inner turmoil, and she glanced through her wet lashes at the rest of the troupe. Sergei and most of the younger dancers played on their phones. Viktor paced back and forth muttering at a sheaf of papers—probably their itinerary. Alexei leaned back in a chair with his hat over his head. Katherine and Fyodor stood in line at a coffee shop. Though Iryna wouldn't pass up a cup of tea, she didn't see how anyone would want caffeine this time of night. To think that one of them wanted her dead felt surreal.

She shuddered and closed her eyes. No, that was worse. She opened them again. Her heart rate increased, and panic clawed at her mind. Normally, she would be talking and chatting with everyone, but her fear made her withdraw. Everything that had happened caught up with her again, and she felt more alone than ever. *I wish Karina was here! At least I would have someone to talk to—someone I could trust.*

Trust me. I will preserve you. A soft voice spoke directly to her heart. Not a real, audible voice—more like a hand reaching into her mind for a buried truth and recharging her soul with it.

Iryna recited the verse she had read the night before. *No matter what anyone does to me, they can't destroy my soul.*

Slowly, her shoulders relaxed, and she released enough tension to allow her lungs to inflate. She had been leaning on people more than God, if she had been leaning on Him at all. Her jacket buzzed, and she jumped. *My phone!*

After fumbling through her pockets and dropping the slippery device on the floor, she finally got ahold of it and saw a notification of a text message. It was from Rick. She connected the dots on the lock screen to form an English capital *R*, and the message popped up.

> Made it home safely. How are you?

Iryna jabbed at the digital keyboard, her fingers touching all the wrong letters in her haste. Eventually, she typed a mostly correct sentence: *I am glad you are safe. I am lonely.* She erased that. *I wish you were here.* No, she didn't want him to come running after her when they'd agreed he should stay there. *I am safe too.* That was okay, and true enough.

> I am trusting God to preserve my soul, no matter what happens.

She reread what she had written then pushed the little triangle, hoping that would send the message to Rick. When it moved the message up to the chat, she felt a surge of triumph and glanced around, almost expecting someone to notice. It wasn't too much different from a computer email program, just harder to type.

Her phone vibrated, and words appeared on the screen almost immediately.

> Sometime, you will have to explain to me
> what that means.

> I am not sure myself. But that is all I have left
> to do.

> I know what you mean. It's hard to be so out
> of control.

> Yes. But if God is God, He is in control, so my
> worry does nothing. I can trust and let go
> because there is nothing I can do. Do I make
> the sense?

> Yes, darling, you make the sense. I want to
> trust God also, but I'm not sure I'm there yet.

Seeing him call her *darling* in print made her tingly. How could she help him with the rest of it? Losing Cassie so young had left him doubting God's goodness, but she didn't know what to say to make it better. He might have to arrive at the truth on his own, as she had reconciled with Natalia's death, though she did not understand it.

> That's okay. God will be there when you
> arrive. And so will I.

> Don't forget, we have a FaceTime
> appointment as soon as you finish rehearsal
> tomorrow.

> I won't forget.

I will be thinking of you every moment until
then.

Me too.

Thinking of you, not me.

LOL. Try to get some rest. So will I. "See" you
tomorrow!

Rick always lifted her spirits. Now, instead of tears, a smile tugged at the corners of Iryna's mouth. She would get through this. Everything was going to be okay.

CHAPTER 19

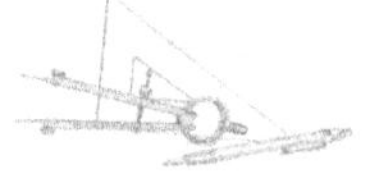

Somehow, Rick made it through his morning at the office. Saying goodbye to Iryna last night had hurt like an unmedicated tooth extraction.

I can't continue a relationship while being constantly afraid of losing her. Even if we weren't being hunted by a vengeful murderer, there are accidents, illness … cancer. He ran his hand over his face. *I have to talk to someone.*

He opened a new page in his browser and searched "churches near me." Scanning through the results, the word "evangelical" in a description caught his eye. Iryna had mentioned that term. Before he could change his mind, he dialed the number.

"Hello, uh," he stammered when the receptionist answered. "Could I get an appointment to speak with a pastor? Sooner rather than later?"

"Certainly. Are you a member?"

"No, do I need to be?"

"Not necessarily. What is the nature of your visit?"

"Um …"

"Marital counseling, searching for God, interest in baptism, personal counseling, questions about Christian living, managing a budget …" The receptionist listed options in a cheerful, businesslike tone.

"The church helps people with their budgets?" Rick asked, momentarily distracted.

"Being a good steward of what God has given is important. We offer classes."

"Oh. Well, I guess a combination of searching for God and personal counseling." He had a vague sense of *déjà vu,* like he was ordering coffee.

"All right. Pastor Shane is in the office this afternoon. How about four o'clock?"

Rick glanced at the clock and calculated how much time he would need to finish his tasks for the day and travel to the church. *Do I really want to do this?* "I can make it. That would be perfect."

The receptionist recorded his appointment, and he thanked her and hung up. He dialed Peters's number and asked him if he could pick him up an hour early. "I'm going to church."

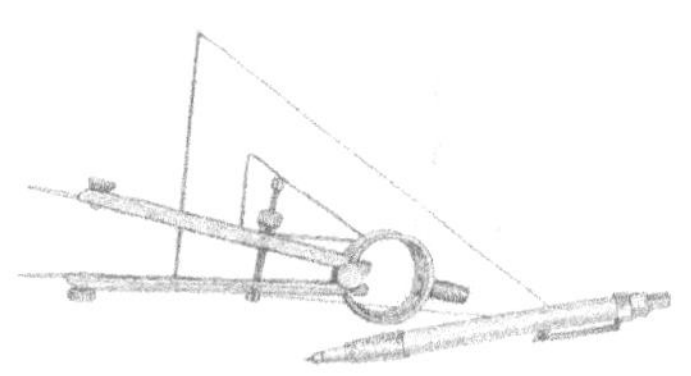

"Good afternoon!" said Pastor Shane with a hearty handshake. "Nice to meet you, Rick. Come on in."

Rick followed the pastor, who was younger than Rick expected, into his office. On one side of the room sat a pair of comfortable leather easy chairs. The pastor sank into one, and Rick sat in the other. The informal arrangement, as opposed to the large wooden desk taking up the other half of the room, invited conversation. The modern structure and décor of the building resembled a business or a library more than a religious institution.

"So, what can I help you with? I don't think I've seen you here before."

"No," Rick said hesitantly. He sucked in a breath like he was about to dive into a pool of ice water. "I haven't been to church in fifteen years," he admitted.

The pastor rested his chin in one hand and leaned against the arm of the chair, waiting. Rick told him all about Cassie, her illness, their prayers, and how he and his parents couldn't understand why she was taken away from them.

The pastor nodded in sympathy, taking his time before answering. "This is the question I get most often. 'Why do bad things happen to good people? God must not really love me if He let this happen.'"

"Exactly." Rick's shoulders sagged in relief that the pastor understood.

Pastor Shane leaned forward. "So, why are you asking now? It's been fifteen years."

"Because …" Rick choked up and grew nervous again. "Now there's this girl, and I think I love her, or I could love her if I let myself, but I'm afraid. What if something happens to her? I don't think I could bear it."

"Well, it looks like there are two questions you need answered. One, where does the pain and suffering in the world come from, and two, is it worth it? I can tell you what the Bible says about the first, but only you can decide the second."

"Okay," Rick said.

The pastor leaned back in his chair and gazed at Rick earnestly. "When God made the world, everything in it was good. The book of James says, 'Every good and perfect gift is from above,' and in Romans, 'In all things God works for the good of those who love Him.' God doesn't want to cause us pain or torment us. He loves us like a father. He loves you. He loves Cassie."

"But then why …" Rick still struggled to understand.

"Because God gives us choices, and those choices have consequences. Sometimes we choose Him; sometimes we don't. We call that sin. Now"—Shane put his hand up to stop Rick's protest—"Cassie's cancer was not a result of *her* choice. Or your parents' actions. It goes way back to the beginning when Adam and Eve chose to disobey God, and the consequence was death —for themselves and everyone who came after them. We are all going to die." His eyes softened. "Cassie died younger than most. Now you have to answer the second question. Was it worth it?"

"Sir?"

The pastor leaned forward again, his eyes boring into Rick's soul. "Would you rather that Cassie had never existed, or would you take what time you had—with the pain—if you had it to do over again?"

Memories of Cassie flooded his mind—laughing at a story he acted out with their toys, her golden curls bouncing, crying over a doll whose head had come off and thanking him for fixing it, squealing at a bear at the zoo, lying in a hospital bed.

"I would do it again," he whispered.

Pastor Shane nodded slowly, his eyes mirroring the emotion in Rick's words. "Jesus felt the same way. Man's sin caused death and separation from God, but Jesus loved us enough that He endured the pain and suffering of the cross to die in our place. His original plan was, and still is, eternal life with Him, if we choose to accept it." He paused to let his words sink in.

Rick had never heard it explained this way. It made sense, but he still had questions. "But sometimes God does heal people. He's able to."

"Yes, sometimes. Why heal some and not others? We can't answer that question. We must trust Him. Jesus wept at the death of Lazarus, one of His best friends. He felt the grief of Lazarus's sisters, Mary and Martha. He felt grief Himself. But He didn't heal Lazarus to ease anyone's grief or pain. In fact, He delayed reaching them until after Lazarus had died. Martha blamed Him for this, as we blame God for our pain now, thinking that He doesn't care, but He cares intensely."

Rick frowned, searching his mind for the story. "Didn't Jesus eventually raise Lazarus from the dead?"

"Yes." The pastor nodded. "But not only because He loved His friends."

"Why, then?" Rick asked, empathizing with Martha.

"He raised him as a testimony of His power over death, proving that He could raise Himself, and us, to eternal life. Lazarus had to die again, later. Jesus gives us the opportunity to live forever. A life after death."

The first ray of dawn shone in Rick's soul. "So, God doesn't fix everything now because this is all temporary anyway. Heaven is the goal."

"Essentially. There is more to it than that, but perhaps we can save it for another session."

Rick nodded. "Yeah, I need to chew on this for a while." He stood and held out his hand. "Thank you, Pastor, for meeting with me."

"Anytime. Thanks for stopping by."

They shook hands, and Rick left. He nodded at the receptionist as he passed by but didn't stop to make another appointment. He wasn't sure when or if he would be ready to do that.

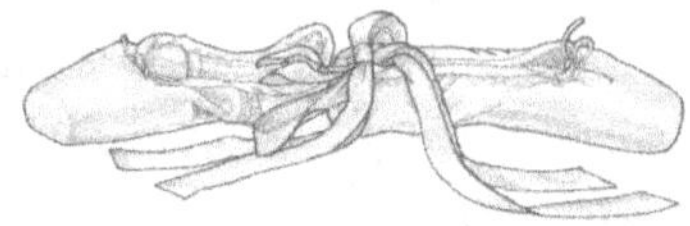

Iryna sat in her hotel room, clean and tired, but the good kind of tired. Dar had set motion sensors by the window and the entry and slept in the double bed nearest the door. With the assurance no one could enter undetected, Iryna had enjoyed a mostly restful night's sleep. She had a couple dreams of being chased in the dark, but at least she slept.

Rehearsal went well despite some miscommunication with the local dance company, and Iryna felt good about the upcoming performances. Now she only had to decide what to wear to FaceTime with Rick. *He's already seen me in my robe.* She blushed at the memory. Slipping the robe over her pajamas, she sat on the bed and checked that the towel around her hair was still in place. Then she carefully followed Rick's instructions for video calling. She glanced across the room where Dar lay on the other bed staring at her phone. This was the most privacy Iryna could expect.

Rick appeared on the video screen, and her heart skipped a beat. A wide grin spread over her face.

"Hey there. Don't you look cute in your towel and robe."

Iryna flushed. "Is it not appropriate?"

"It's fine," Rick assured her with a grin. "Your dinner dress was more revealing than that."

Iryna rolled her eyes, trying to put into words what was different about the various articles of clothing and situations. And wet hair.

While she sat speechless, Rick continued. "In fact, your ballet costume—what is it, a tutu?—left much less to the imagination."

"Rrriiick," she pleaded as she flashed the screen toward Dar to remind him they were not alone.

"Ah, well, comes with the job. All right." He relented and leaned back against a chair she didn't recognize—maybe one from his bedroom. "How was your day? Did rehearsal go well?"

"Yes, although the local company thought we needed twenty male and eight female dancers when it's actually the other way around."

"Uh-oh. That could be a costuming nightmare."

Iryna wrinkled her nose. "Well, they are fixing it. The local ballet coordinates with us on costumes, so that is not usually a problem. They may have to send some extra from New York with the rest of them."

"The costumes don't travel with you?"

"No, they have to be cleaned and packed. Our—what is it? —clothing—no—wardrobe supervisor and props manager stay an extra day to see to those things."

Rick sat up. "Wait. Not everyone flies at the same time?"

"No—oh!" Iryna sat up. "All the dancers flew from Ukraine together, but many of our support staff came the next day." She slapped her forehead. How could she have forgotten those who worked behind the scenes? No one said the killer had to be a performer. "And Olena and a few others got bumped, so they also took the next flight."

"We'll have to find out exactly who flew when." Rick ran his fingers through his hair, making Iryna's fingers itch to do the same. "I never actually read the flight manifest myself. I made assumptions. If Natalia was killed about the same time you left, anyone who flew the next day could have done it."

Iryna groaned. "I can't believe I didn't think of this before."

"I didn't either. We've been investigating everyone for

motive, but other than Masha, we haven't been looking for opportunity. I gotta tell my dad." Rick jumped up and walked with his phone, the background blurring as he sped across the hall. "Stay on the phone," he told her.

Rick knocked on his dad's door, and Iryna heard Mr. Carter's voice, though she couldn't see him. Rick repeated their conversation.

"You know, I asked for a passenger list," Mr. Carter said, "but I never even looked at it, not realizing its importance. There's a whole other set of people besides performers who have backstage access. We'll have to get everyone's flight information. I'll get on that right away."

Rick walked back to his room. "You hear all that?"

"Yes. Maybe he will find something useful."

"I hope so. Did you have time to read over the list of everyone's belongings? Peters and I didn't find anything suspicious, but you might since you know everyone better."

"No, not yet. I can do that now." She set the phone down on the nightstand while she rummaged through her suitcase.

"Just keep the phone where I can see you."

Iryna smiled as she balanced the phone on one leg while sitting crisscross on the bed and setting the list in front of her. She was gratified he needed the connection as much as she did. Other than a quick call to her parents when she arrived in Pittsburgh, she had kept mostly to herself. She was a people person, and it was hard to wall herself off from everyone, but caution compelled her into seclusion.

"Toothbrush, toothpaste, Yegor uses whitening strips—I wonder if I need whitening strips?"

"Your teeth are perfect."

"Your opinion does not count. You are biased."

Rick huffed. "Your boyfriend's opinion is the only one that should count."

"Nonsense. It is a girl's friends and her publicity ... person

… that count. And what about your mother? You can't tell me her opinion doesn't matter."

"Okay, mothers can count. Let's get back to the list."

"Katherine has a *lot* of smoothie ingredients. I don't know what they all are."

"Peters looked into those. They're legit."

"Legit?" Iryna was unfamiliar with this word.

"Legitimate. Real. Um … kosher, genuine—"

"Ah, okay. Video games, item redacted?"

Rick explained Peters's reasoning, and Iryna shared her interaction with Maxim at the airport.

"Steer clear of that guy, for multiple reasons," Rick cautioned.

Iryna nodded and kept reading. "Everyone has clothes and personal items, of course. A book (I thought Masha hated reading), a framed photo, magazines, a what? Ew."

"Yeah, keep going."

"Some of this I do not need to know." Iryna scanned the rest of the list and tossed it aside. "I don't see anything of importance."

"Well, if anything strikes you as odd after you think about it, let me know. Put the list away so no one will find it."

Iryna got up and put it back in the pocket of her suitcase. She covered her mouth and stifled a yawn.

"I'd better let you go so you can get some rest," Rick said.

Though she hated to end the connection, she had to agree. As an athlete, she kept a rigid routine, and she needed to be on top of her game now more than ever. "Thank you again for the phone. It is so much better to see you than just to hear you."

"Of course." His voice grew husky, causing her to tear up. "I wish I could kiss you."

"Me too." She pressed her fingers to her lips and blew a kiss toward the phone. He pretended to catch it and hold it against his heart, making her smile.

"Talk to you tomorrow."

"Tomorrow," she agreed and ended the call. Why was such a little thing like pressing a button so hard to do? She stared at Rick's picture on the screen for a moment before plugging it in and setting it on the nightstand next to the photo of her parents she always took with her. Something about the photograph nagged at her, but she didn't know what. She turned out the light, hoping her brain would puzzle it out while she slept.

CHAPTER 20

Rick and his father sat studying flight schedules and passenger lists while his mother removed the remains of their Tuesday evening dinner. He hadn't realized how many people it took to put on a huge performance like *Swan Lake*. In addition to a dozen support staff and both choreographers, Fyodor and Maxim had flown on the second flight, arriving late Saturday afternoon.

According to Vasyl, the first flight was overbooked, and Alexei, Olena, Fyodor, and Maxim were bumped. Most of the late arrivals didn't attend the welcome party, but he had seen them around and knew their faces. Matt summarized everything they'd learned and printed it with each person's passport photo.

"There's one more important piece of information." Matt slid a stapled document across the table.

"What is it?"

"The results of Vasyl's search for unsolved murders with a matching MO."

With rising excitement, Rick scanned the report. Only one case was listed.

14.11.2015, Igor Smirnov, former KGB, age sixty-one. Hit

over the head with a glass bottle in an alley behind a bar in
St. Petersburg.

"It doesn't say what kind of bottle," Rick observed.

"There's a picture." Matt glanced up as Beth left the kitchen and waved his hand to indicate Rick should turn the page.

At the top of the second page was a photo of the corpse, then an ID photo that looked like a mug shot, but Rick stiffened at the image at the bottom. The label on the shards of glass was clearly visible.

Matt leaned forward. "His service record is classified, but Vasyl remembers him. They were in Poland at the same time."

Rick met his dad's gaze. "Did he know Vasyl was a double agent?"

"If he did, Vasyl would be dead. Smirnov was a KGB hitman. Which leads us to the most important piece of information—the one that started it all." He slid over a printout of a press release from 1982. Another murder—a woman.

"Was she working with Solidarity?"

Matt nodded. "As a financier. The government froze a lot of Solidarity's assets after that. It set us back, though we won in the end."

"So"—Rick pieced the stories together—"we're looking for someone who wants to avenge the death of"—he glanced at the paper again—"Fadeyushka Tarnovskyy? Why do they blame you?"

Matt leaned back and spread out his hands. "Who knows? Because we persuaded her to become involved? The news report doesn't mention the brand of bottle. I don't think I ever knew, though Vasyl may have. One of his contacts dug up Smirnov's case, which fills in some of the gaps."

Rick frowned. "But how could anyone even connect you to her?"

"We don't know." Matt sighed. "Technically, I wasn't undercover. I was officially employed with the embassy, so anyone could find out I was there with a little digging. Natalia's father was with the Polish secret service, also a public position. What was unknown was that we were secretly assisting the Solidarity movement."

Rick left that alone to focus on their suspect's profile. "So, this person must be related to Tarnovskyy. Did she have a family? Husband, children?"

"No children. Married, but estranged. Parents are deceased, and she was an only child."

"But the article says she was expecting, so there had to be someone if it wasn't the husband."

"No one with any legal ties." Matt stared at Rick over the rims of his glasses. "And Iryna is not to go name-dropping. We don't want to set this guy off or make him desperate."

Rick nodded. He wouldn't want to put Iryna in greater danger than she already was. He drummed his fingers on his coffee mug while his father drummed his knee.

"Dad, there's something else I'd like to talk about."

The corner of Matt's mouth turned up. "Shoot."

Rick gave a half smile. "Not Iryna."

"Okay." Matt drew out the word.

"I'm going to visit Cassie's grave."

His dad's eyes shuttered, and his shoulders tensed. "We do that every year."

"Yes, I know." Rick leaned forward and spoke insistently, his words coming out in a rush. "But that's obligatory. We stand there in awkward silence for five minutes and leave. I need some closure."

"Closure?" The word came out harshly. "How much more closure can you get?"

Rick's grip on his mug tightened, but he kept his voice even. He had to get his point across. "I mean … I need to accept that she's gone. To say a real goodbye." A sudden surge of sympathy for his parents flooded his heart. The pain etched on his dad's face saddened him. "I'm taking tomorrow off and going first thing in the morning. You and Mom could go with me."

Matt turned away, his jaw tense. "I'll think about it."

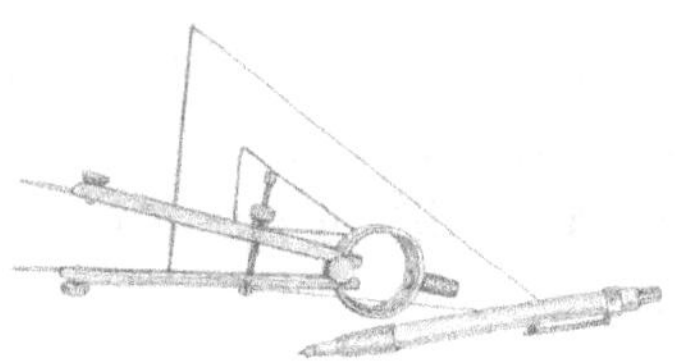

Normally, Rick treated his mother like a rainforest orchid—fragile and beautiful. Perhaps keeping tough things from her did her a disservice. It certainly made it harder for him to seek her advice.

This morning, he was determined to be considerate but open. This trip could be good for all of them. He helped her into the back seat of the sedan and scooted in next to her while his dad sat in front with Peters. His parents' presence warmed his heart. Though he would have gone alone, it meant more that they were with him.

"Tell me again why we're going today?" Beth twisted her scarf around her thumb.

"Because I need to." He'd explained his plan to Iryna the night before, and she wholeheartedly supported him. Trying to explain his thoughts to his mom was harder. "If I can't make peace with Cassie's death, I can't be free to fully live my life. I'll always be holding back."

"You can live your life without forgetting your sister." Her pitch rose.

"I won't forget her, Mom. Not at all. I just ... need to acknowledge that she isn't here anymore. She's somewhere else." He put his hand over his mother's to try to comfort her. "I don't need you to do anything, but I want you to know I'm moving on."

"All right. We're here for you." Her voice wobbled, but she offered a brave smile.

"Thanks, Mom."

They rode the rest of the way in silence. Peters drove them through the cemetery and parked as close to the family plot as he could. After opening the door, he lowered his voice and told Rick, "I have my own grave to visit."

Rick nodded as Peters headed in another direction and let his mother take his arm to walk across the grass. His dad followed, his expression grim.

When they reached Cassie's grave, he walked forward alone and knelt beside the stone marker. "Hello, Cassie." His throat closed, and that was all he could get out. Though it had been fourteen years since her passing, all his memories of her came flooding back as if it had been a day. It felt like she was right there with him, smiling, laughing—ready to play.

"I miss you, Cass," he finally managed. Then the words tumbled from his mouth like an avalanche. "For a long time … I was angry that you were gone. Not angry at you, but I didn't understand why you were taken away. Later, I was angry at God for letting you die, but now that doesn't make sense. If God is real, then Heaven is too, so how can I be angry at Him for taking you there? As a friend of mine said, 'it's either that or believe in no god at all, which would be sadder.' I have to believe that's where you are, that there's life after death, or I'll be too afraid to live."

A low laugh escaped him. "You know that friend I was talking about? It's Iryna. Iryna Ballerina. She's still dancing. And we're dating. I know it's fast, but I think I'm falling in love with her."

As he said this aloud, he became certain of what he needed to do next. If he truly loved Iryna, for better or worse, he needed to be with her. Fear had dictated his actions for too long. He should never have let his dad talk him into staying behind. Regardless of his safety, he didn't want her to be alone. Determination and, surprisingly, courage flooded his heart once he'd made the decision. He stood.

"Bye, Cass. I'll see you again."

He turned, and his mom hugged him, but he looked over her head and met his dad's gaze. "I'm going to Iryna."

Mr. Carter clenched his jaw, but his eyes softened. "Take Peters. He can drive you. You'll get there in six hours."

"Thanks, Dad."

By noon, they'd dropped his parents off and crossed to the mainland.

"I think you're doing the right thing," Peters remarked as he navigated through traffic.

"You do?"

"I was married once. She was an aid worker in Lebanon."

Rick blinked as his mind processed the information.

"We were married five months before she was killed in a bombing," Peters divulged. "If there was any way I could spend more time with her, I would."

"Wow" was all Rick could say.

"Yeah."

"How did you know she was the one?"

"She told me," he chuckled.

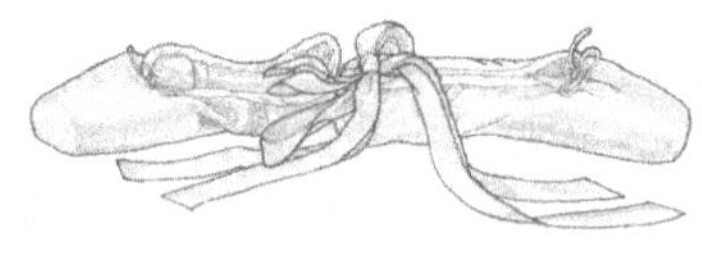

Iryna crossed one foot over the other and stretched toward

the floor until she wrapped her hands around her ankles. The choreographers were working with the American dancers on the lake scene, so all she had to do was stay warm for her cue. Warm up and think.

Lists, names, and faces whirled through her head. So many facts, but so few of them helpful. Making sense of it all seemed impossible.

Her thoughts returned to the photo of her parents. What was it about that picture? Her friends teased her for taking it everywhere she toured. No one else carried photos anymore. Everyone had a phone. Would she stop carrying the photo now that she had one too?

No, because it meant something to her.

Then everything fell into place in her mind. That's why the photograph in the list had struck her as odd. No one carried photos anymore. Not unless it was an old photo—one that meant something very specific. In the case of the killer, a photo of someone who was dead.

Iryna's heart pounded. She knew! She knew who it was. Rather than comfort her, the knowledge made her more frightened than before. Before it was vague, but now the enemy had a face. She wanted to point her finger and accuse the murderer, to yell and scream that she knew, but she didn't have all the proof. And she didn't want Natalia's killer to get away. *I have to tell Rick!*

As casually as she could, she walked around the lines of dancers and found her duffel bag. Her heart hammered so wildly she feared she would pass out. She was about to grab her phone when Viktor walked over and glared at her.

"What are you doing? It is not time for a break," he growled.

Katherine saved her from creating an excuse by wheeling in with her cart.

"Now it is."

Viktor stomped off as Fyodor, Alexei, and Olena appeared at

Katherine's side to help pass out the drinks. The dancers gathered around the cart, glad for a breather.

Iryna turned away. *Maybe I can give Dar a signal.*

She tried to catch her eye, but Dar had set down her thermos and was rinsing her lid under the water fountain before refilling it. Several of the locals lined up behind her, also eschewing smoothies.

A terrible screeching noise filled the air. It sounded like someone had stepped on a cat's tail.

Several people jumped and released startled exclamations. "What is that?" asked Yegor.

Dar strode toward the middle of the room, scanning the occupants while shielding Iryna. The noise came again.

"It's a phone," said Masha in an annoyed tone. "Where is it?"

Everyone glanced around and shrugged. A few pointed at the far side of the room. Masha and several others rooted through the bags stashed along the wall.

"Here it is!" Sergei held the offending device aloft. "It's Maxim's." The iridescent purple case was distinctive.

Masha grabbed it from him and swiped the screen. "It's an alarm, not a call."

"Where is that slacker?" shouted Viktor. "What makes him think he can leave in the middle of rehearsal?" He grabbed Fyodor by the shoulder and shoved him toward the door. "Go find him!"

The crowd thinned around the cart as the dancers retrieved their drinks and subtly distanced themselves from Viktor. Masha stood with her hands on her hips, glaring at the room in general. Dar retrieved her thermos and screwed the lid back on while Iryna distractedly grabbed her smoothie. Since she and Yegor preferred a wheatgrass blend, Katherine always labeled their cups. As she brought the cup to her lips, goose bumps broke out on her arms. *Why does this whole scene feel choreographed?*

Dar approached and took a huge swig from her thermos.

"Something feels off," she whispered as if agreeing with Iryna's thoughts. "Stay alert."

"I need to tell you—" Iryna broke off as Masha walked up to Dar.

"Did you see Maxim leave?"

Dar nodded. "He left as soon as his part was over." She chugged more water.

Masha opened her mouth to ask another question, but Iryna didn't stay to listen. If she couldn't talk to Dar, she had to text Rick.

Iryna slurped her smoothie and sidled back to her duffel bag. When she picked up her phone, she saw there was a text from Rick and one from her father. She entered the pattern lock and read Rick's first.

> I talked to Cassie, but I want to tell you about
> it in person. Peters and I are driving to
> Pittsburgh now. We'll be there just after 6:00.

Iryna's heart leapt at the words. Rick was coming! Though she worried about his safety, the news filled her with relief.

Anxiously, she peered at the time, but the numbers were fuzzy. She blinked then rubbed her eyes, but if anything, the screen was even blurrier than before. Stifling a yawn, she wondered why she was looking at her phone. With a frown, she stared at the screen, unable to recall what important thing she needed to do.

She heard a thud across the room. Iryna turned to see Dar sprawled on the ground.

Masha knelt beside her and felt her pulse. "Call a doctor! Someone get help!"

Those nearby snapped into action. Everyone started yelling. Overcome with dizziness, Iryna backed into the wall, and her phone slipped from her hand. Someone grabbed hold of her before she crumpled to the ground, and everything went black.

CHAPTER 21

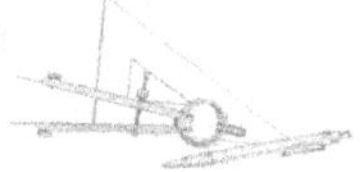

Traffic in downtown Pittsburg slowed to a crawl. Horns blared and people shouted while Peters expertly maneuvered the black sedan through the crowded streets. Rick checked his phone for the thousandth time, but it showed no text alerts.

I shouldn't be concerned that Iryna hasn't replied. She's busy rehearsing. She's not even used to having a phone and might not think to check it. The tracking app showed she was right where she was supposed to be. Worrying would not speed his arrival, and constantly staring at his screen would cause eyestrain. The hours on the road had done nothing but increase his blood pressure.

"Here's the theater," said Peters a few minutes later, pulling up in front of a large building. "I'll check us into the hotel and come back."

Rick barely heard him as he leapt out of the car and bounded up the steps.

"Hold on—where are you headed?" A security guard blocked his path.

Rick dug out the pass he had used in New York and held it out for two seconds before replacing it in his pocket. "Where is the Ukrainian ballet company practicing?"

"That way, but—"

Rick raced ahead, following the strains of music floating down the hall. He skidded around a corner and paused to get his bearings.

"Help!" someone yelled. "Call an ambulance!"

With his heart in his stomach, Rick followed the voice through an open door where a group of people huddled around a prone figure. Momentarily paralyzed by fear, his mind struggled to process the scene until he recognized the bodyguard on the floor.

What happened? Fighting panic, he wove through the crowd, searching for Iryna. He spied her slumped against a wall, her eyes glazed. As he reached her side, her phone slipped from her hand and her eyes rolled back into her head. His heart stopped.

"Iryna!" He caught her before she fell to the floor, easing her down and cradling her limp form in his lap. "Iryna! Stay with me!" He pulled out his phone and called 911.

Someone knelt next to him. "They are on the way," Masha said. Rick barely heard her. His ears rang and his vision blurred. He had to breathe. *God, how could You let this happen just as I'm starting to trust You again?*

People crowded around Iryna. Something told him to keep them away, but his voice didn't work.

"*Vidiydit vsi!*" Masha barked, saying what he couldn't. Katherine stooped and reached for a half-empty smoothie cup. "Leave that alone! Don't touch anything!"

Katherine jumped when Masha yelled at her, but she obeyed. As everyone backed away, Masha leaned over and felt Iryna's pulse. "She's alive," she said, letting out a breath. "But her pulse is weak. Lay her down."

Rick's heart pounded so loudly he was sure he wouldn't be able to feel anyone else's. He realized the 911 operator was talking to him. He had to keep it together for Iryna's sake.

"Do you need fire, police, or medical?" the voice repeated.

"Medical. And police. I think someone is on the way, but …

we have … we have two victims." He answered the questions as best he could. He briefly handed his phone to one of the local dancers so they could give the address.

"Iryna, babe, stay with me," he murmured in her ear as he laid her on her back. With trembling fingers, he stroked her cheek. Her breaths were shallow and far between. *God, please don't let her die.*

Emergency personnel soon flooded in, and three paramedics with a stretcher headed to the bodyguard.

"Over here!" Rick yelled, waving frantically.

One of the medics hustled over and immediately checked Iryna for a pulse. "What happened?"

"I don't know. I got here right as she collapsed. She started to fall, and I caught her."

"She was drinking this." Masha gestured to Iryna's smoothie. "It could contain drugs or poison."

Another team of paramedics entered, and the medic waved them over and caught them up to speed. "Let's get her some oxygen." He asked Masha a few more questions, which she answered with cool professionalism.

Rick stood to the side as they strapped an oxygen mask on Iryna's face and prepared an IV. His eyes glazed over as they worked on her. He wanted to pray but couldn't form a thought other than *God, help!*

The police arrived just as they laid her on a gurney.

Masha leaned over to him and whispered, "You go with her. I will stay to talk to the police."

Rick would have followed Iryna anyway, but he couldn't help giving Masha a curious look. Why was she doing this?

"Keep everyone away from her," she added insistently.

Understanding dawned. "You're Vasyl's spy."

"Hush!" She put a finger to her lips and glanced around. "No one can know."

Rick nodded and turned his attention back to Iryna. The gurney moved forward, and Rick followed close behind.

On the way out, Peters caught up to him. His eyes widened as he took in the situation, but he snapped into action. "I'll bring the car around."

When they reached the ambulance, they hustled her in, closed the doors, and took off. Rick knew he wasn't allowed to ride with her, but seeing her being driven away—unconscious, possibly dying—brought him back to that feeling of utter helplessness and lack of control he'd experienced when Cassie was sick.

When Peters pulled up, Rick jumped in the car. Peters peeled out before he even closed the door. *I gotta tell Dad.* He pulled out his phone and sent a text.

> Iryna's been drugged or poisoned, the bodyguard too. Iryna's alive, but on way to hospital. Tell Vasyl. Do whatever you need to do to make sure the hospital will talk to me and let me see her.

He searched for the hospital's address and sent that as well. *I wonder how the bodyguard is doing. I don't even know her name. God, help her too.*

His phone buzzed with a text from his dad.

> On it.

When he read the text, relief washed over him. Someone competent—someone with resources—was handling the situation. Something clicked in his brain as he thought about it. *That's the way it is with God. He's on it.* Just like his dad, God might not solve the problem instantly, or the way Rick wanted it solved, but He heard. He listened.

Peters pulled up to the ER entrance, and Rick hopped out and raced inside to speak to the desk clerk. "Iryna Shevchenko was just brought in by ambulance. Please let me know when you hear anything."

"And you are?" asked the clerk, her fingernails clacking on her keyboard as she typed in information.

His phone buzzed. "Hang on."

> Vasyl sending you email with legal docs and
> insurance. Faxing to hospital.

Rick checked his inbox and scanned the email. "Fredrick Carter. I'm her legal medical representative. I have power of attorney." He held up his phone. "The records department should be receiving a fax. I can forward an email as well." He didn't even want to think about why Vasyl had the information ready so quickly. Rick felt the heavy responsibility of being entrusted with Iryan's care.

"Go ahead and have a seat, Mr. Carter. I'll inform you as soon as I know anything."

"Thank you."

He found a chair next to Peters, who had already claimed a spot in the corner. Before Rick could catch him up, his phone buzzed again. His stomach twisted when he saw it was Iryna's number.

The text was short and sweet:

> you are the next one

CHAPTER 22

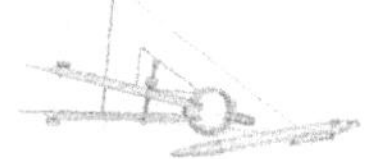

The murderer's daring use of Iryna's phone chilled Rick to his core. Who was close enough to pick it up before it auto locked? A lot of people had been crowding around, and he'd only had eyes for Iryna.

And Masha. How had he not known who she was? Now it all made sense. Why the ballet company kept her around despite her mediocre dancing. Why she joined the company the same time as Iryna. Why they switched her with Karina. Vasyl pulled strings to get her there so she could keep an eye on his daughter. The book in her luggage was probably for decoding ciphers.

But none of that mattered right now. Every five minutes, he badgered the nurses at the check-in station, hoping for an update, but there was no news yet. He tapped his fingers on his knees. Rick was thankful that Peters kept silent. He couldn't hold a conversation right now. All he could do was repeat his prayer. *Please, God. Let her live!*

He thought about his initial reaction to seeing Iryna collapse, how he had questioned God. He still had no answers, but he had to admit the timing was more than coincidence. If he hadn't arrived when he did, someone else might have gotten close to Iryna—someone who could have finished the job. If he hadn't come, no one would be here for her at the hospital.

Rick had spent plenty of hours in hospitals visiting Cassie. Just being inside of one made him sick to his stomach. *Remember, Cassie's in a better place. She's no longer in pain.*

Two heavyset men in black slacks and polos with expensive shoes and gold chains entered the emergency room through the sliding doors. One of them went to the counter while the other glanced around the room as if looking for someone. When the man's eyes settled on Rick, he homed in on him. Rick stiffened as the man approached. Peters shifted in his seat.

"You are Rick Carter?" The man spoke with a heavy Slavic accent. From his complexion, he suspected the man was Georgian rather than Ukrainian.

"Yes." He leaned forward, preparing to stand, but the man took the empty seat beside him.

"I am Vladymir. My comrade, Yuri, and I are here for Darla Miloshenko. We will wait with you."

"Okay. You work for the same … company as Dar?" Vasyl had a long reach. He made sure his family and the people who worked for him were taken care of.

Vladymir smiled. "We are—how you say—part of the same network."

"How is Dar? I haven't heard anything."

Vladymir's face fell. "It does not sound good."

Yuri joined them. At the same time, a man in scrubs and a woman in a white lab coat approached. Rick and the others rose in unison.

The woman spoke first. "Hello. You are here for Darla Miloshenko and Iryna Shevchenko?"

"Yes," Rick and Vladymir both answered.

"We're still awaiting the full results from the tox screen, but it appears that both Ms. Miloshenko and Ms. Shevchenko ingested a large dose of Gamma-Hydroxybutyric acid, also known as liquid ecstasy. I am sorry to inform you that Ms. Miloshenko didn't make it. Her airways had already collapsed, and she stopped breathing before the paramedics arrived. As there is no antidote for GHB, we were unable to revive her."

Rick held his breath, barely able to process the doctor's words. The phrase "didn't make it" echoed in his ears before it sank in that she'd said "Miloshenko." His adrenaline spiked, leaving him jittery. *What about Iryna? If there's no antidote, will she die too?*

"We will need someone to fill out paperwork for Ms. Miloshenko," the doctor was saying.

Yuri raised a hand with a grim expression, and the doctor handed him a clipboard.

"What about Iryna Shevchenko?" Rick rasped.

"You are Fredrick Carter?"

"Yes," he answered.

"If you will come with me, I will take you to Ms. Shevchenko," said Dr. Barrett. "We've put her in a room."

"How is she? Will she be all right?" If he didn't get a definitive answer in about two seconds, he would surely be admitted for heart failure.

"Ms. Shevchenko is stable." Dr. Barrett offered a faint smile and turned to the others. "Only Mr. Carter is allowed in the room. You must remain here."

"Text me if you need anything," said Peters. "I'm not going anywhere."

"I will be close," said Vladymir, without further explanation. A glance and a nod passed between him and Yuri before he strode off in another direction.

Rick hustled through the heavy double doors after the doctor, trying to comprehend the implications of the term "stable." "Will Iryna be all right?" he repeated.

"We're monitoring her, but it appears she will be fine. She's on oxygen but breathing independently and has not required intubation. She didn't ingest as much."

"Is she awake?"

Dr. Barrett shook her head. "It may take up to six hours for her to regain consciousness. When she does, she may be disoriented or have some temporary memory loss. The good news is the recovery time for a GHB overdose is minimal. She should be able to leave within a few hours of waking."

Overcome with relief, Rick's knees wobbled, and tears pressed behind his eyes. The doctor opened a door, and he rushed in.

Seeing Iryna in the hospital bed nearly undid him. This was his worst fear—seeing someone he cared about at death's door again and being unable to do anything about it.

A single chair sat in a corner of the dimly lit room. He dragged it as close to the bed as he could and grasped Iryna's free hand like a rope in the dark. With the oxygen mask covering half of her face, she appeared small and fragile. Her slow, shallow breaths tore at his heart, and he worried the doctor could be wrong.

"You're going to be okay, Iryna. It's going to be okay," he said, as much to reassure himself as Iryna. He leaned over and kissed her clammy forehead.

His phone buzzed, and a text from Peters came through.

> FYI, your dad got word from Vasyl that Yuri
> and Vladymir are legit.

Rick replied with his thanks, grateful Peters had the presence of mind to check on them. His mind barely functioned at the moment, and nervous energy had built up like a shaken soda can. The constant beeping of the machines did nothing to help.

The minutes ticked by, and soon an hour had passed. A nurse came in to check Iryna's vitals and fluids.

"Is everything all right? Is she doing as expected?" The words sped from his lips like a lion pouncing on its prey, but the nurse took them in stride.

"Her oxygen levels are good," she replied, studying the machine. "She has plenty of fluids left, meaning she was already well hydrated. If she keeps this up, she should come out of it in a few hours."

Rick let out another sigh of relief. Since Iryna's condition remained the same, he calmed enough to manage a few coherent thoughts. "The doctor said Iryna ingested liquid ecstasy. Do you know how it was administered?"

The nurse pressed her lips together and glanced at a clipboard. "The source of the drug is unknown, but it would have been in some kind of drink. It's colorless and tasteless, so it's easy to slip into any liquid."

"Where do you get it?"

The nurse grimaced. "Unfortunately, as with many illegal substances, it can be easily obtained on the streets."

Rick nodded, unsure what to do with that information. When the nurse left, he turned back to Iryna, trying not to focus on the "if" in her prognosis. *Iryna is confident she will see her friend Natalia again. She thinks we'll see Cassie again too. If anything happens, I want to be sure. I want to be sure this isn't the end.*

All his prayers to this point had been pleas for help, requests for comfort. The pastor said God wanted everyone to enjoy eternal life with Him. Rick lacked the specific words necessary to accept that gift, but he had to try. Hopefully, the Lord would accept his heart regardless of his floundering.

With some trepidation, he clasped his hands and leaned forward to rest his elbows on the bed. *God, You know I want You to heal Iryna, but if You don't ... I have to know I will see her again. I can't go on like this, afraid of losing everyone I love ...* He choked on a sob, the scars on his heart tearing open again. *I don't know the exact words to say, but I want eternal life. If that means following You, obeying You, that is what I will do. Even when I don't understand, I'll trust that You love me. That You love Iryna. Forgive my unbelief and doubts. Please help me.*

As he bowed his head, a deep sense of peace filled him. He shuddered as the tension in his body suddenly released, and he gasped in surprise at the change. *Thank you, God!* Tears of joy streamed down his cheeks as the assurance that God loved and cared for him entered his soul. For the first time, he truly believed God was in control, that he could trust Him. Knowing he didn't have to be the one in control gave Rick a profound sense of freedom. He reveled in the feeling, breathing easier than he ever had in his life.

By the time Rick glanced at his phone again, another hour had passed. The tracking app on his home screen caught his attention. Curious, he opened it. Iryna's phone was still at the theater. *The killer would be pretty dumb to keep carrying it around.* It would have shocked him to see it had moved—unless the police had confiscated it and taken it to the station.

With Iryna's recovery in God's hands and Peters's and Vasyl's hired security guarding the lobby, Rick allowed his weariness to overtake him. He slouched in the chair and closed his eyes, eventually nodding off to sleep.

CHAPTER 23

Iryna tried to open her eyes, but they were glued shut. Oppressive weight swaddled her body like the wrappings on a mummy, preventing her from moving. She couldn't even wiggle a finger. *Where am I? What's happening?*

Feeling trapped, her pulse raced. In the background, beeping noises and raised voices added to her panic.

"Iryna! Iryna, can you hear me?"

She sensed pressure on her hand as a familiar voice cut through the fog in her brain. She couldn't quite place it. With concentrated effort, she lifted her eyelids for a moment before they fell closed again.

"Her blood pressure's rising. She needs to stay calm," said a new voice.

"Iryna, it's all right. You're going to be fine. I'm here," the first speaker said. A name came to her—*Rick*. His voice reassured her, and her heart rate slowed. The weight holding her down slowly lifted, and she gave Rick's hand a faint squeeze.

"She squeezed my hand!" Rick exclaimed. Iryna's chest warmed at his concerned delight.

"Good," said the other voice.

Iryna felt something being removed from around her head. She struggled to open her eyes again, blinked twice, and managed to keep them half open. She lay in a bed, Rick sat next to her, and a man in green pajamas stood next to a computer monitor. There was something she needed to remember, something important, but the pajama man was talking. A dense fog settled in her brain, and she couldn't understand anything.

"Rick," she managed to say with a tongue that felt too big for her mouth.

"No, babe." He smiled. "That's my name. What's your name?"

Iryna frowned.

"Can you tell me your name?" the man in green repeated.

Iryna understood him this time. He wasn't in pajamas. They were … something else. *I'm supposed to answer him.* It took her a moment, but finally, she said, "Iryna Shevchenko." Yes, that sounded right.

"Very good. Who is the president?" the nurse—or doctor—asked.

"Petro Poroshenko."

There was a strange pause, as if that was the wrong answer. She thought it was right.

"He's the president of Ukraine. Iryna's Ukrainian," said Rick.

"Ah, I'll take that. Well, young lady, it looks like you're back with us. We'll keep you here until the morning just to make sure everything's okay." After giving a few more instructions, which didn't sink in, the doctor left, dimming the lights as he went out.

"Iryna, honey, I was so worried." Rick lifted her hand to his lips and kissed it. "You scared me."

"What happened?"

Rick gave her a quick recap. "What was the last thing you remember?"

"Rehearsing. I was … watching everyone." Her words stuck in her dry throat. "I need some water."

Rick reached for a cup sitting on a tray. He held it to her lips while she tilted her head forward to take a sip. The slight effort exhausted her, and she leaned back against the pillow.

Something buzzed.

"Someone's texting me," Rick said, pulling out his phone. "Peters says Viktor is making a scene in the lobby. He insists on seeing you, but the hospital is under orders to let no one back here."

Iryna frowned. Something was wrong, but she wasn't sure what. If only she could remember.

Rick stared at his phone then jumped from his seat. He put the phone to his ear and paced. "Iryna's phone is here! At the hospital!" He paused, listening, but Iryna couldn't hear the other person. "No," Rick continued, "the location isn't that precise. Okay."

He lowered the phone and looked at Iryna. "Peters and Yuri are going to question Viktor and try to find out if he has your phone."

"My phone?" Iryna asked, confused. "What about my phone?"

Rick opened his mouth to explain, but then his phone rang. "Yeah?" He listened intently.

The door to the room opened, and a figure in a lab coat entered, silhouetted in the bright light from the hallway. The dark outline struck terror in Iryna's heart, and her memory flooded back. Fear paralyzed her as the figure lifted its arm and light glinted off something sharp and shiny. Rick's back was to the door. She couldn't let him get hurt. Iryna screamed.

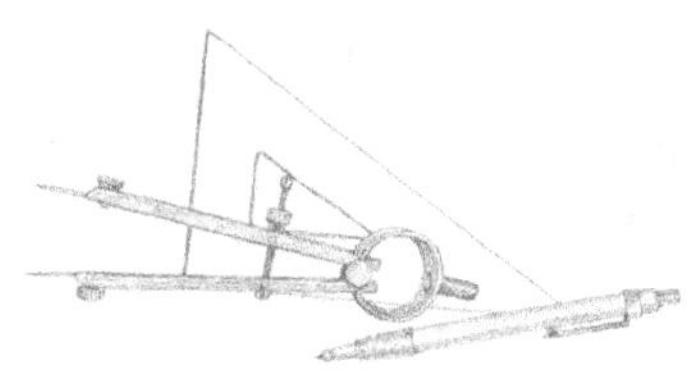

"Look out!"

At Iryna's scream, Rick whirled around to see a man creeping behind him with a knife, poised to strike. His phone clattered to the ground as he sidestepped and threw up his arms in defense. The figure lunged at him, grazing his forearm. Stinging pain overrode his senses, but he kicked the attacker's knee, the sole of his foot connecting solidly. The figure stumbled, falling to one knee, and clawed at the frame of the hospital bed. Rick grabbed a tray from a rolling table and whacked the attacker's hand as the knife slashed at him.

The attacker rolled across the floor, the light from the open door illuminating his features before he popped to his feet with remarkable agility. Rick barely had time to register recognition as the man sprang toward him again. Using the tray as a shield, he stayed between Iryna and his assailant. He couldn't let the man get past him.

Still holding the weapon, the man stabbed at Rick's torso. Rick deflected the strike with the tray and aimed another kick, but the attacker spun away. However, a second figure now loomed in the doorway. The attacker's spin took him out of reach of Rick's foot but into the arms of the new figure, who grabbed his knife arm and bent it back with a sickening crack. The newcomer slammed a fist into his skull, knocking him to the floor.

Noise and yelling preceded a flood of people filing into the room. A security guard entered and flicked on the lights to reveal a somber Vladymir standing over the crumpled form of Alexei. The choreographer wore a white lab coat and a stethoscope, probably scrounged from the theater props. A doctor entered and knelt beside him.

Time slowed, and Rick's pulse thrummed in his ears as he staggered to Iryna's side. "Are you okay?"

Tears streamed down her cheeks as she nodded and raised a trembling hand toward him. He sat on the edge of the bed and hugged her. Iryna let out a sob and clung to him. He shuddered and trembled as the heat of the moment subsided, leaving him cold.

"It's all over now. It's over. Everything's going to be all right."

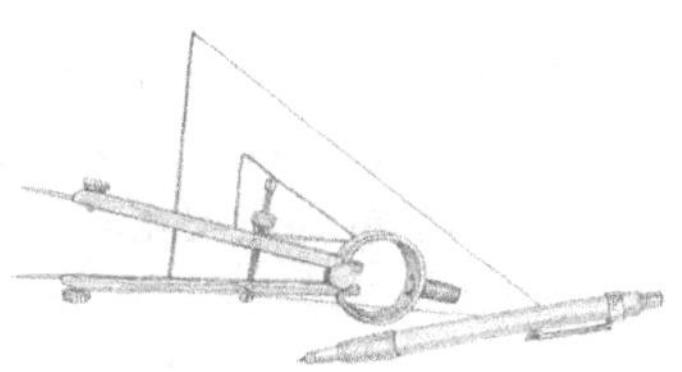

Hours later, once Rick's arm had been stitched up and they'd given their story to the police, Iryna was discharged. Peters drove them to a vacation rental house booked by Matt, who was to meet them there. When they pulled in, a dark-haired stranger in a suit stood next to the driveway instead of his father.

"*Tato!*" Iryna flew from the car and threw herself into her father's waiting arms.

Rick hung back, unable to understand the swift words they exchanged. Vasyl Shevchenko looked far less intimidating than he had imagined until he loosened his hold on Iryna and turned an appraising gaze on him.

"A pleasure to meet you, sir." Rick held out his hand and was rewarded with a firm grip.

"Thank you for taking care of my *Irynochka*. I am relieved you are both well."

Matt emerged from the house and beckoned them inside. Rick gratefully sank onto a leather couch and put an arm around Iryna as she sat next to him. Over copious cups of tea and coffee, they recounted their story again.

"How are you feeling?" Rick asked Iryna when they finished. "Do you want to rest?"

"I have been sleeping long enough. I slept for hours. What I want is to know the other side of the story. How was Alexei mixed up in all this? I think we deserve to know."

Vasyl and Matt exchanged a glance, and Matt nodded. Vasyl sighed and settled deeper into the overstuffed armchair. "After decades of oppression, in the early 1980s, many people were dissatisfied with socialism. The system was failing. Matt and I were both stationed in Poland, which was considered a key to toppling the entire Soviet Union. Natalia's father, Bogdan, was also there.

"In various capacities"—Vasyl cleared his throat—"we all worked to undermine the government. Hiding Solidarity's money was crucial to keeping the movement afloat. I had a university friend, a financier named Fadeyushka, who pledged to aid our cause. When she arrived in Poland, she was murdered by the KGB. Since they suspected one of their own was involved, the hit was kept secret, and I had no way to warn her."

Vasyl closed his eyes and rubbed his temples. "She had been estranged from her husband for some time and was rumored to be having an affair, but I never found out who with. They were careful, as her divorce was still pending. I felt guilty about her death and swore I would do everything I could to protect my friends and family from then on."

No wonder he is such an overprotective father, Rick thought, *placing a spy in his daughter's dance company and hiring bodyguards.* Considering recent events, it was not unreasonable.

"Bogdan and I survived the upheaval of the next few decades. Made new lives for ourselves. Alexei, who had been having affair with Fadeyushka, struggled with depression and alcoholism after her death. He never married or had children. Then a chance meeting in a bar brought him face-to-face with his lover's murderer, the KGB agent sent to eliminate her and prevent her from assisting Solidarity. Alexei must have drawn some information from him over a bottle of vodka—the same bottle he killed him with—enough to set him on our trail."

"This was right before he took the job in Kyiv," Matt inserted. "Before that, he was with the Moscow Ballet."

Vasyl nodded. "Once he was installed in Kyiv, it was an easy leap to connect me and Bogdan through your friendship with Natalia." He canted his head at Iryna. "The tour to America was already scheduled, so he bided his time to gain the chance to hit all three of us. Once he'd tasted revenge, he wanted more."

"People like that want to justify their actions," Matt explained. "They want their victims to know why they've been condemned. That's why he sent the poster and slipped you the matchbooks."

"So he was avenging the death of his mistress and their unborn child," Rick recapped. "But how did he know anything about who was involved? I thought the KGB never found out you were a double agent, and there was nothing to connect my dad to Solidarity." Rick gestured toward his father.

"But Bogdan's part is well known in Poland." Vasyl waved a hand dismissively. "Alexei may have overheard a phone conversation between me and Fadeyushka. She was careful, but maybe she trusted him with part of the story. Iryna staying with Matt was just luck."

"And since Natalia was also a dancer, it was easier to go after her than her brothers or sister," Iryna said with a shiver.

Rick squeezed her hand. "So, what now?"

"Your part is done," Matt pronounced in a firm tone. "Alexei has four murder charges to face—two in the US, one in Ukraine, and one in Russia. He will be punished for his crimes, rest assured."

"Two in the US?" Rick frowned.

"The dancer, Maxim," answered Matt. "They were rooming together. Maxim had obtained a stash of illegal drugs, including GHB. Alexei helped himself to the stash and slipped Maxim a fatal dose, planning to frame him for the murders. They found Maxim in a dressing room."

Iryna cried out. "How awful!"

"Where will Alexei be tried?" asked Rick.

Vasyl scoffed. "Not here. This state has not executed anyone for nearly two decades. I will demand he be extradited to Ukraine. If not …" The meaning of his unfinished sentence was clear.

Mr. Carter raised an eyebrow and cleared his throat. "The only question now is what will happen with the ballet. Viktor received my number from the embassy and has been texting me every five minutes asking when you will return to work. Masha and Sergei are filling in tonight, but he wants you back."

Iryna smiled. "You can tell him I will be there for tomorrow's show."

Rick worried it was too soon, but he knew better than to doubt her. "I will stay here in Pittsburg until you move on."

"I have to fly home tomorrow," said Mr. Carter, "but Peters will stay here with you." The family chauffer was resting after a long night on watch.

"I'll be in town for a few days, then I'll stop by the embassy." Vasyl directed a pointed look at Rick, who squirmed. To Iryna, he said, "You may not feel tired now, *Irynka,* but you will tomorrow if you don't rest. Go to bed."

"Yes, *Tato.*" Iryna rose with a smile, kissed Vasyl on the cheek, and headed to her assigned room.

Mr. Carter yawned. "I think I'll head to bed also." He gave Vasyl a knowing nod.

"So"—Vasyl laced his fingers behind his head and narrowed his eyes at Rick—"it's time you and I had a little chat."

"Yes, sir," Rick replied. Though he didn't know how Vasyl would respond, he knew what he would say. Now that he'd made peace with God, he felt a confidence he'd never known before. Since God had brought him and Iryna together again and kept them safe, he trusted Him to lead them forward, whatever that would look like. If it was up to him, it would look like forever. He hoped Vasyl would agree.

CHAPTER 24

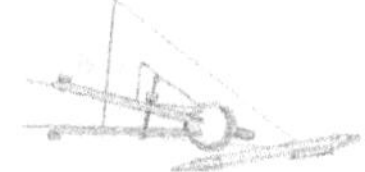

Rick wrapped his arms around Iryna, and she leaned against his chest as they said goodbye near the airline check-in counter at JFK airport. He kissed the top of her head and rested his cheek against her hair. He'd spent every weekend of the last ten weeks with her, but when she boarded the plane for Europe, things would change. He would have to trust God to bring them safely back together.

"When will I see you again?" Iryna whispered in his ear.

"I have a ticket for the end of March."

She nuzzled his neck. "That's so long."

"It's going to take that long to finish up the jobs I've committed to. By then, Mark will have his architect's license, and I'll sell the business to him."

Iryna leaned back with a gasp. "What? You are selling your business? Why?"

"How else can I move to Kyiv and help you with your studio?"

"You are moving to Ukraine?" Iryna gaped.

"And just so you know—so you can be prepared—when I get there, I plan to ask you to marry me."

Iryna laughed. "You sound so certain. Why wait until then?" She tilted her head back to gaze at him, eyes sparkling.

"Because asking now would be rushing it a bit, don't you think? At least, your father thinks so."

"Hmm. Perhaps. He likes you, you know."

"I didn't figure he'd give me his consent otherwise."

"Well"—she raised an eyebrow—"just so you know—so you can be prepared—I will say yes."

EPILOGUE

Feb 12, 2022

Iryna locked the door of her studio and pocketed the key, blinking back tears. Rick put one arm around her shoulder and grasped the handle of the baby carrier with the other. Their three-year-old daughter, Natalia, took her mother's hand.

"You are a wonderful instructor, darling. The children in Brooklyn will be lucky to have you," Rick said.

Iryna sniffed. Though they were blessed to have a new home and good jobs waiting for them, she hated to leave Kyiv and all the children she had taught there. She hated to leave her parents behind. But with a Russian invasion imminent, her father could not leave, and though she dreaded being parted from her grandchildren, Iryna's mother refused to abandon her husband.

"I hope we can come back someday," she said.

"I hope so too," Rick answered. "It's in God's hands."

Iryna smiled, a sense of peace washing over her. "Yes, it is."

ACKNOWLEDGMENTS

Thank you to my former student Natalie for checking the accuracy of my Russian and Ukrainian usage, suggesting relevant changes, and ensuring the correct spellings were used to differentiate between the two.

Thank you to School of Tomorrow and the First Russian Christian school for giving me the opportunity to work with Russian and Ukrainian students in the US and abroad.

Thank you to my beta readers, Heidi, Emmy, Casey, and my mom, to Karly for helping with ballet terminology, to Suzanne for her input on life in New York, to Brandy for checking my theological and biblical references and helping me fine tune the spiritual message, and especially my critique partner, Anna, who has read each version of my manuscript and provided valuable encouragement and feedback.

To God be the glory for giving me the inspiration.

Any inaccuracies are my own fault.

ABOUT THE AUTHOR

Ever since I was a little girl, I have loved to read. One of the first books I remember reading was a Wonder Book version of *Cinderella*. It was in my kindergarten reading station, and I loved the illustrations. I would pick that book every time, so my teacher removed it from the shelf to force me to expand my horizons. Now I own a copy.

Richard Scarry's *Busy, Busy World* also influenced me artistically. It told a story of two painters who painted a mural of a large sun inside someone's house. I thought the idea was genius, so I drew a large sunshine on my wall with crayon. It was scrubbed off, but I continued to have a desire to express myself.

When I was not reading, I spun stories in my head, but I never wrote them down. Drawing and painting interested me more than writing. I have since painted numerous works of art, including some large outdoor murals.

Over the years, I have had trouble with insomnia. I heard if you recorded your ideas, it would enable you to sleep. That didn't help, but I did complete my first novel! Recently, I was diagnosed with narcolepsy, and understanding my sleep patterns, along with scheduling a nap during the day, has greatly improved my quality of life. The line between dreaming and wakefulness for me is often blurred, and some of my ideas come straight from dreams.

My goal is to write entertaining stories packed with danger, adventure, and romance that are also uplifting and heart-warming. The characters face difficulties, endure trials, and make mistakes, but everything is resolved into a happy ending.

Failed Protocol by Cindy Bonds

Olivia Lloyd has left the U.K. to work in Texas as head of security for a tech firm. Her training in the British Army had given her a chance to get into the SAS—Special Air Service. But she washed out, with the help of her uncle and his contacts. Now, she was here at her uncle's request—miserable and lonely after running away from her last life-altering loss.

Kenton Matthews' Recon days are over as he now works as a detective in Dallas, offering assessments for security when high-value targets come to town. But a request from an old friend has his heart pounding, as the threat to the large tech firm holds more than just a breach of security.

Kenton is determined to battle the failed mission from long ago and will do everything he can to protect Olivia from facing the same torturous man her uncle did. But can Olivia trust the one man her uncle deems more than worthy?

Get your copy here:

https://scrivenings.link/failedprotocol

Death Under the Ice by Deborah Sprinkle

Trouble in Pleasant Valley—Book Four

When Homeland Security Analyst Claire Green's brother urges her to come visit, she clears her desk in Chicago and heads for southern Ohio. But when she arrives, the house is deserted and her brother, Alan, is missing.

Claire enlists the help of Alan's neighbors, Madison Zuberi and her husband, Captain Nate Zuberi of the Pleasant Valley Police Force, in the quest to find her brother. But she's in for two surprises.

First, Alan has been keeping secrets from her—secrets that may have gotten him killed and put her life in danger.

Second, Private Investigator Rafe O'Connell, the only man she ever loved—and lost—is a close friend of Madison and Nate, and they ask him to be part of the investigation.

Claire needs their help, but can she put past hurts behind her as she not only tries to find her brother, but stay alive?

Get your copy here:

https://scrivenings.link/deathundertheice

Stay up-to-date on your favorite books and authors with our free e-newsletters.

ScriveningsPress.com